Make Me Hot

Make Me Hot

Marissa Monteilh

KENSINGTON PUBLISHING CORP.
http://www.kensingtonbooks.com

DAFINA BOOKS are published by

Kensington Publishing Corp.
850 Third Avenue
New York, NY 10022

All Kensington titles, imprints and distributed lines are available at special quantity discounts for bulk purchases for sales promotion, premiums, fund-raising, educational or institutional use.

Special book excerpts or customized printings can also be created to fit specific needs. For details, write or phone the office of the Kensington Special Sales Manager: Kensington Publishing Corp., 850 Third Avenue, New York, NY 10022. Attn. Special Sales Department. Phone: 1-800-221-2647.

Dafina and the Dafina logo Reg. U.S. Pat. & TM Off.

ISBN 0-7582-1120-1

First Kensington Trade Paperback Printing: January 2006
10 9 8 7 6 5 4 3 2 1

Printed in the United States of America

This book is dedicated to every woman who at times, just hasn't felt as though she is . . . enough. Not light enough, dark enough, skinny enough, thick enough, tall enough, short enough, young enough, old enough, sexy enough, bootylicious enough, hot enough, or just plain old pretty enough. I feel you. Know that you are beautiful . . . and that confidence has nothing to do with cup size.

ACKNOWLEDGMENTS

For this fourth book, which personally hit home, I'd like to thank those who were part of my makeover to this point and acknowledge the part of my life that led to where I am today, and to where I'm going. Whether the connection was painful or pleasurable, it was necessary and destined because it's all God, and so I thank God for my life. I'm also thankful for all of my defining moments—AND SO IT IS.

I want to thank all of those middle school kids at Monroe Junior High School who teased Marissa McLin—the tall, skinny, quiet, gifted child (my how things have changed, except for the tall part ☺). I couldn't have written *Make Me Hot* without you. And to my middle English teacher at the same school who singled me out in front of the class and told me I was destined to be a writer—thanks! Now, that was a defining moment.

To my kids who are all grown up and all living in different states, doing their things, preparing for their grand life experiences—I thank you for your patience, support and love, always and in all ways. And to my sweet angels, my grandchildren, who remind me to celebrate the simple things in life, like bananas, you make Mimi proud!

Thanks to all of my loving friends (you know who you are), but especially to my best friend who I met five years ago, you lift me up, so I can stand on mountains. Your friendship is as rare as your heart. See you at Starbucks!

A BIG shout out to my wild, supportive, and very special fantastic touring divas: Lori Bryant-Woolridge, Victoria Christopher-Murray, Nina Foxx, Carmen Green, and Jacquelin Thomas. We are the

ladies of FemmeFantastik who while on tour, have shared sometimes steamy, sleepless discussions on any given highway across
the country, six deep in an SUV. What a blessing! Please check out
our blog at www.femmefantastik.blogspot.com.

To all of the media, the booksellers, the reviewers, and my fellow
authors—your kindness and time and support are invaluable.
Special thanks to Jimmy Vines, Book-remarks.com, the fine and
talented A. J. Mason, (voted the official "Hot Boy" 2004), and all of
the enthusiastic book clubs—especially Special Thoughts Reading
Group, Ladies of Color Turning Pages, Velvet Slippers Book Club,
Turning Pages in Oakland, and Legal Divas in Atlanta. Thanks for
having me!

And to the readers . . . those of you who take the time to come
out and meet me, e-mail me, sign my guest book on my web site,
and most importantly, tell a friend. Without you, there would not
be Marissa Monteilh, the author. Your anticipation of what comes
next, and your undying love of characters and story, make this
journey worth it in every way. Thanks!

Last but certainly not least, much appreciation to everyone in my
new Kensington family, especially Walter Zacharias, Steven Zacharias, Karen Thomas, Nicole Bruce, and Lydia Stein. Originally, I'd
sent Karen my manuscript back in 1999, but she politely rejected
the submission. I thanked her for her time and said that one day
she was going to be my editor (no, I didn't stalk her and I didn't
actually tell her that . . . but I thought it and I claimed it and I let it
go). Well, five years later, Karen did indeed make an offer. I take
pride in being able to finally say "Karen Thomas is my editor." It's
a dream come true! As Yolanda Adams sings, "Don't ever give up
on you."

I'm off to finish the next book. So stay tuned! It'll be hot!!

PROLOGUE

"I'll bet you'd screw the heck out of her if no one was looking." The smoky clouds hung low as ten-year-old Morgan Patrice Bayley heard the older schoolboy speak those tainted words behind her young, slender back as she made the long trek to her classroom after recess. The volume of their voices pierced her tender eardrums. The intensity made her ears sting. Her young palms contracted and grew clammy. The weighted statement, almost a dare, carried even more of a load upon her young shoulders than her bulky, army-green backpack. The puberty-ridden boy and his jovial friend passed her in the circular patio. Each snickered as they pointed to her lanky, skinny legs, made worse by her clingy, white support kneesocks, which was part of her Catholic-school uniform back then. In the fifth grade in 1975, pants were not acceptable for young schoolgirls, especially in Morgan's conservative private school.

In the seventh grade the esteem-shattering taunting continued. "Did you break your nose?" a chuckling boy asked Morgan in the cafeteria. She held tight to her tray at lunch period as she slid her goose-bumped thighs onto the cold glossy beige table bench. The old sticks-and-stones saying banged around in her head, but the words seemed without value. She made sure to sit near the very end of the table, as far as possible from the group who was staring through her very being. She felt isolated and extra alone today because her best and only friend, Tyra Bolden, was playing hooky to hang out with her cute boyfriend, the most popular boy in school.

With dread, she quickly flashed her eyes at the group. "No, I didn't," Morgan answered softly without a glimmer of apparent emotion. But the emotion, dominant and acute, was there indeed, on the inside. On the outside, as usual, she shielded her unusual face from the world with her hair as best she could. Her long, wispy bangs and forward-brushed pageboy didn't overpower her face as much as she prayed they would. But from under her hairdo, she tolerated their words. She'd learned to be an actress. It was a survival ploy.

"I'll bet she can smell invisible," one kid joked while a couple of other junior high schoolers high-fived him, holding their bellies and pointing in sheer amusement. She took in the resonance of their torturous laughter but dared not lend the group her eyes a second time.

Morgan aimed her focus down at her plate instead and remained seated. She began eating her lunch, taking a quick bite, and then lowering her fork as she chewed in slow motion. For the long moment, chewing seemed to be the only action she could perform to distract herself, raising and lowering her teeth to chomp into her food. It seemed like a dreaded job. The special of the day—baked chicken, mashed potatoes and gravy, and apple crisp—was her favorite meal. Today, it all tasted the same: like dry, gray cardboard. All she could think about was how much she'd pay to fast-forward the final bell of the day so she could go home. She swallowed with force. Her stomach accepted delivery of her lunchtime nourishment, but it was in knots, as usual.

Even back in preschool, other youngsters used to point and stare at Morgan. They wondered why her nose was on the "wrong way." "Why is it so crooked, so long and so curved?" they'd ask. Even though her verbal response was that she was born that way, her internal response was that one day, her nose would be powerless. One day, no one would notice her Roman nose coming down the sidewalk first. One day, they would notice her for who she was on the inside. Even more important, one day, even *she* would find out who she was . . . if she could just get out from behind her bo-dacious snout.

"Morgan, you are beautiful, no matter what the other kids say. Remember to take constructive criticism seriously but not per-sonally. You are special and God blessed you with a uniqueness you should cherish and embrace." Morgan's mother was good at trying to boost her self-confidence. *Easy for her to say,* Morgan thought, being that her mother was perfect in every way, the epit-ome of beauty and grace. Her mother always smelled of Shalimar and had an ebony-brown complexion, chiseled features, major curves, and an ample chest. Morgan never bought into her mom's assessment of why God decided to bless her with such a distinc-tive look and boyish, scrawny body. After all, kids listened to the opinions of their peers at that age, not their parents. But instead of wallowing in the visual aspect of who she was, and buying into the media portrayal of what teenage girls should look like, Morgan focused on her schoolwork. Each year she consistently made the honor roll, always in the gifted classes, always surpassing all oth-ers when it came to academics. And she did all of this in spite of the fact that she had many grown-up challenges at the tender age of thirteen.

It was a tall, cute, soft-spoken boy who offered to walk her home in the eighth grade. To her, he was a mixture of youthfully geeky and full-fledged studly. Morgan lived in a two-bedroom home in Inglewood, California, on 85th Street, where she shared a cramped room with her younger, easy-on-the-eyes sister, Olympia Annette Bayley. It was a small white house with a burgundy front porch, red-and-white awning, and off-white shutters. After exiting the school bus, Morgan and the boy were stride for stride with few words being exchanged, intermingled with long moments of awkward silence. For the past two days he'd seemed charming, sweet and very attentive. It was almost as if for the first time since she'd met him earlier in the year, he really saw something in her.

They stepped into Morgan's home through the side kitchen door. "Would you like some lemonade?" Morgan asked him demurely as she crossed the threshold with him inches from her back.

"Yes," he said, as he closed the screen door behind them. Morgan dropped her book bag on the black-and-white linoleum floor, took a plastic cup from the cupboard, opened the side-by-side refrigerator and poured from the lead-crystal pitcher. She turned from the refrigerator once she'd replaced the chilled pitcher onto the shelf. She closed the door and instantly the cup containing the cold refreshment fell onto the kitchen floor as she felt the sudden pressure of the boy's hormonal body against hers. He didn't bother kissing her. He just pressed his hands to her shoulders and began to grind. Against her forehead, she felt his hot breath as he exhaled through his nose with force and pumped his way up against her. She pressed her fists into his stomach with a sudden burst of resistance, but he grabbed her wrists and firmly held her hands above her head. Morgan squirmed and asked in an alarming tone, "What are you doing?" He remained deafly silent.

Morgan's heart began to race like a Formula One car as he pressed up against her. He awkwardly maneuvered his knee into her pubic bone. She felt the force of his leg between her thighs and her breathing quickened. He released one of her wrists and grabbed both wrists with one hand. He raised her rayon plaid skirt and immediately located her underwear, pulling the white cotton fabric down just enough to place his trembling fingers along the outline of her private part. He quickly inserted his middle finger, and Morgan grunted. He removed his finger from the tightness of her virginness and tried again, and again, and again, each time at a slower pace. His breathing quickened too.

As though with a mind of their own, Morgan's eyes closed to protectively shut out the vision. But before the boy knew it and to Morgan's surprise, she appeared to be easing his maneuvering with her own syncopated grinding, pressing back toward his hand as if to assist. He released her wrists and her arms fell limp beside her. He fondled her tiny nipples with his young leathery hands and started to kiss her neck with his ChapStick-deprived, full lips. The heels of her tennis shoes gave way to the slippery liquidity of the spilled chilled lemonade beneath her rubber soles. She eased downward along the refrigerator door as though she had been poured from a glass herself.

Eyes now open, Morgan found herself lying on the cold, wet floor as the lemonade greeted her back, thinking to herself that this must have been how her buddy Tyra felt when she had had sex two months before. As he lay on top of her, smelling like he'd neglected to take a shower after PE class, she thought to herself, *Oh my God, I'm doing it.* It felt like sex was supposed to feel, or so she thought. She thought he must have been excited by the way he was sweating, by the depth of his breathing, and by the hardness behind his zipper. His scent seemed strangely intoxicating. She took in a long nasal breath and felt high. Then, just as he'd done before, she copied him and bent her own knee upward, making a point of meeting her thigh to his private part. Then he slipped both hands down to remove her panties, lifted her skirt and unbelted himself. He slid down his pants and underwear all at once, and before Morgan knew it, he was poking her with his stiffness at the very perimeter of her unexplored opening. Morgan wondered how his largeness was going to fit inside of her. She opened wide and held her breath while he fingered her again, and then slipped it in, one inch at a time. It felt weird. It hurt. It was painful, as though he was bursting his way through her bulging hymen to make room for his entry. She scooted up and back, and he paused. Then he tried again. And she scooted back again. He tried again, this time more gently. This time, she did not scoot back. She took it. Before she knew it, he'd eased in, nearly halfway, and then he groaned and froze. As quickly as he had started, he was done. He fell onto her chest and laid still. He still reeked of a salty smell, but she inhaled his essence with her quick breaths that mirrored the beat of her young heart. Morgan stared up at the stained glass ceiling panels, looking dazed and feeling a mixture of emotions as if she had been both violated and welcomingly deflowered.

He stood, looking as though he'd purposely excluded her from his realm of vision, and pulled up his disheveled, damp clothing, while all Morgan could do was notice how wet she felt in between. Nothing but wet. It felt like he'd spit on her, but she knew what it was—a word she'd learned in health class: sperm. It reminded her of the scent of bleach, she thought. She felt ashamed just lying there, so she turned her face, almost as if in regret of her own actions against him, got up, and suddenly ran into the bathroom, covering her mouth and nose. She then heard the back door close. Thinking her mother had come home early from work, Morgan's hands shook with each beat of her heart while bolting toward the kitchen only to find . . . no one. No new lover, no mother, just a quiet stillness and the spilled remains of the refreshment for her guest, splattered upon the floor. By now the telltale liquid almost outlined the shapes of their bodies prior to their departure. It framed their ex-virginity.

Morgan reached for a roll of paper towels, and fell to her knees to clean up the puddles. Her eyes filled with puddles of their own. At that moment, a voice interrupted her mental calamity.

"Do you need help?" her mother asked with two brown bags of groceries cradled in her arms, noticing her daughter on all fours.

Morgan kept her face hidden and wiped her eyes. "No, Mom, I'm fine."

Morgan's mother placed the bags on the kitchen table, looking as though another question was to follow. But it did not. Any question she could have come up with would not have helped her clean up the mess her daughter was in. Nine months later, Morgan gave birth to little Corliss Victoria Bayley. Morgan was now a mother herself. Her mom convinced Morgan that abortion was never an option. It was, she said, one of the biggest sins a woman could make.

Around nine o'clock one evening, two weeks before her high school graduation, Morgan put her three-and-one-half-year-old daughter, Corliss, to bed, and then reached for the ivory Princess phone in the hallway.

"Yes, this is Morgan Bayley. Excuse me? Whose mother? My mother?" Her voice grew louder. "No, that cannot be." She tried to swallow. Her breaths accelerated. "You're mistaken. She's at work. I'll call her there now. She's where? I'll be right there."

To her horror, Morgan, her father, sister and daughter arrived at the hospital to the news that her mother was dead. Morgan burst through the hospital room door leading to the Intensive Care Unit to see for herself.

As she hugged her mother's cold, stiff, lifeless shoulders, Morgan's tears dripped onto her mother's bruised chest like melting ice cream. Morgan vigilantly examined every feature on her mom's familiar but pale, still-perfect face, just to make sure they had the right person. She kissed her beloved mother's hard, chilly lips, and then heard her own daughter ask from the hallway, "Where's Grandma?" Morgan's heart sank, drowning from the wrenching pain of her loss.

Immediately, Morgan ran to her grieving family and the group hugged and cried in disbelief, wracked with sorrow and unanswered questions. One thing was for sure: Morgan's mother did not die alone. An older male companion had been behind the wheel of his new blue Cadillac. Morgan's mother was a passenger. And Morgan's father was an eyewitness.

CHAPTER 1

Unlike my opinionated father, my boyfriend, Jabril Montgomery, never laid a hand on me. But at times, his words did tend to rip and cut into my very being. At least that's how my "higher level of self" felt. I tried to allow spirit to guide me. I listened to Dr. Phil tell me how I should acknowledge my defining moments and cherish my life experiences. But for me, most of those moments focused around the negativity of my looks.

Yes, it was strange that Jabril was a carbon copy of my chauvinistic father. And what was even worse, through it all, it was eerily comfortable, like a zone that was all too familiar to me. Even at the age of thirty-nine, after five years of being Jabril's woman, I would still allow him to control me, and berate me, almost as though I deserved it. And the side of me that hated it, the little girl in me, was deep inside, unable to stand up for herself.

It was an overcast, marine-layered morning, even though it was nearly eleven o'clock. The fog hovered over the top of the towering palm trees that lined my cul-de-sac street. It was LA so it would surely clear up by the afternoon. I liked to take in the view of my neighborhood before I got ready to head out. The sight of the newly constructed tract homes was a beautiful thing to see. As I stood before the bay window of my master bedroom, I struggled to remember when my dad first started being so angry, so gruff, and so cruel. When Mom was around, perhaps her warmth and positivity served as a buffer to his esteem-shattering comments. Like in the eighth grade when he couldn't find something to write with. "Hey, Morgan, can I use you as a pencil?" he joked. Or when I gained weight after my daughter, Corliss, was born and he said, "Maybe now your body will catch up with your nose." Or better yet, when I tried to breastfeed and he told my mother, "Buy her some ready-made formula because that baby will surely starve at Morgan's bosom."

But Mom always did the damage repair. "Morgan, baby, he didn't mean it. River, you apologize to that child."

"Oh, woman, she knows I'm just kidding."

No, I didn't.

But for sure his cynical remarks became more potent once the anger set in after Mom died. He never, ever talked about it, but I was almost certain he was embarrassed by her infidelity. He knew she was seeing that man she was scheduled to meet in that grocery store parking lot, no telling how long before their accident. Even if he did try to tell us this man was just a coworker. Dad's anger was mixed with grief. That much was as apparent as any physical flaw that I may have had. He just wore his flaws on the inside.

Dad was still asleep, as usual. He always slept late. I was letting him stay with me for a while because he'd had a bout of bad luck for about twenty years straight. The last straw was when he suffered a mild stroke last year after stressing over finances. He kept it to himself that he'd lost the house, the same house I grew up in. I could have helped him save it, but it was too late to stop the trustee sale. As usual, he just had too much pride.

So, living on Social Security, he moved in with me. No matter what, he was my dad. And Jabril thought my father was so cool. He actually encouraged me to take him in. The two of them spent more time together than I did with either one of them. They liked Lakers games, beer, and boxing. They were like two peas in a pod.

Ever since Corliss got her own place—after she got her job at an HMO as an esthetician—it had been me against the testosterone kings.

"Cookie." That was Jabril speaking, coming from his morning

audition, headed upstairs after using the spare key I gave him. Sometimes he'd hang out at my house all day, even while I was out doing my job. Cookie was his pet name for me instead of calling me Morgan. "Morgan is a man's name," he'd say.

I decided to momentarily kiss my bit of reflective solitude good-bye and see to my man. Turning from the window toward the direction of his distinctive fragrance, I replied, "Yes, sweetie. I'm in here."

"Hey, Cookie! How are you, baby?" He stood before me and planted a kiss on my forehead. He was all decked out in a black nylon Jordan sweat suit with his hat to the back.

"I'm fine. How are you?" Sometimes he'd slip and call me Crookie. I hated that stuff he pulled. He swore he didn't throw that in as a jab at my nose, but I knew he did.

"Cool. What's for dinner later tonight?"

"What would you like?" I asked.

"How about your baked whiting and asparagus with hollandaise?"

"No problem," I said with a smile.

"Great! And hey, can I use your computer right now? I need to research more auditions."

"You know you don't have to ask," I assured him.

"Thanks, Cookie. By the way, I booked that gig for Chevrolet. It shoots next week. You know, that commercial I told you about where I play the tough guy driving a Blazer."

My face beamed. "Congratulations! They booked the right guy for that one."

He walked away in the middle of his next sentence, looking down at his cell phone. "Right, right. I'll be in your office if you need me."

"Okay."

I watched his manly frame from behind as he departed, and then I returned back to the neighborhood view. He was the fourth man I'd ever been with in my entire life, if you included the two one-timers. But he was only my second relationship. The first one lasted a little more than two years. The brother politely announced that he was leaving me for a younger woman he'd gotten pregnant six months earlier. I hibernated for about eight years after that. But Jabril seemed different. He seemed pretty devoted and he did appear to live up to his commitments.

Physically, I don't know what in particular he saw in me. We met one morning while we were each driving down the street in our cars. He was driving his black 520i and me?—I was driving my pearl-white Expedition. He surely didn't hit on me for my body because he couldn't see below my chest area and that wasn't much to see. We were at a traffic light and he actually got me to pull over. He approached with a swagger.

"Hello there. My goodness, look at you. You have such gorgeous, full lips. And your hair, did you just get it done?"

He was charming and funny and he smelled like a real man. His scent crept through the driver's side window. It was spicy and clean and earthy. He called that night and we went out the next day. We've been an item ever since.

Jabril is handsome as all get out. He is way over six feet tall and I am barely five-five. He has a body like a running back, with big biceps and big legs. His complexion is as fair as mine is dark. His features are model quality.

I guess you could say I have some physical assets. You'd think I wear false eyelashes they are so long. I have to pluck my eyebrows and shave my legs all the time with my hairy self. The good part of it is that I have a head of hair like a lion. It's thick and dark and flat ironed just past my shoulders with long, thick bangs.

Unlike my best friend, Tyra, I grew out of my skinny stage years ago. I've had hips like Beyonce and booty like J.Lo ever since Corliss was born. But because I was skinny for so long, I didn't dare talk about losing weight. My thing was my nose. I'll tell you . . . I'd have paid good money to have a nose like Jabril. His is classic, defined, and sexy.

Jabril said he loved me as I was, but he never ever told me I was pretty. He had a habit of dating average-looking women for some reason. Trust me, I've seen pictures of his many exes. Perhaps so-so-looking women make him look better, or maybe in my case he just couldn't handle the competition of other men staring at me like they stared at my foxy baby sister, Olympia.

"Cookie, telephone. It's Olympia," Jabril yelled. I didn't even hear it ring. Now the brother was answering my phone.

I stepped away from the plantation shutters and grabbed the cordless next to my bed. "Hey, Sis. What's up?" I heard a click indicating that Jabril had hung up.

Olympia's tone was obvious from the first word. "Not much. And why is he picking up your home phone? It sounded like he was on the other line."

"Because . . . I don't know. Maybe he was."

"Is he living there?" she asked, accentuating the question.

"No." I began pacing the floor.

"Then why is he always there? Does he still have a place of his own or did he lose that?"

"You know he does."

"Maybe not. Even Daddy fell onto hard times and lost his roof."

Sitting upon my queen size bed, I grabbed an *Essence* magazine from my nightstand, flipping through the pages backwards. "Well he didn't. I was just over there last week. What else is up?"

"Damn, I forgot why I called you now. That Negro burns my butt. He's so damned controlling. He probably answers on purpose just to try and bust you."

I tossed the magazine onto the bed. "Nothing to bust me on. Anyway, you're not dealing with him, I am."

She could be heard programming her microwave. "You've got that right. But you won't be dealing with him either if I have anything to do with it. And you know Corliss feels that same way. We just don't like how he treats you and you can't even see it."

"I appreciate your concern, both of you, but I'm fine. When are you going to find yourself a man anyway?"

"Oh, you know I'm back with Kenyon."

"No comment." On that note, I was back to pacing.

"At least he doesn't use me and abuse me."

"I seem to remember him . . . Do you remember why you called yet?"

The microwave beeped. "Whatever it was, it certainly wasn't more important than talking about drop-kicking Jabril. Anyway, I've wanted to tell you this face-to-face but—Corliss and I are going to hook you up on a blind date and there's nothing you can do about it. Corliss has someone in mind so be nice when she tells you about it. Just do yourself a favor and cooperate."

Struggling to keep my voice low, I headed back to the window. "Now why would I do that? I'm not available."

"Oh yes you are. And you'll do it because you know you need to." Olympia started smacking on her food, smack dab into my ear.

"No I don't, Olympia. You can just forget it."

"We will not."

Breaking from the familiar view, I headed toward my walk-in closet. "Anyway, I've got to get dressed for a property inspection. I'll talk to you later."

"Okay, Sis. But think about what I said. And tell that poor ex-cuse of a man to keep his evil hands off of your phone."

"Later."

CHAPTER 2

Jabril sat at my oblong desk in my home office, giving the flat screen of my computer his full eye contact. From my bedroom directly across the hall I could hear the sound of the keyboard as he typed each letter. "Cookie, come here. Now!" His urgent tone was startling.

"What?" I said, headed his way from the closet with a pep in my step.

My eyes tracked his long, pointed finger to a file icon on my computer screen. His voice was deep and strident. "What's this file on your desktop? You downloaded a document on breast enlargements? Haven't we talked about this before?"

Glancing away from the screen, our expanded eyes met as I crossed my arms. "Yes, we did. But I wanted to find out more. That's all. It's no big deal."

He scooted the leather chair back and spoke authoritatively. "What more could you possibly need to know? It's a no. Now that's that. What's up with you, downloading this madness?" he asked and commented at the same time.

My hands rested on my hips. "Jabril."

"What?"

I leaned down toward his face. "I'll be back. I've got a meeting."

He backed away. "I mean it now, Cookie. I love your little rosebuds just as they are. After all, if it's more than a mouthful it's enough, you know."

Giving him a "get real" look, I proceeded to chase his cheek and placed a big wet one on his face. I exited my office and went back into the bedroom to change. *Rosebuds? This is a perfect time for some work-related space.*

Before I knew it, the day was winding down and it was time to head back home. The property locations that I'd scouted were part of my responsibilities for my position with the South Central Revitalization Project (SCRP) which was created after the Rodney King riots. I meet with investors and ask for money, but most of our funds come from the government. We provide housing for the homeless, teenage mothers and AIDS patients. It's the most rewarding aspect of my life because it allows me to share in the healing of those who are disadvantaged, underprivileged, or just going though momentary challenges. It pays well and allows me the freedom of being out in the field as opposed to being in the office. It also allows me the opportunity to pay my mortgage on time. I live in the same neighborhood I grew up in. It is not a mansion by any means, but it's a two-story, four-bedroom home and it has a small oval pool and redwood Jacuzzi.

"Hey, baby! I was just thinking about you." It was Corliss, my heart.

"You were? That's eerie. Hey, Mom. I only have a little time left on my lunch getaway between patients but guess what?"

"What?" Oh here it comes. I heard her car stereo bumping the local rap station. "Now don't hit the roof of your car. Not that you ever do. You are alone and in your car, right?"

"Yes."

"Promise you'll stay cool?" she asked, accentuating the first syllable.

"I promise."

"There's this guy who's been coming in for treatments for the past two months. His name is Marcus Coles and he's an attorney for Sky Media, the company that owns the TV and radio stations. And he's just about your age, okay a little younger. He's thirty-eight, single, and I know for a fact that he's handsome. Handsome like an older Shemar Moore."

"And what does that have to do with me?" Caution accompanied my sentence.

She laid it on the line. "I set up a lunch for the two of you this weekend."

My response could only have been, "Why?"

"Why? So you can get to know someone other than Jabril the ogre. You don't even know how you should be treated, Mom. You wouldn't know how to act if a man complimented you and cherished you and gave to you, now would you?"

"I've had that before."

"Well you don't have it now. Don't you even care that Auntie Olympia and I can't stand the way he treats you?"

Here we go again. "Corliss, I appreciate your concern, but I'm just fine."

"Tell me you plan on marrying him one day."

There she was, testing me as only she could do. "It's not that serious yet."

"Yet? It's been, what—five years now? Mom, you're not getting any younger. And he keeps such close tabs on you, it's like you're in prison."

A beep indicated a waiting call. "Hold on a minute, honey. Hello."

"Hey, baby. Where are you? Aren't you done with your meeting yet?" Jabril asked, sounding impatient as he unloaded two questions at once.

"Yes, I am. I'm on my way. I had to stop at the grocery store."

"Where are you exactly?"

"I'm on the 10 transition to the 405. It won't be long."

"That should be fifteen minutes, or twenty at the most."

My finger hovered over the talk button. "Something like that, depending on traffic."

"Well, I'm waiting so hurry up. And I'm starving."

"Okay, I'm doing my best. I've got to go, I'm on the other line."

"With who?"

My words quickened. "With Corliss. See you soon."

"She just called here. I told her you were in the car."

"Good. Good-bye."

"Love you," he proclaimed just to postpone my disconnection.

"Okay."

"Okay?"

"Love you too. 'Bye," I said, half-getting my closing word out before I clicked back over. "Sorry about that. Now Corliss, think about it. Do I look like I'm in prison to you? I hold down a job, take care of my home all by myself, and care for my dad. I have friends and I have interests. He's not my whole life. I'm doing just fine, dear."

Her radio seemed two notches louder. "You talk a good game but I don't believe you're happy. You're just not quite selling me. Worst of all, that man teases you about your looks. Mom, now don't deny it. I heard him the other day when he said you put the N in nosey."

I found myself talking louder. "That's because I was snooping in his pockets when I washed his pants."

She pressed air through her lips. "Oh please, I know what he meant. And let him wash his own clothes. Why are you so accommodating? You spoil him like you're his mom. That man will never let you leave him. He knows he'll never find another woman in the new millennium of liberated babes who'll spoil him like you do. I sure wouldn't do it."

Her comment made me smile. "No, I know you wouldn't. You got your independence from your auntie."

"I'd like to know where you got that pamper-your-king-at-any-cost mentality. Surely not from Grandma."

Suddenly, my smile turned upside down. "You don't know how your grandmother was, Corliss. And I've heard enough of this. I'm not interested in this Marcus attorney–patient of yours. I'm in a long-term relationship and I believe in fidelity. I'm doing just fine. Now I need to focus on the road and get home so I can make dinner. Are you coming by?"

"No, Mom, not tonight," she replied at a low volume.

"Well, I'll make extra just in case you change your mind. You're always welcome."

"No thanks. Anyway, I'm sorry I brought it up. Have a good night."

"Corliss, I appreciate your concern, dear. I really do. But please call your auntie and tell her I said no thanks. Maybe you can hook him up with her?" I suggested.

"He's too old for her. Besides, she has a man now."

I reminded her, "And so do I, dear."

"Mom, drive safely." She exhaled with obvious vigor.

Disconnecting, I shook my head and looked at myself in the rearview mirror. Through my jeweled FosterGrants, I took in an eyeful and wondered if I'd even be attractive to anyone if I wasn't with Jabril. I'd have to get used to the whole getting-to-know-someone again. The thought of it made my head hurt, and my dang feet throb. I reached down to undo my ankle straps so that my toes could breathe, and proceeded home to my men.

As I walked in the front door with five plastic shopping bags filled with groceries, my spike heels met the hardwood floor with resounding, clopping sounds like I was wearing horseshoes. I was dead tired. Dad and Jabril were watching a Lakers game, munching on microwave popcorn and swigging on cold bottled brewskis as I walked by.

"Do you need help?" my dad, named River Bayley, asked as if he had eyes behind his head.

"No, I've got it." The handles of the bags were making weighted imprints into the creases of my fingers.

Jabril yelled out, "Damn, that Kobe is nothing but net every time."

Dad replied, "He earns every penny of those millions that's for sure. What's for dinner?" he asked me.

"Jabril requested whiting."

"That sounds like a winner."

Jabril asked, "You sure you're okay with that, Mr. B?"

"I'm okay with that. Look at Shaq on that Miami team, man. I thought he went to free-throw school. He's less than fifty percent from the charity stripe again this year."

While leaning upon the kitchen island I finally took off my

heels. My toes were grateful. I watched the two peas in a pod. It was almost like Dad gave birth to Jabril himself. They were even starting to look alike. Same height, same distinguished faces, same strong hands and muscular build. But Dad was just a couple of shades darker with a head full of graying hair. Seemed I was just comfortable in this zone. I suppose what's familiar might not always be good for you or to you, but it just seemed common enough to deal with.

That night, Jabril decided to stay. In bed he was—completely opposite from how he acted when he was vertical. It was as though he got off on what he could do to me. Maybe our orgasmic sessions were what kept me bonded to him, even through the insults and controlling demands.

Imagine the statue of David. That would be my man's physique. He was built like he'd been sculpted to perfection. Generous and skilled, Jabril always had his bag of tricks close at hand. It usually consisted of textured condoms, massage oil, and his tiny vibrating massager that looked like a small penis.

He preferred that I didn't wear deodorant after I showered. And I knew why, so I wasn't complaining about skipping that step to my grooming. Jabril approached as I exited the bathroom. He picked me up with ease, like he was about to carry me off to an erotic wonderland. He laid me on my back upon the down comforter and picked up his bottle of almond oil.

He poured a few honey-colored drops onto his palm, rubbed his hands together to create a bit of warmth, and worked his magic touch over my breasts. I always joked that I had more nipple than boob, but he worked them good, and then moved up to my shoulders. He inched his way down to my stomach, and then past my hips to my legs. Jabril loved to rub my feet into ecstasy, adding pressure to the arch of my foot, and then pulling and squeezing each toe with focus. He turned me over, adding more oil to his palms. This time it was a royal butt massage, deep into the muscles of my rear end, and then down the back of my thighs. Jabril placed his manly hands under me and lifted my hips. He

brought his mouth to my rear thighs and the curve of my but-
tocks, gently flicking his tongue. But this time, I felt a different
sensation. It was a cooling feeling that lit up my skin.

"What's that?"

I looked back as he stuck out his tongue to expose a clear
lozenge. He pointed to the dresser. It was a package of Halls icy-
cool mints. Damn, that boy was creative. My body belonged to
him. He melted my heart like a hot knife through butter. I shut my
eyes through the orgasmic feeling of his skilled tongue action.

Jabril turned me over again and licked up the side of my waist,
traveling to my sensitive hip bone, and then raising my hands
above my head, coming up to tongue my armpits. He placed his
flat, stiff tongue under my arm, licking me firmly, and then lightly
biting my skin. I squirmed with pleasure and my head grew dizzy.

Before I could even begin to reciprocate, he reached for the
massager, turned it on, positioning himself in between my legs.
He spread my opening apart with his left hand, and rubbed the
massager over my peak with his right hand. He introduced his
tongue inside. I closed my eyes and moaned, assisting his intentions by grooving my hips along with him. My body was an inferno
as I grinded into his face. All I could do was surrender, contracting
from head to toe, expelling a wild rush of wetness ending with a
long, feminine grunt.

Jabril grabbed a magnum condom and placed it over his hardness. He inserted himself, joining my heat, working his size all
through me. I was in heaven. He was moving his hips but good.

"Baby, oh I love the way you do this," I purred lustfully.

"You deserve to feel good. You're my lady."

"Yes, I am. And I love you."

Jabril was good at stopping himself from reaching a climax. He
paused momentarily, stood up and pulled me to my feet. He faced
me and lifted me up, making sure that my legs wrapped around
his hips while he stood. He held me in midair, bucking all through
me as I peered over at the closet's mirrored vision of his mascu-
line physique, intertwined with my feminine frame, opposite skin
tones contrasting. His well-defined leg muscles flexed while he

worked, and his ass cheeks contracted at a hurried pace. I leaned my head back and took the ride, enjoying it, needing it, welcoming it, accepting it, and again, pulsating through his every thrust.

"Okay, here we go. That's what it takes, right there," he moaned through his teeth. But he stopped. He took two steps forward, leaning me back onto the bed while still inside of me. As he pulled my legs all the way back, I felt his thrust deeper and deeper. I let out an erotic, muffled sound. And then he released his baritone scream into the pillow. We came together. It was beautiful. He kissed me. I kissed him back.

He immediately lay on his back while carefully adjusting the still-fitted condom. "I met this lady at Staples today who's going to put me in touch with her agent." He stared toward the shadow of the brass ceiling fan while the cool air blasted our sweaty bodies.

Still panting, legs coming back to normal from an orgasmic shiver, I replied, "Oh really." I hoped it was I, and not she who'd motivated his performance.

"Yes. We're going to have lunch after my audition tomorrow morning."

"Okay. That's nice of her to offer to do that. But what does she get out of it?"

"Just one starving actor helping another." He stood up, and then headed to the bathroom.

"Right." This time, my eyes locked on the ceiling fan too.

CHAPTER 3

Early the next day I threw on my nightie as Jabril left for his audition, and gave in to the lure of the unmade bed, cuddling back under the covers, basking in the afterglow of our morning hello. I had a little more time before my first meeting. I tried to pull the flannel sheets up to my chin and doze off again.

"Morgan, wake it on up now. Tyra's here." A blurred vision of my dad hovered over my bed as he shook his head in amazement. He mumbled out loud. "That girl looks better and better every time I see her." *No, he didn't say that. And what's he doing up so early?*

My eyes quickly adjusted to the light of day delivered through the sheer beige curtains. I swear I must have been dreaming, rubbing my swollen eyelids wondering how my sixty-two-year-old dad would dare comment about my thirty-eight-year-old friend. Certainly not out loud and certainly not to his own daughter.

"Thanks, Dad. I'll be right down," I said, preparing to toss the covers and sit straight up.

"No, stay in bed, girl," Tyra said in her anchorwomanlike voice, walking in quickly as dad walked away. He gave her a weird, full-body once-over. She continued to speak. "I'm too excited to even wait for your slow self to creep on out of that heavenly looking poster bed anyway."

Butter pecan Tyra, a personal trainer, was tall, slender, and curvy like a pinup girl. She had long, healthy, brown real hair and big dark eyes. Tyra always looked as though she pampered herself, what with her colorful acrylic nails and flawless skin. She had a lot of juice in her caboose, or as the men said about her booty: she had a history behind her. She'd always been cute, even back in elementary school. But somehow, the older she got, the foxier she looked. And obviously, Dad noticed.

Tyra jumped onto Jabril's side of the bed and sat up, wearing black-and-white boots, black jeans and a white men's dress shirt.

I sat up, half-covering my mouth. "Girl, I haven't even brushed my teeth yet." After a quick whiff, I also realized that not putting on that deodorant last night was not a good idea.

"Just stay on that side of the bed." She spoke rapidly like she had a major news flash. "That is if you do decide to react to what I'm about to say. But for now, I'll do all of the talking. Just listen." I watched this woman who I'd known for so long, my loving girl who always had my back. It was like she was my second sister in a way. She was someone who I thought I knew extremely well. "Remember all of the conversations we've had about how much it would cost to get our breasts done . . . yours and mine?"

I replied, still feeling a little short on sleep, "Yes, and we came to our senses and spent that money on property instead."

"True, but Morgan, you also thought it would be cool to get your nose done, remember that?"

Peeling the covers from my legs, I prepared to stand up, but paused. "I was just fooling around with that idea. I would never have a bone broken on purpose. That's some major surgery."

"I know it is, but how long have you been feeling awkward when people make stupid-ass comments out loud? How many rear ends have I had to threaten to kick when some chick teases you and bruises your ego with some lame insult?"

Impatiently, I looked her way. "Where are you going with this?"

She leaned in closer. "Tell me you've never really wondered what your life would be like with a new nose and big tits, Morgan. Your whole image would change. Maybe even your whole life."

Her words caused me to stay put. "Tyra, please."

She took a deep breath. "Morgan, I took one of our pictures from New Year's Eve and sent it to KJAZZ radio."

"One of our pictures for what? Please tell me it was not for what I think you're about to say."

"They're having a Soulful Renewal contest, kind of like an Extreme Makeover, but over the radio."

"What's the point of doing it over the radio? You can't show your face over the radio."

Tyra spoke unhurriedly. "They'll have the winner appear on TV all over the country to show off their new looks. It's a big promotional thing where you enter with a story and a photo, and then when they call you, you have to name the last three songs they played. I've been tuned in 24/7 since last week. Well, Morgan, they called me this morning, I named all three songs, and you won."

"What? I won?" I asked in a high-pitched voice.

"You won the contest based upon my submission. They're going to hook you up with a plastic surgeon who will do anything you want done, for free. And, I mean anything."

Throwing the covers back up over my legs, I leaned against the headboard. "Dammit, girl. You . . . Tyra. Why didn't you just ask me instead of trying to surprise me?"

"You would have said no. I know you all too well."

"And what if I say no now? Don't you think they want people entered in this contest who want to do this type of thing? I am hardly a willing participant." I shook my head no. "I'm not interested."

"Morgan, come on now. This means tens of thousands of dollars' worth of surgery by a Beverly Hills cosmetic surgeon. You would never be able to pay for this on your own."

I raised my hand, flexing it her way. "It's not about the money. You know I've worked on accepting my image all my life. I lived in anguish from being called Olive Oyl for years. But God saved me from that insulting name when I gained all this weight, which I wouldn't trade for anything in the world. They couldn't suck this fat out of me if you paid me a million dollars. Tyra, it takes a lot of self-love to appreciate a big booty and thighs. I love my body and I have a man who loves it too, itty-bitty titties and all."

She scooted her body to face me. "Morgan, this is Tyra you're talking to. You are not fooling me by talking all of this self-love crap. I've been there, even when your family wasn't. And I know for a fact that you'd like a smaller nose."

"But I won't kill who I am to get it. What if they screw it up and I end up looking like an alien or something? Plus, I never want to change my overall look. There's no guarantee I won't look totally different, and that would not be cool. They can't guarantee enhancements. I'll be forty years old next month. I can live the rest of my years with what God intended me to have."

"Morgan?"

"Look, I really, really appreciate what you tried to do. And I understand why you did it, truly I do. But I do not want plastic surgery. I don't want fat sucked out, implants inserted and cartilage chiseled. I hate surgery anyway. You know that. I even hate hospitals. Really, Tyra, I am fine. Why don't you take the prize and get your breasts done? They're smaller than mine," I kidded.

She looked down at her chest. "They are not."

"Are too." I looked at her chest as well.

Tyra touched my forearm. "Morgan, they chose you, not me, so I can't simply walk in there asking for bigger boobies. The whole idea is about a drastic change."

"That's what I'm afraid of . . . it being drastic. No thanks, girl. But I do appreciate it." I took a peek at my digital clock radio. "I've got to get up and go now anyway."

She looked let down, glancing around for her plaid purse. "What am I supposed to tell them?"

"That you didn't check with me first and I declined."

Tyra stood. Her shoulders were slumped. "Fine, Morgan. Just make me look like a fool."

"Better than making me look like one." I stood up too and walked over to her. I placed my hand on her shoulder.

She shined me on and searched her purse for her keys. "I'm going to run now. I'll call you later. Are you sure you don't want to think about it or talk to your family first?" She gave me her baby-doll face that had moved mountains before.

I took my hand back. "No, I know what their reactions would be. No . . . just like I said."

"Good-bye, Morgan."

"Good-bye, Tyra." I hugged my best friend without a full effort in return, and then headed straight to the bathroom to brush my teeth. I heard her shut the front door.

Cupping my mouth with my hand, I checked my own breath. Poor Tyra had to deal with my morning mouth. Standing there with a lopsided hairdo in my short, sheer navy blue nightie with the shoulder straps sliding down my arms, I rinsed and spit. I caught a glimpse of my profile in the side medicine-chest mirror. My nose had somehow become my friend, my overbearing buddy that I'd grown to love. It was almost my trademark. As I checked it out from the front-on vanity mirror, it was definitely big, and hooked, and almost angular. But it was mine. I covered my nose with my hands and right away, my big eyes stood out, and my high cheekbones, and my plump lips that I accented so intensely as a way to distract from the feature that lived directly above. I was sort of pretty, almost like my mom, sister and daughter. I just plain old had a big nose.

I released my hand and there it was. My nose. My whole life it had always had top billing on the marquee of my face. All assets paled to its power. It really did overwhelm my face. It was, it was . . . hideous.

The weekend was my time with family and my man. No work allowed. I usually tried to make dinner so that everyone could get together and bond over a meal, like Mom used to do when we were young. What took the fun out of it was times when Corliss or Olympia butted heads with Jabril, when he said something chauvinistic that they interpreted as a put-down to the female species. He'd promised to do better. And I had faith that he would.

"Hey, come on in, baby girl," Dad said as he greeted Corliss at the door on a Sunday night. "How are things going in the world of haircare?"

She strolled in wearing a tan tailored pantsuit. Her two-inch-long, reddish-brown hair was trimmed and styled to precision. Corliss looked a lot like my mother, with her ebony complexion, high cheekbones, beautiful stature and full chest. "Grandpa, it's preventative skin care."

"I know that. It's all of that. Cosmetology, right?" Dad said as though she'd missed his real intention.

"Yes, but I work as a licensed facialist in a doctor's office. You make it sound like I do weaves."

"Girl, you're just like your Auntie Olympia. Feisty as a dang alley cat."

Jabril joined in. *Could he have been trying?* "Oh Mr. B, Corliss was just making sure that you know more about what she does for a living."

"Hello, Jabril." Corliss did not offer him a hug.

He offered no hug either but continued to speak. "Hey there. I hope you're hungry because your mother cooked up roasted chicken, macaroni and cheese, and mustard greens."

Olympia caught his sentence as she walked in with a plate in her hand. She hugged Dad. "Oh really? Did you request that menu?" she asked Jabril with a raised eyebrow.

"Actually, she did ask my opinion."

"Thought so," said Olympia, wearing a short, hooded velour dress.

Dad's face beamed with pride at the sight of her. "Now there's my girl." He hugged his youngest daughter like he hadn't seen her in twenty years.

She returned his embrace. "Hi, Dad."

He stepped back and checked her out from head to toe. "Don't you look gorgeous?" He spoke in Jabril's direction. "Man, I had to fight the boys off with a stick when she was young."

"I'll bet," Jabril replied.

Olympia looked like she'd heard all of this before. She almost seemed uncomfortable with it. She turned to her niece with a hug. "Hi, Corliss sweetie. You always seem to glow. Any new man in your life?"

"No, not right now, Auntie Olympia."

"I know you have many opportunities," Jabril interjected.

"Sometimes." Corliss walked toward me rolling her eyes just before I could make my move to save her. "Hi, Mom. It sure smells good in here."

"Oh thanks. Hi, sweetie," I replied with a kiss on her lips. And I grabbed Olympia's hand as she walked up. "Hi, Sis. You look pretty. I hope you all enjoy what I made."

"We always do," said Olympia. "And here, I brought a lemon cake for dessert."

I took the plate. "Thanks so much. You didn't have to do that."

Jabril agreed, "Yes, Morgan was preparing to make a 7 UP cake."

"Well, now she doesn't have to go through the trouble," Olympia told Jabril as though he should get a clue.

"That's true. Those lemon cakes sure are good," Jabril replied in semisarcastic agreement.

The three of us ladies walked away hugged up like Destiny's Child. Dad and Jabril took over the sofa.

"I'm starving. When will dinner be ready?" asked Dad.

"In about fifteen minutes," I told him.

"Well hurry up. I could eat this couch," Dad added.

"Dad, try not to do that, okay? At least wait sixteen minutes," joked Olympia as she peeked inside one of the skillets on the stove. Corliss and I couldn't help but laugh.

Dad frowned. "Don't be giving me that smart-talk crap. Just because you're the baby, don't get all spunky on me now. You and Corliss need to be more like Morgan and chill out. Not every comment a man makes is meant to degrade your womanhood."

"Don't try to figure it out, Mr. B," said Jabril. "We're from different planets."

"Yeah, chauvinistic Mars," Corliss remarked with a snicker.

Olympia high-fived her niece with her eyes.

Jabril spoke right over her comment. "Cookie, I'm starving too."

"Okay, it won't be long," I told Jabril.

Corliss shook her head at me with consternation as she and her auntie set the table. Actually, it was a look as though she could have pimp-slapped me.

CHAPTER 4

"Gotta go, Sis, but thanks for dinner," Olympia said as we hugged. "I've got a hot date with Kenyon," she whispered. Kenyon was her not-so-ex-boyfriend. The two of them had been playing break-up-to-make-up games for years.

"Thanks for coming. I'll call you tomorrow."

"Okay. Good night everyone."

"Good night," we all said as I watched her walk to her car, shutting the door as she honked.

Dad, Jabril, Corliss and I agreed to watch the *Brown Sugar* DVD and sip on some brandy while we ate our lemon cake.

Corliss leaned back on the loveseat, took off her Escada heels, and put her feet up, cozying up with a red wool throw over her legs.

"You're going to miss the movie, baby girl," Dad told her, lounging on the recliner.

"I'm not dozing," she replied, sounding exhausted.

Jabril said, "Yeah, don't fall asleep because you'll be there all night and you've got to get up to go to work in the morning."

"And if I do I can still make it home in time to get dressed. Do you work tomorrow, Mom?"

"Yes, I do," I replied, and then looked at my man. "Jabril, she still has a few clothes here anyway. She'll be fine."

"Yeah, but she shouldn't sleep on the couch like that."

"And why not?" Corliss asked, sounding confused.

"I just mean it's not good for your back and your neck."

"I'm fine," she said. But then her tone shifted into the annoyed zone. "I can go upstairs to the guestroom if you don't want me to ruin my mom's sofa."

Jabril responded, "I didn't say that."

She sat up. "No, you think I'm going to get makeup on her off-white couch, right?"

Dad spoke up. "Baby girl, he didn't say that. You can lay wherever you want."

Jabril continued with his opinions. "When I grew up, we didn't put our feet on couches where people sit."

Corliss had irritation spelled out across her forehead. "Well, this is not where you grew up and this is not your house. This is my mom's house where I lived."

"Yeah, I hear you. This is not my house, right, I got you." Jabril said, sounding cynical.

"Exactly. But it's funny how people can put their butts on something that they can't lay their feet upon. That makes no sense," she said, making the comparison while she shook her head side to side.

Now I know what a referee feels like. "Jabril, Corliss, come on now. Let's just enjoy the movie."

Dad added, "Actually, Jabril, since my grandbaby had a few sips of brandy, I'd prefer that she stays over anyway. I wouldn't want her driving home tonight feeling a buzz."

"Okay, then I'll get her room ready," said Jabril.

Dad was firm. "No, you won't. She'll lay wherever she good and damned well wants to lay." He looked smack dab at Jabril as though he was wishing for another comment.

"Morgan?" Jabril looked to me.

"Corliss, honey, you probably would be more comfortable upstairs if and when that time comes."

Dad looked at Jabril. "But for now, she's staying where she is."

"Mr. B, I don't really care where she lays. I was just looking out for her." Jabril tried to play it off.

"Yeah, right," said Corliss.

Dad wasn't having it. "I'll look out for my own family if you don't mind."

Corliss hissed, "Now you've ruined the whole evening with your opinionated comments. Who gives a damn what your family did? When we come to your house, then you can lay down the law according to your Walton's clan rules."

Dad scooted up to the edge of his seat. "She's right. This is the last time you come here trying to tell people what they should do."

"Dad," I said with a visual request for him to back off.

Dad spoke with firm control. "No, Morgan. His comment was meant to provoke and control. This is your house."

I tried again. "Okay, now everyone, let's . . ."

Corliss stood up and slipped on her shoes. "You know what? I'm leaving anyway. I don't even want to stay here. I've got my own house to go to."

Jabril stood up too. "You stay right where you are. I'll go." He headed upstairs, taking weighted steps until he reached the top.

Corliss picked up her purse and headed for the door. "One day, Mom, you're going to give him his walking papers to the front door for real, not simply up those stairs. I think he pulls that crap on purpose."

Dad was still frustrated. "He acts like people are just supposed to take his nonsense. Not everyone is you."

"Dad, what do you mean by that?"

"I mean you let him get away with far too much. This is your own daughter, Morgan. It's like he can do no wrong in your eyes."

"I think the whole thing just got blown out of proportion," I tried to explain.

"How?" Dad asked.

"With that makeup comment. I know he didn't mean that."

Corliss turned as she put her hand on the doorknob. "Oh, so it was my fault?"

"I didn't say that."

"You know what, Mom? I'm going to go now. I can't be around that Jim Jones brotha'. Thanks for dinner."

"Corliss?" Dad spoke up.

She pulled the door open. "Grandpa, I'm fine. I actually only had one sip. And I'm just right down the road. Talk to you later."

Dad approached and gave her a hug. "Drive carefully and call us when you get home."

"Good-bye, honey," I said.

Corliss shut the door without looking my way.

Dad followed me into the kitchen. "Morgan, Jabril can be annoying and you know it. But he'll charm his way out of this one as usual."

I was thinking, *You should know his motus operandi. I guess it's just like having a mirror to your own face, huh?*

I turned on the dishwasher. "Actually, Dad, you used to have your moments too and Mom didn't kick you to the curb."

"Don't try to compare what you two have to the years I spent with your mom. And leave her out of this anyway."

"Sorry, Dad. I'm going upstairs." I turned off the kitchen light.

"And I'm going to restart this movie. Good night." He fidgeted with the remote.

"Hello. Okay. Good, Corliss. I'll let her know. Good-bye." Dad yelled upstairs. "Hey, Corliss called. She made it home."

"Thanks, Dad."

I wasn't quite sure how the night ended so badly but it did. Dad and Jabril had never butted heads before, even when Jabril had gotten controversial. In particular, Dad didn't really defend anyone against Jabril. Sometimes the two of them would laugh out loud about the ladies' reactions. I guess Dad was in the mood to rescue Corliss tonight. But I thought gentlemen were always supposed to come to the rescue of damsels in distress.

"I'm going to bed, Jabril." I stood in the doorway to my office wearing my baby-doll pajamas.

His jaws were tight as he glued his eyes to the computer screen. "I'll tell you one thing, the next time your dad gets on your man, you'd better stand up and support me."

"Support you? What did I do?"

"Nothing, that's just it. How many times have I told you to stand by your man, Morgan?" He squinted his eyes my way.

The chime of an AOL Instant Message sounded. I could see that the person asked, "Are you still there?"

Amazement prompted me to take a step inside. "Who are you talking to?"

"What do you mean who am I talking to?"

"Who are you chatting with?"

He turned from me to the screen. "Do you mind? I'm on my own account minding my own business."

"On my computer?"

The chime rang out again. My eyes didn't fail me. The name was Platinum Babe.

A second later he clicked the image to minimize the IM box, and the Web site he minimized was Beautifulgirls.com. "Since when has that been a problem?"

My hands found their way to my hips again. "It's not a problem, but if you're talking to women in my house . . ."

"Then what?" He glanced at me as though he dared me to complete my sentence.

"Then . . . why, Jabril? What does that do for you?" I asked, pointing at the screen.

"These are my friends."

"Have I met them?"

"Morgan, you're really crossing over into a red zone that you don't want to enter. I'm with you every night. Not out in the streets. So you need to be happy I'm here and go to bed."

I stuck my head out toward him to bring my ears closer. "I need to be happy you're here while you chat?"

He replied with a resounding cockiness, "While I enjoy my space."

"Space with whom—prettier women, sexier women, women whose pictures you find attractive? Is that it? Are these women . . . pretty?"

He spoke to the screen. "Good night, Morgan."

My hand was now flailing about. "How would you feel if I did that? Sit up chatting with men all night?"

"Go right ahead."

I made an about-face. "Okay, I will."

He finally turned my way but spoke toward my back. "Oh please. You're never on this damned thing."

"I will be. Starting tomorrow night."

"Why?"

I prepared to take a step toward my room. "Because something or someone on there is keeping you from coming to bed with Morgan Bayley, your woman, who you say you love. There must be something intriguing about instant messages."

"I'll ignore that nonsense and tell you you're not going to sit up here and chat."

"Watch me," I said, putting one foot in front of the other. I heard and felt his pounding, quick-paced footsteps behind me as the IM chimed again.

"Morgan, I forbid you from playing this tit-for-tat game." He was on my heels.

I made a beeline dash while I spoke. "Your Platinum Babe is calling you." I closed the bathroom door and immediately turned the lock.

"Open this door now," he demanded, trying the knob.

"No."

"Morgan, I'm warning you . . ."

"You're warning her what?" said my dad in as deep and menacing a voice as I'd ever heard. "Boy, you have lost your damn mind tonight. I suggest you back away from that door and get back to what you were doing before I decide to make you back away. Leave my daughter alone. Now get!"

Jabril sounded as though he was willing to surrender. "Chill out, Mr. B. It's just a friendly little couple's disagreement. Morgan and I were just discussing her place."

"Not while I'm staying at her place."

I heard heavy footsteps heading away and saw the shadow of what I hoped was my dad's feet from under the door.

He said nothing. I said nothing. He walked away. A glimpse of the gentleman in my dad shone through for a moment after all . . . and all for me, Morgan Patrice Bayley.

Staring at myself in the bathroom mirror again, I grabbed the wall phone. As if they had a mind of their own, my steady fingers entered Tyra's number by touch.

Determination prompted me to say, "I'm in."

"In?" she asked. "In what?"

"I'm ready for what we talked about. Please make it happen."

"Are you sure?" The sound of muffled voices could be heard.

I did not skip a beat. "I'm sure. Please do it right away. Are you alone?"

"No," she replied with a combination of reserve and elation. "I'll call tomorrow morning before you change your mind."

"Good night. Sorry to interrupt. And thanks."

"Night." Her voice smiled.

I exited the bathroom to lie down. Jabril walked past the bedroom door slowly. His eyes found me. I expected him to ask who I was talking to. But he didn't. He broke his stare and walked back toward my office and closed the door. I got up and closed my bedroom door too. *So, I need to know my place, huh? I should be glad, huh? Okay. Now it's time to make it happen. Now it's time for you and everyone else to look at me and refer to me as beautiful.*

CHAPTER 5

Those low-waist jeans always make the crack of my rear appear to play peekaboo. When you have to bend your knees to put on your jeans, they say that's a sign of draggin' some serious wagon. I tossed clothes from my closet like I was digging dirt from a ditch. I just couldn't seem to find the right outfit to wear to my meeting. I looked at myself in the mirror, and realized it wasn't so much the outfits as it was me. I'd gotten used to the fact that what could really make me look better from the neck down did nothing from the neck up.

My meeting was at a local coffeehouse with an investor. Sometimes I wear a nice pair of jeans and a casual tee with a blazer. But in order to wear the Brazilian jeans that Corliss talked me into buying, I'd need to keep my blazer on the entire time. Maybe they weren't made for the nearly forty sisters.

Jabril left last night without saying a word. He never even bothered to come in and say he was leaving. But wherever he had to go was obviously more important than staying with me, I supposed. He really needed to . . . "Hello," I said as soon as my cell rang.

"Hey, baby. Good morning." Speaking of the devil.

My voice was low-key. "Good morning, Jabril."

He sounded serious. "I've been thinking about you all night. I didn't get a lick of sleep."

"I see."

"Morgan, I want you to understand something."

"What's that?" I asked as I parked and exited the car.

"I have to admit that I was probably in a bad mood last night before dinner because I got this phone call."

"From who?" A lady opened her car door and it grazed my driver's side door. I looked at her and she actually had the nerve to give me the finger. *What the—?* I forced a burst of air through my mouth that blew upward, gusting through my bangs.

"The call was from my agent. I didn't get that gig I wanted with the car company after all. The truth is I was on hold for it and they hired someone else."

I felt a tad bit of pity but continued to sound bland. "I'm sorry. Why didn't you tell me?"

"I just didn't want to talk about it. It felt like I'd failed after I told you I'd booked it."

"I would have understood, Jabril. I know how that business is." A man let the coffeehouse door close right in my face. I opened it myself with extra muscle. *What a mean world we live in.*

"I know, but I think it was in the back of my mind all night. That's why I was so on edge with Corliss, and with you. I'm sorry."

"No problem, Jabril. I understand."

His energy level seemed to switch into fifth gear. "I'll have to apologize to your dad later on. How about if we go out tonight? We haven't been out to dinner and a movie in the longest time."

"I'd like that." I replied, almost automatically, while filing in behind the ten-deep line of fellow caffeine addicts.

"See you around eight o'clock."

"See you then."

"I love you," he exclaimed.

"Love you too." *Why do I let him do that?*

A conservative-type man walked in, looking around, looking lost. He wore a dark golf shirt and dress pants. We were both wearing sunglasses, even inside of the coffeehouse. His hair was graying at the temples, and he was slightly overweight, but tall enough to pull it off. He stood behind me. "Hello, are you Mr. Watson?"

"Why yes."

"I'm Morgan Bayley." I extended my hand.

"Nice to meet you." His shake was dead-fish weak.

Why was I getting a cold Clint Eastwood stare? He got in line behind me. I took the lead on all conversation. "So, did you have trouble finding this place?"

He responded while scrolling through his Blackberry. "No. I've been here before."

"I see. It's a hot one today, huh?" I asked, glancing out of the window.

"Yes, it is," he said nonchalantly.

"How long have you owned The Watson Corporation?" I inquired.

"Oh, about ten years." He still looked down.

"That's great. I've heard a lot about you and your company. You have a great reputation."

"Thanks." He watched a young, attractive lady walk by with coffee in hand.

"I appreciate you taking the time to meet with me."

"You know, I'll be right over here at this table. I already had my morning coffee at home."

"Okay, I'll be just a second."

Within minutes, I paid for my venti white chocolate mocha and took a seat across from him, making sure to remove my shades before I sat down.

"So, Mr. Watson, I want you to know that our organization has been extremely supportive of programs for the homeless and for AIDS victims. Being associated with SCRP will indeed reflect well for you as an active supporter of humanitarian-rights issues." I couldn't see his eyes though his dark Aviator lenses.

"I'm sure it would, Ms. Bayley, however, five million dollars exceeds my single-charity limitation. Actually, I rarely invest more than six figures."

Cautiously, I sipped on my fire-hot brew before I spoke. "I understand. This is an investment, as you said, and not a donation. You will see your dollars multiply and you will be helping others with your generosity. We invest your dollars into real estate in areas where your equity will grow."

"How will I know there will be any equity after, let's say, five years? That's not something you can guarantee." He glanced down at his phone as it rang. Surprisingly, he didn't answer it.

My fingers completely embraced the coffee cup, absorbing the welcomed heat. "Then we can place a time limit on your loan so that you receive a percentage after that period of time, with an option to return your monies."

"I would not want my funds mixed with others though. That's something that my accountant warned me against."

"Oh no, we would never do that," I assured him.

Suddenly, the female worker walked by to clean off a table next to ours. Mr. Watson finally took off his sunglasses and his attention totally shifted to her lower body, somewhere around her leg area. Actually, straight up the back of her thighs as she leaned over the next table.

In an attempt to regain his attention, I spoke again. "Mr. Watson?"

"Ahh, yes." He returned to the present. "Well, Ms. Bayley, let me think about it and see what I can come up with. I'll talk it over with my financial person and get back to you. Is that okay?" He stood up and shook out his pants leg.

"That's just fine," I replied after taking another sip.

"Well, I must get going now."

"I'll stay for just a second. I need to go over some papers before my next meeting. I'll give you a call, say next week?" I asked.

He stepped away while he spoke. "I'll call you soon and we'll talk. Thanks so much and you take care."

"You too." Not even an exiting handshake.

I bet if I had taken off my blazer and went to the counter in my skintight stretch jeans to lean over and grab a couple of packs of raw sugar, he would have been willing to stay longer and talk about it. I've always said I'd be damned if I'd resort to the casting-couch scenarios where you get more bees with honey than water. Well, my water was about to get a lot sweeter. I'd had it with the blank looks at my face yet in their eyes I could see their thoughts spiraling around as they wondered how they could be talking to a woman who sounded so sweet and tender over the phone, yet had a face only a mother could love. I continued reviewing my files at my office away from my office.

Before I could even get onto the main street after pulling out of the parking lot, my cell rang. Sometimes I wished they'd never invented cell phones. The ignore button had to be the greatest feature on the darn thing. But this time, I smiled at the caller ID.

"Hi, Mom. Where are you?" Corliss sounded brand-new.

"Just getting ready for another meeting before I head home."

"You're never in the office anymore." I heard someone talking. "I'll be right there," Corliss said to her.

"This was part of my new deal. Ninety percent of the time I'm in the field and I work from home. Are you having a busy day?"

"Marcus Coles just called. He's coming in this Friday."

"And?"

"And I think you need to come in for that new skin treatment you wanted."

I was not surprised at her. She was persistent if nothing else. "I don't need to come in for that so soon. I just had one not long ago."

"Mom, please? I think I'll die if you stay with that poor excuse for a man another day. Jabril is like a caveman, just dragging you by the hair."

"Hardly. But I am sorry about last night, baby girl."

"Mom, he's so damned opinionated."

"I know."

"How do you stand it?" Corliss asked, sounding like she could just puke.

"He has his good qualities too."

"Anyway. I think you need to take me to lunch on Friday. How about it?" she asked.

"Oh, okay, that sounds nice. But I'll meet you out somewhere. I'm not coming up to your office, Corliss. No funny business. Just lunch."

"Just lunch."

"It's a date," I told her.

"I'll talk to you later on."

"'Bye, sweetheart." I turned on the jazz station and tapped my fingers as I cruised down the freeway.

Walking in through the door that led from the garage to the kitchen, I noticed Dad sitting on the sofa, channel surfing. He was sipping Coors from the can. "Hey, Dad. How was your day?"

"It was quiet. That man of yours called to apologize to me for him getting all in your face last night. I told him he needed to apologize to you."

I placed my purse and keys on the kitchen table. "He did."

Dad put down his beer and eyed me. "Morgan, I don't know about him. He's starting to worry me. He's like a bomb waiting to go off. What in the hell is he going through that's making him so uptight?"

I left my spiked pumps by the back door. The coldness of the tile floor greeted my feet but the coolness was welcome. I needed to be welcomed by something, or someone. "Nothing other than regular actor's ups and downs. He'll be fine."

"Just don't you think I don't hear you two around here some-times when he decides he's unhappy about something. Most of the time I stay out of it but last night was just ridiculous. I know you can handle yourself, and this is your house, but sometimes I'm glad I'm here."

And that felt welcoming too. "Why is that?"

"I just need to keep an eye out for you, that's all."

With an internal grin, I sat on the arm of the sofa. "Dad, I'm fine." I patted him on his back and he momentarily flashed half of his teeth. "Listen, can you believe that Corliss wants to introduce me to someone? One of her patients."

"Oh Lord." He sat back and crossed his ankle over his knee.

"Oh Lord, what?"

"Your own daughter is trying to play matchmaker."

"I told her not to."

He thought for a minute. "Well, I guess I can't say that I blame her considering how she feels about Jabril. But I don't think it's such a good idea. Just make sure you close one door before opening another. As bad as Jabril might be, you're with him for a reason and until you decide to break it off with him, you need to live up to your commitment with him as his lady. After all these years, you two owe each other at least that much. And cut out all of that arguing. Life is too short for that madness."

"I agree, Dad."

He sounded like he was speaking from raw experience. "Good. Now I'm all for you doing what you need to do to make sure a man is treating you right. But don't play with a man's emotions. Men love hard you know, contrary to popular belief. No man wants to see another man with his lady."

"And no woman wants to see another woman with her man either. Dad, Jabril is chatting online with other women and I just don't think it's right."

"I don't know about all of this chatting and this high-tech stuff. But think about it, where is he every night? With you. If he wanted to be with them, he'd break it off with you and be out there. And you seem to be giving him all of your time too. That's a great thing. All of this creeping on folks to be with other people only leads to broken hearts and unhappy endings."

I gave him a love tap on his leg and stood up. "I know. Thanks, Dad. I appreciate your feedback and advice."

"No problem. By the way, Tyra just called. Said she couldn't reach you on your cell for some reason. She sounded pretty excited so give her a call."

"I will."

"What are you doing tonight?" he asked.

"Jabril is taking me out to dinner."

He picked up his beer and the remote. "Smart man. You two lovebirds enjoy yourselves. I'm going over to Sierra's house."

I headed toward the stairwell. "Sierra. I haven't heard you talk about her in about six months."

"Yeah, well she called yesterday and asked me to come by so we can talk. I said, hey, why not?"

"Good. You two lovebirds enjoy yourselves too."

"I'll be back late so don't wait up," he advised me.

I yelled back toward him. "I won't."

"Tyra, what's up?" I asked as I held the phone to my chin while running the bath water, preparing for a luxurious escape.

"Oh, Morgan. There you are. I need to talk to you. By the way, that foolish dude I decided to kick it with was over the other night when you called and he had the nerve to wait until I was ready to make love, climbed on top of me, and then this Negro grinded his way into busting a nut. It was all over my stomach. I heard of waxing that ass, but waxing that stomach?"

I laughed inside. That's so Tyra.

"And that was just from grinding. I don't remember him being the one-minute man before." She then spoke away from the phone. "I'll have a bacon ranch salad and a plain hamburger."

"Plain hamburger?" I asked.

"I just can't handle salads alone. I need me some meat, girl, and I don't mean chicken. Thanks." She then spoke with a whisper. "Anyway, I gave him head and he got ready again. But he put on his rubber and came again within five minutes. No foreplay, no getting me lubricated, no kissing, no nothing. Just dry-walling me with his big stuff. I mean no oral on his part whatsoever. These guys are tripping big time out here. Now I know why I'd stopped seeing him before."

I added more bubble bath under the flow of the faucet. "Tyra, wow. He must have been really excited to see you if he came that fast. You need to talk to him about that."

"I did. I asked him what the hell was up. He said, 'What? I'll get it up again,' and then he commenced to snoring. My goodness, how selfish can you be? Plus he's young."

"I'm sorry about that."

"There's nothing worse than a man who can't hold out long enough to give a woman pleasure. Damn bastard. I need me an older man, like sixty, to put me first and take his time. They make foreplay, eight-play, so I've heard. They make sure they stop them-selves just before they come so they can go down on you again. Now that's a real man there."

"Yeah, but then the old buzzard would need Viagra to get it up."

She spoke louder. "I'd rather have that than the three-second man. And the funny thing is, when he first came in the door, he asked if he could take a shower. I heard the sound of the water, and he sang along with the oldies station on my radio. An old Bloodstone cut. And then he shaved in the mirror and all I could smell was his Cool Water cologne, consuming the walls of my bathroom. It had been a long time since I felt that way. I lit lilac candles and lavender incense and put mango cocoa butter all over my body and baby oil on my bareness. All that like we were headed to Love's Paradise. And then five minutes later, he was apologizing. I need to find me a man."

"Sounds like you do."

"Oh I'm sure you don't have that problem, what with Lover Brotha' Jabril and all. Can I get extra ranch dressing, please?" she asked the drive-thru person. "You know, I felt like a whore. He ac-tually left me a few hundred dollars on my dining room table when he left."

"What? What was up with that?" I didn't know how she stayed in such great shape with extra ranch.

"I think he left the cash because we were talking about me pay-ing my car note in person because it was late. I guess he felt guilty for his poor performance. He's not getting back in my place, money or not."

"But you spent it, right?"

"Yeah, but I'm tired of that. Remember when I was dating fine-ass Cedric Roberts with the LA Dodgers and he used to place an envelope under my pillow for me to pay my rent?"

"I sure do. He was taking good care of you."

"That always made me feel so cheap though, Morgan. I'm older now and I'm making my own money. When am I going to find a man who can bring his own to the table, who can please me in bed, and who's faithful?"

I did a bath-water temperature check and added more hot water. "Well, after all, Cedric was a major playboy."

"Major. That money was supposed to keep me quiet and give me incentive to put up with his crap."

"Yeah, but that only lasted about, what . . . six months?"

"Yeah, I had to kill that noise. But he could throw down in bed though."

"I remember."

"But that's not why I wanted to talk to you. Girl, I talked to Toni Mack at the radio station and they are thrilled. They'll be calling you to set everything up, but they'll want you to come in next week to talk about it."

"Next week?"

"Yes. And they've scheduled the surgery with the doctor for next month, on the third."

"Tyra, come on now, that's my birthday. You know that."

I could hear the loud snap of her fingers. "Oh, hell, I forgot. They made it seem as though the doctor sees patients overseas and in Los Angeles. I guess his schedule is pretty tight. That's the only day he's offered them for his services." She took a breath. "Actually, if you think about it, that's a great thing that it's been scheduled for your birthday. I think it's meant to be."

"Meant to be, huh?"

"Meant to be."

I turned off the bath water and swirled my fingers along the fragrant tea rose bubbles. "Well, if I'm going to do this I might as well shed this skin and get on out there, ready to talk about it and ready to open myself up for a blessing."

"Have you told anyone?"

"Not yet. I was waiting for you to confirm."

"Well, consider it confirmed. I think you need to get the word out amongst those who are closest to you. And damn what that Jabril says. You need to stay focused on the fact that you are doing it for yourself. Your dream is about to come true. Dammit, they didn't put pickles, or catsup or anything on this burger."

"Excuse me, but you did ask for a plain burger. That's what you got." I could hear the bath water calling me.

"Those chumps."

Dimming the lights, I slowly stepped into the Roman heavenly tub. "Tyra, you got what you asked for."

"And so have you, girl. Congratulations. By next month, Morgan will have had the makeover of her life. Love you," Tyra exclaimed while she smacked the sound of a kiss.

"Love you. 'Bye. And thanks." I disconnected the phone, sat back against the inflated bath pillow and surrendered, closed my eyes, and forced long, deep cleansing breaths. *The makeover of my life, huh?*

CHAPTER 6

Jabril stood at my front door. "You look great, Cookie. That's my favorite dress." I knew that. It was a simple, black, knee-length number.

"Thanks. You look handsome yourself." He wore a bulky brown sweater and brown cords with his tan suede Timberlands.

"I thought we'd go to Crustaceans for dinner, and then to see the second showing of a play over at the Wiltern Theatre, called *My Lady, My Lover*." He held open the car door.

"Oh, that sounds like fun. I heard it's pretty good." He loved watching his fellow actors do their thing live onstage.

He was blasting his new Brian McKnight CD while he placed his hand on my knee as we interlocked fingers. Automatically, we always held hands when he drove. Before I knew it, he had pulled up to the valet at the restaurant.

We followed the hostess to our table. I love that restaurant because they had a magnificent fish aquarium under the floor, so you walk on thick, beveled glass while the royal blue and vivid orange tropical fish dart about under your feet. It is such a trip.

The restaurant was crowded and trendy-looking. Along the way, I spied a table of four gorgeous ladies who glanced our way. Or should I say they were glancing Jabril's way? He was walking behind me as usual, which kind of bugged me. I could never see what he was doing back there. Sometimes I wanted him to lead the way, holding my hand until we reached our destination, but he always said, "Ladies first." I turned for a second to try to catch his facial expression, and I saw him coming out of a big smile in the direction of the ladies. I turned back toward the hostess and stopped at our table.

Jabril pulled out my chair as I took my seat. Facing the ladies who were still giving him attention, I continued to look over until they finally decided to focus on each other and not my man. I can't say that I blamed them, but I did hope that one day he'd have to deal with men staring at me in that way.

He took his seat and the waitress handed us the menus. Another waiter brought us two glasses of ice-cold water with lemon. All I could think about was telling him what I'd done. That I was about to have a dream come true . . . a new face, a new look, and a new lease on life.

Jabril spoke while perusing the drink menu. "Where was your dad? I noticed his car was gone."

"He's over Sierra Jacob's house. You know, the lady he met a couple of years ago but had a hard time getting close to."

"I remember her. Actually, she's the only one I remember."

"She's the only one period. Other than her, Dad hasn't dated anyone since Mom died." I sipped my water.

"Sierra really liked him from what I remember."

"She did. But she let him go because he said he had so many demons to deal with. I don't blame her. He just wasn't ready. Mom was still all up in his head after all those years."

"I guess it's long overdue for him to settle down, Cookie. Twenty plus years is long enough."

The young, pretty waitress approached. She smiled as she spoke to Jabril. "Can I get something to drink for you both?"

"I'll have a 7 UP and she'll have a Cosmopolitan."

I gave an approving nod, but actually wanted an Apple Martini. Jabril thought he knew me so well. He thought I was predictable and safe and easygoing. He was about to friggin' flip.

The waitress replied after she wrote on her pad, "Yes, sir. I'll be back for your order in a minute."

"Thanks." Jabril closed and placed the dinner menu on the table and turned his focus back to me. "So, what else is going on?"

I crossed my arms along the table. "Not much."

"Are you hungry?"

"Kind of." I perused the room.

He tilted his head to the side. "Morgan, what's up with you?"

"Why do you ask?"

He studied my expression. "I know you."

"I'm just looking forward to our fabulous night out together. I love this place." I continued to look around the room.

Jabril was persistent. "Good. Nothing else is going on, right?"

Picking up my menu, I pointed toward the seafood section. "No, just trying to figure out what to eat. This looks good."

"How about if I get you the shrimp scampi you like?"

He did actually take the words right out of my mouth. "That would be good. I'll have that."

"And I'll have the Porterhouse steak." He never even needed to read his menu. He knew what he wanted.

Within the hour, we were done. He escorted me out of the restaurant, again walking behind me the whole time. We stood outside as he gave the valet the ticket. I looked to my right as Jabril hugged me and saw one of the valet guys staring at me. When he caught on that my eyes were focused upon him, he quickly looked away. He gave an elbow to his buddy, who gazed over toward us too, and then he looked down. The two of them sneered until a man walked up handing them his ticket. What in the hell was that? It felt like I was back in junior high school. The only difference was, some adults have learned to not say anything. But the looks I'd get every now and then spoke volumes.

As we entered the packed theater after purchasing tickets for the play, Jabril followed me to our seats. He decided to head to the bathroom so he excused himself. I watched him walk away. I was really so proud of him for planning this evening to show his love for me. I just couldn't seem to bring myself to tell him about the major reconstructive surgery I was about to embark upon. The words just wouldn't come out.

After the play, we arrived back home and before I knew it, Jabril went upstairs. He put on a Take Six CD, lit some lavender candles, and began to run my bath water, even though I'd already had one. He called me into the bathroom and stood directly in front of me, pulling my dress over my head and stripping me down to my birthday suit. He picked me up and actually carried me to the tub, placing my bare body down into the warm, sudsy water.

He used a dab of my lemon body wash and began to rub me down with a large loofah sponge, starting with my neck and moving down to my chest. He massaged my hard nipples with his fingertips. He kissed my neck as I lay back, and then he lowered his hand deep into the water, finding my opening and inserting his index and middle fingers gently inside, allowing the water to enter and rinse me at the same time. He continued to give me a finger ride that sent my head spinning as though I'd downed a full bottle of wine all by myself. He moved down to my legs and rubbed his hands over my thighs, knees, and down to my feet.

He stopped for a moment, leaned his face down to mine and kissed my nose. He kissed the bridge of it, the tip of it, the side of it, licked around my nostrils, and even rubbed his nose to mine, kind of like an Eskimo kiss. He proceeded down to my mouth, smacking his full lips to mine and giving me his tongue for my tongue to dance with.

Jabril brought me to a standing position, escorted me out of the tub, and patted me down from the knees up with an ebony-colored towel. Suddenly, he bent my left knee and placed my foot along the side of the tub. Jabril knelt down and leaned into my middle section. He pointed his tongue to lick my peak, and then he slipped his tongue along the side of my lips. I closed my eyes and took in this pleasure, feeling myself becoming hotter and hotter, and wetter and wetter with each flick. Jabril stood up and again picked me up, carrying me to the bed. He spread my legs to finish the job. I screamed his name while he gave me his moustache again. I released all of my juices and he gently kissed my throbbing split as he backed away.

He came up to mount me, now naked as well, and entered me slowly. "It's always been so damned tight," he said upon taking over my insides. I gasped. It felt so good and so right. No matter what, Jabril inside of me was like magic. Nothing else mattered. Maybe it was the Scorpio–Pisces connection, but horizontally, we fit like a glove. Vertically, it was another story. We reached our point together and he whispered in my ear, "You're my lady, and I am your man, no matter what. That will never change." He kissed me. I kissed him back.

He rolled off of me while I lay flat on my back. We lay side by side in silence from the afterglow.

A good orgasm always sent Jabril into deep-sleep mode. Tonight was no exception. But he usually woke up very early in the morning trying to get in another round. With all my heart I wanted to tell him. But I just couldn't ruin the moment. And so, silence rocked us to sleep.

Sure enough, by nearly four o'clock, I felt a hand on my hip. I was half-awake anyway. He slowly rubbed my butt cheek, and then gently pulled me from side to back. That meant he wanted to go down under the covers. He climbed over on top of me.

"Jabril, I'm getting plastic surgery on my fortieth birthday next month." I held my breath.

He immediately scooted off of me and lay on his back. He turned his head toward me. His eyebrows dipped. "What did you say?" Jabril took the remote and turned on the television for some room light. I was just fine telling him in the dark. He clicked the mute button.

"I said I'm going to have surgery next month. Surgery on my face."

Jabril sat up. "Surgery to do what?"

"To reconstruct my nose."

Immediately, he sprang to his feet. "Cookie! No way, I do not believe you're serious."

I still lay flat, looking up at him as he stood over the bed. "I'm very serious."

His tone reeked of anger. "Why would you go and do something like that?"

Suddenly, I remembered that Dad was gone and Jabril and I were home alone. *Oh God, please don't let this man start trippin' out.* "Because I've been living behind this huge dang beak my whole life," I said while pointing to my nose. "I'm tired of being judged by my face as opposed to what's inside."

"So you want to be judged by your face instead of your heart? You want to be accepted for your looks?"

Turning to my side, I rested my head upon my hand. "I knew you wouldn't get it."

He took heavy steps toward the window and then back. "I think you're just trying to get back at me for chatting online, that's what I think. And I knew you had something on your mind last night, but surely not some bullshit like this. And you didn't even have the decency or courtesy to discuss it with me first. You just throw it on out there right before we make love? Cookie, come on now."

"Jabril, the decision has been made and I'm going ahead with it." I sat up in bed, bringing the covers up over my chest and hugging my torso.

"No, you are not!" His expression communicated his firmness.

My eyes flashed a stop sign. "Jabril."

"Cookie, you're not."

"Jabril, yes I am."

Jabril paced a trail from the bed to the bathroom door, rubbing his head as he looked back at me. He pointed my way. "You are not going to do this, Cookie. You were born with exactly what God intended for you to have. Your parents accepted you as you are, just as everyone who loves you has accepted you too."

"Maybe I just haven't accepted myself." My sweaty hands choked the covers.

"Well you need to. And maybe that's not something that cosmetic surgery will teach you. You're a smart woman. When you look in the mirror, you see what you believe yourself to be. That's what you need to work on. A nip and a tuck will not give you self-esteem." He started walking back toward my side of the bed, naked as can be, with his member hanging soft and low.

"But it will give me a chance to be seen as someone aside from my nose, distracting them from their initial approach to me. You don't know what it's like, Jabril. You stand here with your perfect face and hot physique. How can you judge me when I've lived with the taunting and stares my entire life?"

"Forget those people. What really matters is what's inside of you and the people who love you, Cookie. Like your father, your sister, your daughter, your friends, and me. What you seek you can only find within, not on the outside."

"My insides are fine. I want my outsides to match up. It's not rocket science, Jabril. You're making entirely too much out of this. These procedures are very common."

He pointed his finger in my face. "Cookie, I forbid you from doing this."

"You cannot forbid me. I am not your property or your child." I clenched my jaw and waited.

He turned his ear my way. "What did you say?"

"I said, I am not your child, Jabril. I'm a grown woman who has made a decision for my own good. I do not need your permission."

Jabril continued to stand over me, looking down with fire in his eyes, blood rushing to his cheeks and a slight shakiness to his hands. He spoke in a lower range. "If you get this surgery . . ."

Sitting back so that my butt was against the headboard, I braced myself. "If I get this surgery, what?"

"We're through."

I expected that. I couldn't even act surprised. "It has already been set up through a radio station. Tyra arranged it. I won this contest after they saw my pathetic picture, and they voted for me: the lady with the big-ass nose. You might want to stick around for this."

"Stand up and look at me." Jabril yanked the covers off of me and grabbed my arms. He pulled me to my feet. I stood in front of him in all of my nakedness. My eyes expanded as they met his. "A few hours ago, I made love to you. I love you just the way you are. I'm begging you not to have some stranger cutting on you. This nose, this is the nose that you were born with. You wake up every day with the nose God gave you. I cannot imagine you without the nose that makes you so unique. I don't want to look into your face and see another nose, and I surely don't need large breasts to make me love you more so don't even go there. You know how I feel. People who get nose jobs need psychological counseling more than anything. So get it right. After all, have you ever wondered why they call it *plastic* surgery? So you want to look like those women you see in Hollywood? And don't kid yourself. You're not doing this for me. You're doing it for yourself."

He still held my upper arms as I spoke. I looked up at him, speaking more with my eyes than my words. "Well it's about time I did something for me and me only."

"Morgan." Oh no. He called me Morgan. He started to squeeze my arms tighter. "No, you are not going to do this. Now later today we are going to call and cancel."

"No, I am not. Now let go of me." I backed away but his hold was too tight.

"Do you want to lose me?"

"Better than losing myself."

Jabril shoved me back onto the bed and leaned over me as I scooted my legs upward into a fetal position. "Morgan, you'd better . . ." He stood up straight and shook his hands over his head. "I'm gone. Good-bye."

He rummaged around to find his clothes and immediately ran downstairs. All I could hear was the slam of the door, and then his car screeching off down my street.

Lying in the same spot he shoved me into, my mind was going 300 miles an hour. Had I lost the one man who loved me as I was? Would I ever meet anyone again who would accept me with all of my flaws? I could not help but repeatedly glance over at the phone. Would he call to say he understood, or to say he was sorry, or to say he wanted to come back over and stand by me through all of this?

I could not sleep. I could not cry. I could not even feel the realness of this man walking out on me. I was numb. Just before daybreak, I got on my feet and put on my robe. I went into my office, headed straight to my desk, and logged on to my computer.

Upon logging on, I noticed an email sent to me on my AOL account by AfroConnections.com. It read, *Find the mate of your*

dreams. The one you were meant to be with could be out there.
Check it out.

Something inside of me felt guilty for logging on, but before I
knew it, I'd joined and written a profile:

> **LadyMB,** *Pisces, professional, from Los Angeles.*
> *Looking for a man to cherish me. Love to cook, love*
> *cozy dinners, watching old movies, candlelight baths*
> *and traveling. I'm looking for my soul mate. I'm 5' 5",*
> *medium build, medium brown complexion, no pets,*
> *one grown daughter, average looking with a big*
> *heart.*

Within a few minutes of my posting, I had three e-mails:

LadyMB,
You're new, welcome. My name is Bob and I'd like you to
send me a picture.

LadyMB,
Welcome to the Afro world. I'm BrotherMan. Nice profile.
Seems like we have a lot in common. Here's my picture. Can
you send me yours?

Hello, LadyMB,
I too have one daughter. And I'm a fellow Pisces. Your profile
almost matches mine word for word. When you get a minute
to look at it, I hope you decide to reply back. I'd love to get
to know you better via e-mail. My e-mail address is JayJay@
checkers.com.

His profile did read very similar—he liked to cook too, liked
old movies, walks on the beach, and traveling, and he lived in Los
Angeles. Local sounded good. He was looking for his soul mate
too.

Dear Jay Jay,
I'm impressed. I'm new at this so please be patient. You are my first. Well, it does look like we have a lot in common on paper. But how old are you? I'm 39 and you could say that I'm going through an interesting time in my life. I'd love to hear more about you.

LadyMB,
I'm so honored to be your first. You sound at ease with your reply. I want you to feel comfortable and move at a pace that you're okay with. I'm happy that we're both local. I'm the big 4-0, soon to be 41, so it looks like even our ages are the same. I was born and raised in Los Angeles and I work as a chef at a local restaurant. I'm divorced. I love art and museums and anything that is evidence of a creative mind. I'm about to send my eighteen-year-old daughter off to college. If you'd like to know anything else, please let me know. I'll be very open and honest with you. Thank you for writing me. And one day we'll have to tell each other why we were up so very early. Fate perhaps. Feel free to contact me when you see fit. If you don't mind, I will send a message your way tomorrow. Have a blessed day, and thanks for entering the world of online dating with me. You made my day!
Jay Jay.

He sure seemed nice. So that was how the whole online love thing worked. And he didn't even ask me for a picture. But then again, he didn't offer one either.

CHAPTER 7

"Today we have our Soulful Renewal Beauty Makeover contest winner, Morgan Bayley, whose best friend, Tyra Bolden, contacted us to enter her longtime friend in our contest. Tyra submitted a picture of the two of them, which you'll find on our Web site, and a letter as follows:

> *Dear Station Manager,*
>
> *This letter is written to you from my heart, which is right where you'll find my best friend in life, Morgan Bayley. We met in the fifth grade, which was nearly thirty years ago. Morgan endured years and years of teasing and torturous stares from cruel children who made fun of her at every turn. Somehow, she endured the insults and name calling and has become the most beautiful woman I know. Knowing her so well, I am aware of her pain and her internal desire to undergo a physical change as kind of a sweet revenge to those who made it their jobs to make fun of her nose. It would mean the world to me for your station to consider a woman who has made something out of herself, is a proud mother, and a beautiful lady. Please consider choosing Morgan, who always does so much for others. This is the least I can do for her."*

Having heard this letter for the first time, I was frozen in mind and body.

The female dread-wearing DJ, Toni Mack, interrupted my paralyzed state. "Morgan, did you know that your friend had done this?"

Her question spun through my head. The nagging pain from the back of my bruised arms interrupted the processing of my reply. Removing my dark sunglasses, I adjusted my headset and spoke slowly into the long microphone. "Ahh, no, I didn't. She told me after I'd already won."

"That was risky. And what was your reaction?"

I whisked my bangs down to cover my forehead, as though the listening audience could see me. "Honestly, I was shocked that she took it upon herself to do this without telling me. But knowing Tyra the way I do, she had nothing but great intentions throughout the entire process."

Toni seemed to examine my features, leaning toward me and then backing away. Perhaps she was thinking I was hard to look at. But even though I could tell she was trying to get her eyes used to my visual, she had a warmth to her face that was very comforting. "And how was it for you growing up being teased? I mean it could not have been easy."

I fidgeted with my hands and twirled my sterling-silver thumb ring. "It's been tough, but I developed a thick skin. I want kids to know that even though other kids can be cruel, you must believe in yourself and have a high level of self-love. It sounds corny but that is what got me through, that along with a lot of support from my mother."

"So then why now? Don't you think this will teach kids who are in the same situation that eventually they'll need to change themselves?"

"I'm almost forty years old and I'm way beyond living with my looks. I did not run to a plastic surgeon when I was younger because I had a mother who constantly reminded me that I was beautiful and she always encouraged me about my looks. But I've lived life far beyond what anyone could have said to me in words." My fidgeting suddenly ceased as I scooted closer to the microphone. "I've lived life watching and observing people's actions.

People can be very cruel. People do not hesitate to let you know that they find you different. I simply want an opportunity, before it's all said and done, to see how the pretty half lives. I want to see what it's like to have a nose that's less noticeable."

"And is it true that you'll also get a breast job?"

Praying that Jabril was not listening, I just put it all out there. "Yes. I had a baby when I was very young. My breasts could use some help, so this is not about size as much as it is about fullness. Feeling good about yourself and loving yourself sometimes means making changes to feel as good as you can depending upon the specific point in your life."

"But would you recommend plastic surgery to teenagers?" she asked.

"As I said, it isn't something I would have done early on, but if someone feels they really just cannot go on the way they are, I say go for it. Sometimes people can be in such turmoil, especially at an age when our peers can be extremely opinionated. We need to stop judging someone else's level of awareness and image, and support them through their insecurities so that they feel more secure in the long run."

Toni the DJ winked at me. "Well, you are a beautiful person, just as Tyra indicated, and we wish you much luck. We'll be setting you up to meet with Dr. Diamond in Beverly Hills next week for a consultation, and we'll shoot Before-and-After video, chronicling your experience. This will air on BET and we'll host an event, kind of an out party for you, so that your family and friends can see you for the first time. Congratulations, Morgan. And please know that we're behind you in your decision. We'll be seeing you again soon."

"Thank you. And thanks to everyone at KJAZZ for this gift. I could not have afforded it on my own."

"Mom, have you lost your mind?"

"No, Corliss." I secured my shades over my eyes as I approached my car.

"I had to hear this on the radio?"

Briskly turning the ignition, I put the car in gear and pulled off.

"I've wanted to tell you but I was so exhausted from telling Jabril that I just couldn't bring myself to do it again, so please be kind."

She took a cavernous breath. "Mom, I'm all for it. But I never thought you would be. That's why I asked if you'd lost it. I say hooray for you. Just be safe and make sure because there's no changing back."

Another call beeped in but I didn't even look to see who it was. "They have a psychologist who talks to you prior to the day of surgery. I still need to go in and talk to the doctor but I'm one hundred percent sure that I'm ready. I'm actually getting excited."

"I won't even ask about Jabril's reaction."

"He's pissed off, Corliss. There's no denying that. I haven't seen him since I told him."

She sounded animated. "Oh, is that all it took to get him out of your hair?"

My voice was much more low-key than hers. "I'm not happy about it but I won't beg him back."

Office phones rang in the background. "Well, you shouldn't," she replied.

"I won't. But I miss him."

"He should be the least of your problems, Mom. Look, I've gotta go. I suppose I should say congratulations, huh?"

"If you want to."

"Congratulations," she said convincingly.

"Thanks," I convincingly replied back. "See you at lunch tomorrow."

The missed call was from Olympia. She had heard the radio interview too. I owed her a call, but not right now.

Later that next week, the house was quiet again. Dad was over at Sierra's house for the umpteenth time, and Jabril was sticking to his guns with his stubborn self. I found consolation in sipping on a glass of Sauvignon Blanc while logging online.

Hello, LadyMB,
I just wanted to say hello to you, the day after you came into my life. I really like the fact that you have not been online be-

fore, going through all of the rigmarole that I've gone through. I've had a few encounters but obviously they have not panned out. I hope to be able to get to the point where you feel comfortable enough to meet. I noticed you said you were average looking, which is hard to believe, but so am I. I'm tall, with fairly light skin, my head is shaven bald because it was receding, and I'm of average build. You could say I'm nothing to write home about physically, but I am a kind-hearted, giving man who wants to find someone I can give to. I keep telling my best friend that I can be brought down by the right woman. Now that my daughter is about to fly the coop to go off to college in Arizona, more than ever I want to settle down. I hope that doesn't scare you but I want to put that out there just in case we're at opposite ends of what we desire. We don't want to waste each other's time. Well, enough of my rambling on. Please tell me about you. What's your favorite color, favorite flower, and favorite song? I won't ask for your number, I know it's too soon. You can ask me for mine when you're ready, I promise you I am not committed and not married, I'm single and available.

Jay Jay,
Wow, I'm even more impressed. I haven't checked my e-mails in a while so I apologize for not getting back right away. I feel a little guilty because in some ways, I'm not available. I'm in the middle of a standoff with my boyfriend of five years. We are at odds about a decision I've made and he's backed away. To be honest with you, I got up the nerve to do this online thing because he was doing the same thing. It's just that I never expected to run across you. ☺ My favorite color is yellow, my favorite flowers are roses, the red-and-white ones, and my favorite song is *I'm Ready* by Tevin Campbell. Whatever happened to him anyway? My father lives with me for now, my daughter is twenty-six—see, I had her when I was very young, and I work as a project director. I would rather not call each other for now, as you stated, but I'd prefer to keep going via e-mail until I find out where I'm going with my guy

who has just moonwalked. I just want to make sure. I hope you understand and that you are not turned off. But if you are, I honor your thinking.

LadyMB,
Glad I'm online. Good hearing from you. Thanks for your honesty. I wouldn't have it any other way. Take your time to work through that situation. I'm here. No stress, no pressure to talk, no pressure to do anything but chat every now and then. That much I would enjoy continuing with you. Until next time, take care, lady. And know that I look forward to getting to know more about you. That's one thing about the Internet. Nothing gets in the way of getting into each other's head. Good day!

After a long sisterly talk with Olympia, I headed toward the front door to meet Corliss for lunch at Marie Calendars. As I left the house, Dad was sitting on the living room sofa reading the daily paper.

I let out a cleansing breath. "Dad, I want you to know that I'm scheduled for a little procedure pretty soon."

He tossed the newspaper onto the coffee table. "Actually, Jabril called me trying to get me to talk you out of it. I was wondering when you were going to tell me. I just would have thought with you being older now, you would have moved past these self-image issues. I see teens and women in their twenties making major changes so that they can live their lives without having to experience so much criticism and indifference. You know Barry Manilow said bigger is better. Some things are better left alone though, Morgan."

How did I know he'd say that? "Very funny, Dad. That's such a macho statement. Men can have gray hair, bad feet, a gut and bad breath and we woman just tend to put up with it."

"You too have had someone to 'put up with it' . . . Jabril. But you're almost forty. Why now?" he asked, leaning back with his arms over the back of the couch.

Shifting my purse to my other arm, I had a question for him.

"Why not now, Dad? Honestly, when I was a teenager, I could not have seen myself—not even able to imagine what my body would look like in my twenties—having this type of surgery. But I'm old enough now to handle the consequences of my decision, if any."

"I hope so, Morgan. I support you but I just want you to be sure. There's no turning back. This is for the rest of your life."

"I know that. But do I really have your support?" I asked.

"I think you need to do what will make you happy."

My dangling car keys clanked. "This will make me happy."

He picked up the newspaper again. "Then I wish you the best."

"Do you really, Dad?"

"I do."

"That means the world to me."

"Be careful. That's all I can say." He resumed his reading, shielding his face from mine, or mine from his.

"Corliss, I'm pulling up to the restaurant. Are you on your way?"

"I'm just a few blocks away. Go ahead and get a table and I'll find you," she told me.

"Corliss, I actually met someone on the computer."

"You mean on the Internet?"

"Of course that's what I mean."

Her voice was high. "Wow, Mom, what's gotten into you?"

"I don't even know," I said as I parked.

"Save the story, I'll see you in a minute."

Before I knew it, I was escorted to my seat. My eyes bugged at the name on the display as my mobile rang. Deep down I was excited. But I still sent the call straight to voice mail. What could Jabril have possibly wanted other than to try to talk me out of my decision again?

Oh please, there was Corliss walking toward me. Suddenly, I knew I needed to kick her cute little butt.

"Mom, hello, you look so beautiful," she said, surely hoping the compliment would deter me from my desire to choke her in her designer jumpsuit.

A man with her greeted me. "Hello there."

"Hi." I replied, looking up at him from my seat. He was pretty handsome. Conservative looking, nicely dressed, with curly hair and light eyes.

"Mom, this is Marcus," she said, looking at me and then at him.

"Nice to meet you, Marcus." I extended my hand and he did as well.

"Have a seat," Corliss told him, taking a seat herself as he sat across from us. She secured her purse next to her hip. "So, Mom, Marcus is one of my patients, I think I told you about him."

"Yes, you did."

Marcus asked me, "Corliss talked you into coming over here for this lunch meeting, huh?"

I shook my head yes. "She's pretty convincing."

He gave her a look. "Yes, she is."

Oh what the heck, I decided to try to make conversation. "Corliss tells me you live in Emerald Bay near Playa Del Rey."

"Yes, I live on Copper Lane," he replied.

Corliss interjected, "Nice area." Things were dead quiet for a few never-ending seconds. "My mother works for an organization that helps people. She has a big heart like that." That was my little matchmaker daughter.

Marcus's eyes locked onto her while speaking to me. "So how did you end up raising such a remarkable daughter?"

I replied, "Yes, she's quite a young woman."

"Yes, she is." He didn't blink.

"My mother is the best mother in the world. She's my role model, that's for sure."

"Uh-huh," he replied, looking all up into Corliss's very being.

The silence was loud. "Well, let's order, shall we?"

Corliss replied, "Let's."

After a lot of small talk, a few entrees, and a couple of laughs, Marcus excused himself. "Unfortunately, ladies, I have to get back to the office." He took three twenties and a ten out of his wallet and placed them on the table. "It was so nice meeting you, Morgan. Lunch with two beautiful women is a rare occurrence in my life. Even lunch with one lady is rare for me."

"I'm sure you have all the ladies looking you up," Corliss said, trying to give a last-ditch sell as if I needed to know he was a good catch.

He seemed to blush right into his Creole redness. "Not quite." He looked at his gold watch. "Well, I'm outta here. I think have an appointment with you next week. I'll see you then," he told my daughter.

Corliss replied, "Okay, thanks for taking care of the bill, Marcus. And thanks for coming."

"Yes, thanks, Marcus," I added.

"My pleasure. See you later, Corliss," he said, glancing back her way as he walked toward the door.

"He's about to run right into the wall if he doesn't turn around," I said, looking at him with a forced smile. "Corliss, why does he get facials so often anyway?"

"Why does anyone go?" The waiter took the bill and the money.

"He doesn't look like he needs anything done to that face."

"That's the whole point. He takes care of himself," Corliss replied, taking the last sip of her iced tea.

"Looks like he enjoys his appointments."

"Mom."

"Well, from what you tell me, he sure comes in a lot. Every week?" I asked.

"Mom, that's not the point. The question is, what do you think about him?"

"He's very handsome, I'll say that much."

"And?"

"And what? There really wasn't much else going on."

"What are you talking about? I saw him looking at you." She pulled out her lipstick and mirror from her purse.

"So did I, but it wasn't like a wow, look-at-her look. It was more of a stare after I spoke a couple of times, that's all. Mainly, he looked at you."

She spoke as she puckered her lips for a touch-up application. "Mom, you're so sensitive. Not everyone is looking at your nose. He looked at me the same way."

"Well with me, it was like he was giving me the once-over, like a third degree. With you, it was like he was hanging on your every word."

"You know how some men are. They look at nails, feet, hair, everything," she said, replacing her lipstick, and then checking out her manicure. "I need to get a fill."

"Well, he sure did look at everything. He now knows if you need a nail fill as well as how many fillings you have in the back of your mouth."

Corliss looked bored with my replies. "So you still haven't really said yea or nay."

"Nay."

"Mom."

"Corliss, first of all you are not slick. Bringing that man to lunch without telling me."

"You wouldn't have come if I did."

Grabbing my purse, I took my keys in my hand. "You're right. Corliss, I'm not interested, honey. But thanks."

She followed suit. "We'll see what he says, then you'll feel more confident."

"There just wasn't any chemistry, that's all. He seems nice."

"Okay, fine. You must be back with Jabril," she said as though she had it all figured out.

"No, I'm not." The waiter brought back the receipt and the change.

She stood up, leaving it as a tip. "Then you must be smitten by this online mystery man."

I scooted my way out of the booth and we walked to the door. "Not."

"What's his name?"

"Jay Jay," I replied.

"Jay Jay what?"

"I don't know."

"You don't know his name?" she asked.

"No, and he doesn't know mine."

A man held the door open as Corliss led the way. He looked

back at her, staring as we headed toward the parking lot. She seemed not to notice.

"Mom, you need to have someone with you when you meet him now. Be careful."

"Thanks, dear, but we're not even at that point. Yet."

"Knowing you it will never happen and Jabril will be back over tonight."

"Don't be so sure."

"Well, I've got to get back myself. I can walk you to your car," she offered.

Pointing to my car and hers, I said, "You parked right next to me. I guess you didn't notice on your way in, what with your escort and all."

"Anyway. So, Mom, are you ready for this surgery?"

"As ready as I'll ever be."

We both stood by our car doors, pressing the buttons to our remotes. "Will you call me as soon as you meet with the doctor?"

"I will."

"I still can't believe it. I guess I'd better get my last glimpses of you as you are while I can," she said, half-putting her right leg into the car.

"Yes, you should because a change is gonna come."

"For the better, right?"

"Of course!" I replied as we shut our doors and pulled off. She looked good in that silver Volvo.

CHAPTER 8

My mom used to doodle like mad. She'd grab a sheet of paper and pen and squiggle these designs—symmetrical shapes and intersecting squares, circles, triangles and diamonds, with flowers, hearts and arrows. Usually she'd go into doodle mode when she'd talk on the phone or when she'd be in deep, silent, reflective thought.

"Mommy, will you teach me how to do that?" I asked at the tender age of eight.

Mom smelled good every day of her life, like a breath of fresh morning air. "Morgan, you need to put your energy into learning a lot of other things as opposed to perfecting my scribble."

Standing next to where she sat, I peered over her slender shoulder. "But, Mommy, it's beautiful."

"No, baby. You are. Here, how about this?"

And she drew this perfect face with the biggest eyes, longest lashes, most luscious lips and wonderful nose I'd ever seen.

"Who's that, Mommy?" I asked.

"That's you. You're picture-perfect." She giggled.

I sort of frowned. "But it doesn't look like me."

"It does to me. Beauty is in the eye of the beholder, you know." She held it away and examined it again. "Yes, it's you all right."

My heart sped up. "Can I have it?"

She tore the page from the notebook. "Here, baby. Remember, beauty's only skin deep. Now get to practicing from your workbooks."

"I will. Thanks."

Skipping away, you'd have thought I picked the winning lottery ticket. I taped the picture over my dresser mirror until the day I moved into my own place with Corliss.

Today, I spied the masterpiece where it hung over my fireplace with a pale peach-colored mat and gold-speckled frame. Whenever I had doubts about life, when I missed my mom, or felt alone, I'd gaze at it and all was well in the world. Today I felt alone and had doubts, but for the first time, the gazing was not working.

I wanted to cancel my appointment. But I couldn't. I couldn't afford to not experience what it would be like to really look the way my mom saw me. I didn't want to have any regrets about what my life would be like if I didn't go ahead and have the surgery. I'd known for forty years what it was like to live with this face. I decided to take my chances and find out what it would be like to live without it. I just hoped I wouldn't regret it.

My consultation appointment was at two in the afternoon. The renowned plastic surgeon Dr. Daniel Diamond had a beautiful, ritzy-looking office decorated in onyx and light brown. All along the walls there were smiling faces of beautiful people of all races—looking as if they didn't have a care in the world, enjoying their new . . . whatevers. And smack dab in the middle of one wall, in big, bold letters a sign read, "A tent without a strong frame is weak and poorly shaped, likewise the face." *Oh, so now I'm a tent,* I thought.

"May I help you?" asked the stunning Asian receptionist.

"My name is Morgan Bayley. I'm here for a preconsult."

Her face beamed. "Oh, you're the winner of the radio makeover contest, right?"

"That's right."

"Wow, how cool is that? I listen to that station all the time. We've never participated in anything like this before."

I leaned into the tiny window. "I'll bet a lot of business is coming your way from this type of promotional event."

She gathered a few papers and placed them onto a clipboard. "Yes, there've been quite a few more calls lately than usual. But a lot of listeners can't afford the services we offer. I couldn't have either if I didn't work here. It's just one of the perks," she replied with her wrinkle-free forehead and thick lips.

"Oh yes, I wanted to ask, is Dr. Diamond a member of the American Board of Plastic Surgery?"

"Why, yes, he is." She pointed to a seal affixed to the window.

Glancing over, I felt pleased. "Good. Thanks."

"So, Ms. Bayley, just fill out this patient-information sheet and health-history form, and I'll get with you right away."

"Will do. Thanks," I replied as I took the clipboard and sat down.

A wealthy-looking, blonde, classy white lady was already seated. She made a point to look away from the *Elle* magazine while she watched my every move as I sat across from her.

"Radio contest, huh?" she asked. She read the look on my face. "I hope you don't mind my asking. I just overheard."

I looked up. "Yes." She looked good but was one step away from overdone.

"That sure is a great way to beat the cost of this type of surgery. It's pretty pricey."

"I know that's right." I replied with pen in hand.

She spoke through a pair of full, pouty lips that reminded me of Wanda on *In Living Color.* She pointed to her face. "I've already had a forehead lift, cheek and chin implants, nose job, lip injections and a facelift. I'm here today to find out about my breasts and tummy. I think I'm addicted. It's amazing how they can work wonders."

I shook my head to accompany my words. "Oh, no, I just want a couple of things and that's it."

"I tell you, it's addictive. It's like a tattoo. You get caught up in the allure of the knife. Once you have one thing done, you'll want another. When the swelling goes down and you look in the mirror, you'll wonder why you hadn't done it sooner. It has totally changed my life. My husband said he feels like he's married to a woman twenty· years younger. And wow, does it ever spice up your sex life." She raised her eyebrows, looking devilish.

"I'll bet." I tried to resume writing.

"So I guess you'll just have your nose done."

How dare she? She should have been reading her magazine instead of reading me. She was really getting on my nerves now. "Ahh, yes." I cut my eyes in slow motion.

"Oh, I'm sorry. You need to finish your paperwork. I'm just rambling on. I apologize."

"No problem." I lied.

The receptionist spoke to her. "Mrs. London, the doctor will see you now."

"Okay, thanks." She stood up, grabbing her Chanel bag, taking short steps in her spiked leather heels. "Best of luck to you now. And remember, it will totally change your life."

"Just changing my face, that's all."

"You'll see," she said, going into the office through the waiting room door.

Within minutes I completed the extensive health forms and returned the clipboard to the receptionist.

"Oh, so you want a breast job too. I can give you a serious reference. Girl, I had mine done. And I just had a baby. I can breastfeed and everything. And the good thing is they don't ever sag. Don't they look good?" She poked her chest up high, looking proud and busty.

One couldn't help but notice, what with her skintight V-neck sweater and all. "Very nice."

She stood up. "I got me a husband with these bad boys. You can come right on through that door."

I was willing to bet she had a brotha' at home, talking like that.

She handed me a gown. "Leave it open in the front, leaving on only your panties, and then have a seat on the examination table." She smiled as she exited the room.

The room was bright white and small. It was cold as all get out in there. I was freezing actually. I hate doctors' offices. The only times I've had surgery were for a hernia when I was a kid and my C-section. I hadn't been near a hospital since I had Corliss . . . other than when Mom died, that is.

"Ms. Bayley, hello. I'm Dr. Diamond." The attractive doctor entered and closed the door behind him. My goodness, I thought, he looks more like an actor than a plastic surgeon. He could have been a Big Ten quarterback in college. Dr. Diamond is a nice height. It looked like he had a nice build under that white doctor's coat. His eyes are hazel and his hair is light brown. He wears a thin mustache and faint sideburns.

"Nice to meet you."

He shook my hand and put the medical file under his arm. "Well, looks like congratulations are in order. You won out of all of the submissions the station presented to me over the past few weeks."

"You were involved in the selection process?"

"Yes, I was. And your case is classic. The classic case of a beautiful woman, with A-1 bone structure who just needs an alteration on her nose, to start with. You know our noses are the most prominent, defining feature on our faces. It's the first thing people see, other than our eyes."

"I believe that. Sometimes people don't look past it."

"I can imagine." He took a seat and scooted his stool next to me. "Well, I totally envisioned you afterwards and I think you are going to be very pleased with the results."

"I sure hope so."

"But I must ask you, what do you think needs to be done?"

"Just my nose," I told him, touching the very tip with my index finger.

He brushed my bangs to the side with his hand and glanced at my face straight on. "You have frown lines on your forehead, Morgan. You know we can get rid of those with a little Botox."

"No, I don't care about that. Just my nose. That's what's been a nightmare."

"Believe me, I want to try and give you what you want. I'm sure that your nose has affected you growing up, but I want you to be ready for how the world will perceive you after the surgery."

"I'm glad you didn't use the word reconstruction. That just sounds like you're building a skyscraper or renovating a mall."

He smiled and continued to examine my face with his eyes. "In the case of your nose we will redo the areas that are out of synch with your base bone structure by removing the hump and narrowing the bridge. We'll probably lower the tip, and you'll end up with an appealing shape that's in line with your entire face. Even the angle between the nose and upper lip is changed. We call this type of surgery rhinoplasty. It involves reshaping the external application of the nose. So, you'll need to meet with our psychologist at some point before the surgery, just to get you ready for the mental aspects of the postoperative unveiling and beyond."

"Funny, I bet I know what he or she is going to say."

"Probably so, but it's a requirement for my patients." He looked down at the file and then at my chest. "Now I notice that you're requesting a breast enhancement. I'll need to see what size you are now." He scooted over to buzz the nurse to come in and accompany him.

"I'll be right in," she said over the speakerphone.

As she walked in I opened my gown and he continued the exam. "Now, your breasts are, what—a size A?"

"Yes."

"Did you breastfeed?" He asked, lifting underneath my saggy right breast.

"Not successfully."

"I can see where a saline implant would add some roundness. There is enough skin, I'd say, for a C cup. Would that be okay with you?" The nurse handed him a sample implant. He handed it to me. "That would be about this size."

The round, pliable sack looked enormous. "It seems huge."

"It's much different when it's implanted." He pointed to my underarm. "We simply make an incision under your axilla, which is the armpit, so that there is no scaring on the nipple. We'll place it under the muscle so it will look very natural with your breast width and depth."

"Okay. What about deflation? I've heard of that happening. You know, those horror stories."

He explained. "There's a risk for that and a risk of wrinkling or puckering or hardening, but it's a very small risk. There could be decreased nipple sensation and even infection or bleeding but that happens very rarely. Let me ask you, have you ever thought about a tummy tuck?" My bloated, roadmap of a tummy stared back at him.

"Oh, no, thanks. I had a C-section when I was very young. But I'm fine with my tummy. Besides, that's nothing a few sit-ups won't fix."

While he spoke, the nurse took back the implant. "Now, Ms. Bayley, this is not costing you a penny. And it's better to think about everything you need at once so we can do it all in one surgery as opposed to coming back later. I see that happen all the time but mainly for financial reasons. I'm willing to do whatever you want me to do."

"No thanks, Doctor."

He continued running it down as though I had a list of options. "I can even add a new belly button if you'd like. I see that you had hernia surgery and the stitches below the navel are evident which makes the navel look distorted."

"That's the old banana-chip look that I'm famous for. But I still don't think so."

He crossed his arms. "So, just the nose and breasts?"

"Yes, just those two. I can live with the rest."

He walked over toward a small X-ray-type machine with a monitor. "Well, let's see your Before-and-After nose looks on our computer screen. I think this L4 type, slightly sloped image will work. Please turn to the side. Have you ever broken your nose?"

"No. You have no idea how many times I've been asked that question. Why do you ask?"

He explained. "It's just that the configuration of your nose, being tilted especially, is very unusual. Such an abnormal configuration of the cartilage can cause respiratory problems. Do you have problems with breathing or nosebleeds, headaches?"

"No."

"I consider yours to be a congenital abnormality. Do your baby pictures show that your nose was turned like this?"

"Oh yes, this has been my calling card from day one."

"I see." He faced the screen toward me and showed me the Before-and-After images.

Inhaling, I held my breath for a moment too long. Just that slight change without the hook made me look so different. And then he decreased the length. I released my breath. "Oh my goodness. That's amazing."

"I told you you're a great candidate."

My profile with the smaller nose now fit with my other features. It was unbelievable. I looked so much better, so different. "That looks perfect."

"I thought you'd say that." He put his index finger under my chin. "And Ms. Bayley, I'm going to suggest a chin implant, only to bring your receding chin forward to alter the basic underlying structure and make the face look more symmetrical. It's important for balance, proportion and definition. It'll be a noticeable aspect of your profile image and it will bring your lower face into balance with the tip of your nose. You have a slight overbite and your chin has sunken back a bit through the years. It's a simple technique that's not painful at all. We make a small insertion from inside your mouth, where the bone is approached, and the projection of the chin is altered. Afterward, a small elastic dressing is applied. The incision will barely be noticeable, but I think it will just enhance the entire facial structure as a whole. Here, take a look."

It did make a huge difference. "I suppose so." I waved my hand to signal enough. "But that's it now, no more than those three alterations."

He raised his eyebrows. "You're sure about not having the tummy done?"

"I'm sure. But thanks anyway." I closed my gown before he offered up something else.

He made notes in my file. The nurse exited the room. "This operation won't take long at all. I'll need you to take these papers and read them carefully prior to your day of surgery, which is March third, correct?"

"Yes, my birthday."

"Well, what a happy celebration of life this will be."

"You can say that again."

"And my receptionist will give you the appointment time for the consultation with the therapist. No food or water after twelve midnight the night before surgery. No vitamins, herbal medications or Tylenol-like pain reliever fourteen days prior. If you have any questions, please call me anytime." He handed me his business card. "That's about it, unless you have any questions."

"No, I don't. Well, actually one more. Will it be painful?"

"Perhaps right after the anesthesia wears off. And you might have some discomfort, but only for a few days. I'll give you medication for that. For the nose we'll apply a nasal splint and nasal packs and your face will feel puffy. You might even have a headache or two. You'll come back to remove the bandages, and then again in three weeks to monitor you once the swelling goes down and bruising goes away. And then you'll have your major unveiling a couple of months after the initial surgery. No physical contact with family until then, okay?"

Gulp. "Okay. It sounds like I'm going to be a mummy."

"I don't mean to alarm you. It really is fairly simple surgery and it goes very smoothly. You'll be so excited afterwards that a little bruising and swelling will be well worth the rewards. I guarantee you."

"Can I get that in writing?" *Wow, did I just joke?*

"Good one. Any other questions or anything else I can tell you?"

"Doctor, please. Just make me hot."

"I will do my best, Ms. Bayley. Well, I'll see you on March third. Thanks for coming in."

"Thank you."

We shook hands again just before he exited. But then he turned back for a quick second. "Ms. Bayley, I'd think about that tummy tuck if I were you."

"I'm proud of you for going through with this, Morgan," Tyra said as we sat at a little bar on Melrose Avenue for a quick celebratory drink. We used to do that all the time, but ever since I got with Jabril, I'd stopped taking the time to hang out.

"I'm proud of me too. Thank you for hooking it up."

All of a sudden, my message indicator on my cell beeped. I didn't even hear my phone ring.

"Cookie, I can't believe you haven't even called me. I'm so shocked by your decision that I can't even think straight. I keep waiting for you to tell me you've changed your mind. I wish you would. But I know you haven't. Knowing you, you'll do this just to show me that you have a mind of your own. What you don't realize is that I already know that. But, I can't be with you once you do this to yourself. I guess some men would be thrilled that their lady is getting a supposed enhancement to their face, and larger breasts, which I hear from your radio interview that that's what's up, but not me. I love you just the way you are, Cookie. I will not love you more, and I will not love you less. But I just can't look the new you in the face not knowing who I'm looking at. I just can't do it. I miss you. And I hope you change your mind. Good-bye."

Tyra read the look on my face. "That man is actually putting his feelings before yours again."

"You sure know me." I tucked the phone into my bag.

She was sipping on her usual Malibu and pineapple. "Hell, I know him. It's not even about your face, or your body or what you need. It's about control. You're going against his wishes and his ego can't handle it. And you're going to attract a whole new crew of suitors that he can't compete with. That's the main reason. He wants you all to himself because he's the one who's insecure. He needs a personality makeover."

"That's a good one." I chuckled and ordered that Apple Martini I'd been wanting.

"I say you jump on this right now as a hell of a good reason to never allow him to come back. Let him go. He asked for it. Let him live with it."

"Yeah, but I miss him too. He'll be fine once he sees me afterward."

"Believe me, you won't want him afterward. Once the Denzel types start running up on you, you'll be like, Jabril who?" she kidded.

"I don't think so. But we'll see. In the meantime you're not going to believe this. I have actually been chatting with this guy online," I finally confessed to her.

Tyra's eyes bucked. "No way."

"Way."

"No way." She shook her head as if in disbelief.

"Way."

"You! Oh my God, will wonders never cease? Is he nice?" she asked.

"He seems very nice. And he's moving nice and slow."

"What does he look like?"

I replied. "I don't know."

"No picture yet?"

"Not yet. Just a few e-mails."

A man walked up. "Can I buy you a drink?" he asked Tyra.

She didn't even look up at him. "No thanks. I'm sitting here talking to my girl if you don't mind."

"Sorry to interrupt. Just asking." The man tucked his tail between his legs and headed back to a table full of other men who surely felt his pain.

"Girl, he seemed nice. I think you've taken a man offering you a drink for granted."

The waitress brought my drink. "Sometimes they can be so obnoxious. They can at least send the waitress over so they don't interrupt."

"You'd better take a second look at him." I looked back at the dejected man as he took a seat. "He could be that older man you're looking for."

"I didn't notice. Besides, he didn't offer both of us a drink and that's rude. Anyway, like I was saying, you need to know who you're chatting with. At least make sure it's a man and not an eighty-year-old white woman. Girl, you're not even hip to online dating etiquette. That dating highway will eat you alive."

"I'm cool. It's just e-mails." I crossed my legs and took a sip.

"At least talk on the phone so you can hear his voice."

"I'm not ready for that. But I will."

"Girl, and he doesn't even know what you look like?"

"No."

"Are you going to wait—I mean until the surgery?" she asked, seeming as though I was a trip.

"I haven't thought about it. It depends on how long it is before we're ready to see each other." This time I swigged the green liquid.

"Morgan, come on. You haven't thought about it?"

"Well, maybe I have. I'll probably wait. This is the first time that my looks have not gotten in the way, so to speak."

"Girl, you enjoy every minute of chatting with your mystery man. Welcome to the new millennium." She took a final sip.

"Thanks."

She pulled a few bucks from her wallet for the bill. "Speaking of dating, I told you I didn't have much time. I'm off to meet my Internet man myself. We're meeting at Benihana restaurant."

"You're going by yourself?"

"Girl, I'm an old pro at this." She stepped off the bar stool. "I'll be fine. I'll check you later."

"I'm free if you want me to go with you."

"No, it's a public place. I'll be fine."

"Fine, Tyra, but be careful. Call and hang up if you don't like him."

"Gotcha. Ciao."

I grabbed her hand. "Tyra, thanks again for entering me in the contest."

She hugged me. "No problem. It's time you had a chance to bowl them over when you walk in the room."

"No, duh." Sitting at the small bar table, I finished my drink alone. The men in the room outnumbered the women by far. But still, not one of them made their way over to my table. Before long, I added cash to the table and proceeded to the exit. The security guard at the door looked in my direction and then stared. I wondered was he looking at it or looking at me? He smiled. I started to walk to my car and then looked back. He was now eyeing a young hottie with never-ending legs. The initial visual to men is what it must be all about.

The minutes wound into thirty. The freeway was wide open. Tyra did call. She hung up. Another one bites the dust. I thought so.

"Hello, Dad." I said as I walked into the den. This time his beer of choice was Miller Genuine Draft.

"Hey, Morgan. How did everything go with the doctor?"

"Just fine." I proceeded to the kitchen and took a cold bottle of water from the refrigerator.

"So you're going ahead with it?"

"I am."

"Okay, whatever you say. No word from Jabril?"

"Yes, he left a message. He's still not having it."

"That man needs to check himself and support you through this. I don't like that. I actually gave him more credit than that."

"Me too. How's Sierra?" I asked.

"She's fine. She wants to get back together."

"Wow. I figured as much. You two did get pretty close before, huh?"

"I guess you could say that."

I paused a moment, pulling up the spout of the bottle. "So what was your answer?"

"I haven't answered yet. She's just afraid of dying alone." He changed the television channel.

"Dying? She's not that old. But Dad, you know what they say. Life's not that important if you don't have love."

"I'm fine. For now I've got to keep an eye on you."

"And me on you. What do you want for dinner tomorrow?" I asked as I headed up to my room to get comfortable.

He gave the television his stare. "How about your hamburger steaks and mashed potatoes? Your mamma's award-winning dish."

"You're on."

"Thanks, baby."

For some reason, I stopped. "Dad, do you still miss her?"

"Now why do you want to bring that up?"

"It's okay. I know you do."

He stared straight forward. "I'm trying to watch some basket-ball here."

"Okay. But I sure miss her. I wish she was here to see what I'm about to do to myself."

"She is," he assured me. He looked my way with certainty. "She is."

CHAPTER 9

Similar to the feeling of bereavement, a nagging pang shimmied through my gut, all because of the deep sense of loss I had from actually missing Jabril's butt. But I hadn't heard a word from him. Seemed like he was on my mind constantly, from the moment I geared up to the moment I shut down. His disapproval weighed heavily on my mind, but I just couldn't continue living my life trying to please him.

The preop therapist, Dr. Holly Grace, was located on the third floor of the UCLA Medical Center. She seemed to have a laid-back presence. Her movements were slow and fluid. She had a few pale freckles and a high forehead. Her hair was pulled back into a long ponytail, no bangs. She wore stylish framed glasses. Her lips were pink and her eyes were blue. She was soft-spoken, kind of a plain-Jane-looking woman yet very feminine. She sat across the desk in her high-back chair, pen in hand. I leaned forward as I crossed my legs. She spoke first.

"Now, I want you to really think about what it is you want or expect from this surgery."

"Honestly, I expect to look less abnormal. And please don't preach to me about society's standards of normal." I leaned back and applied pressure to my palm. "I know we put those standards on ourselves. I call it institutionalized lookism. But still and all, we must live in this society with certain standards of beauty and expectations of our appearance that affect how we're treated." I squinted my eye. "There was nothing normal about how I was treated in school. People can be cruel. And no matter how strong your level of self-image is, confidence is a mixture of your own level of self, based on the level that society places on you to fit in. I have been excluded and treated differently because of my looks. Screw all of the talk about what matters is what's inside of you and what people think of you is none of your business. It is my business. If it's not mine, who else's is it? I want to wake up and have someone see my eyes, my lips, my ears, my cheeks, my neck, my hands, or my feet before they're bombarded by my nose. I want to stand in the mirror naked and see an image staring back at me that I can say is at its best. I want my saggy breasts to be firm and shapely, just like my hips and my legs. I think more people will see me on the inside if they can get past me on the outside. Maybe I'm wrong, but I'm ready." I felt a bit defensive as I spoke my last word. I grabbed hold of the arms of the chair. She really didn't deserve that barrage.

She looked at me as though she hadn't expected such a rambling, but also as though she got it, or at least I thought so. She read from my file and commented, "I see here that you have a BS in psychology."

"Yes."

"Then you know, Ms. Bayley, that all of the teasing you received from people in your life was because of their own pain. We're meaner when we don't like ourselves. They tried to tear you down to make you feel bad about yourself so that they could mask their own issues. If they'd felt good about themselves, they wouldn't have needed to put their feet on your back. And you also know that you must peel away the layers without masking the truth with an augmentation. I tell all my clients that feeling better about ourselves is a process toward becoming whole. It's about working on becoming whole, one step at a time so you can overcome your insecurities. It's a process, and you're a work in progress. It won't suddenly change for the better the morning after you become a D cup. Do you understand where I'm coming from?"

"I do. And I agree with you. But, I can't live life by the numbers anymore. This is a symbol of my ability to become a brand-new me, through and through. I see this as just one step in the entire process."

She nodded and wrote a few words. She lightly tapped her pen to her chin. "Actually, Ms. Bayley, I think you're realistic in what you expect. But I'm warning you, just be prepared to have to develop a self-assuredness afterward unlike any that you've ever had. It will be hard work." She sat up straight and jotted down a few more notes. She looked me square in the face. "I'll approve your surgery. Just sign these release papers and you'll be on your way. Good luck."

Simultaneously exhaling, smiling, and swallowing, I scooted up to sign my name as she slid the papers my way. I scribbled my Jane Hancock slowly, as though signing my life away, yet signing nonetheless. Surely it wasn't the signature of someone who was just talking so much trash. I wrote the date, March second, and thought to myself, *Today is the last day of Morgan Bayley, the girl with the big nose who boys would screw if no one was looking, the woman who makes men feel secure because no one else would want them. Tonight, that Morgan Bayley was being put to rest. Tomorrow, a new Morgan Bayley was set to be born . . . a new and more beautiful woman whose outsides would be equally yoked with her insides.* I was ready to be the best me I could be, made over and coming out of my shell after forty years, from a cocoon to a butterfly with wings.

Today, on the morning of my very own fortieth birthday, I was actually going . . . under the knife.

"I'm coming, I'm coming," I yelled to Olympia who was sitting outside in her Lexus, honking repeatedly. I dragged my large-sized, overpacked piece of luggage and put it in the backseat.

"I just wanted to make sure you didn't barricade yourself in there and I'd have to come in and get you. By the way, Happy Birthday," she said as I closed the door. We leaned in for a kiss. She was dressed casually, wearing a black velour sweat suit, but on her it looked like a million bucks.

"Thanks. I told you I wasn't going to turn back. I appreciate you taking me."

"Girl, a ride and moral support are the least I can do."

"Maybe when I'm done I'll look like you, huh?"

"Very funny. Where's Dad?" she asked, turning onto the main street.

"He's still sleeping."

"I can't believe he didn't get up to say his good-byes."

"It's okay. He was up late talking on the phone. I'm surprised you didn't wake him up the way you were leaning on that horn. Anyway, Corliss came by at the crack of dawn and Tyra called about fifty times. She's jazzed as all get out."

"That's sweet. What about your e-mail buddy? Have you told him?" she asked.

"I've heard from him, but he doesn't know."

"You're not going to tell him?"

"I will." I pulled the visor mirror down and made certain to only glance at my eyes, checking for residual sleep in the corners. I was cool.

"When?"

"While I'm recuperating."

"You did bring your laptop, right?"

"It's right here," I said, pointing toward the floorboard.

"And what about Jabril? Did you hear from him?"

I flipped the visor back up. "Next subject."

"Sorry, Sis." She did about seventy on the freeway.

"Hey girl, will you do me a favor and say a prayer? You're always so good at it."

Olympia parked in the hospital lot and turned off the ignition. She reached out for my hand. "Dear Lord, we ask that you watch over Morgan today through her surgery. Please bless and keep her and see to it that this procedure is a success. We pray for the nurses, doctors, anesthesiologists, and everyone else who's involved today. And we ask for Morgan's complete satisfaction through the unveiling and beyond. Please come into our lives and our hearts, Dear Father. We love you and we need you and we know that everything is fine. We thank you and claim her health and recovery after this successful surgery, whoever she might be after she comes out of there. AND SO IT IS, Amen."

Snatching my hand away as she giggled, not appreciating her attempt to humor me, I replied, "Ha, ha, very funny."

She patted me on the back. "Just joking. You'll be fine."

From the time we walked into the waiting room, Olympia stayed on the phone handling her catering business calls. After a few minutes, the receptionist called me in.

"I love you, Sis. Now be brave and know that everything will be all right."

"I love you too." I noticed her eyes clouding up. "I'll be fine. Now go ahead on."

"I will." Her pretty face was flushed. She tried to shield her eyes by holding me tight.

"Olympia, go," I said as I pulled away, trying to fight back the tears myself.

"Take care of her now," she yelled as they escorted me to the dressing room. The door closed in her face. "I love you" was all I heard from the other side of the door.

"She's a mess," I told the nurse, laughing.

"How are you?" the nurse asked.

"I'm fine."

"Nothing to eat since midnight, right?"

"Don't remind me. I'm starving."

Within an hour or so, I wore nothing but a nylon cap on my head and a white-and-blue, shirtlike gown. They laid me upon a gurney, strapped a blood pressure cuff on my arm, wheeled me into the sterile, cold operating room and placed me upon the operating table.

"We'll get started in just a few minutes," I heard Dr. Diamond say, putting his comforting hand on my arm.

"Okay." I never looked toward his voice. I stared straight up at the banal, clean, blank ceiling, with rows of bright, full-wattage lights.

Apprehensiveness had a hold on me. What if I just jumped up from the bed and ran right out that door? Right back to my life that really didn't seem so bad now. Would that be the smart thing to do or the coward's choice? Maybe it would be a lot easier than going forward with this multihour operation. But I could only pray that the rest of my life would be richer and more enjoyable afterward.

My toes were curling, my nipples were hard, my eyes were blinking a mile a minute, and my head was starting to pound. I could feel the veins in my temples throbbing. I was hungry. I was thirsty. I was nervous. I wanted to run. But there was nowhere to hide. I'd been hiding inside for way too long. It was time to come on out.

"Hello. My name is Winona Finley," a woman said who started to insert an IV into the back of my hand. "I'm your anesthesiologist. What I'm about to give you, which some call happy juice, will put you under fairly quickly." She flashed a smile, and then prepared to place a needle in the tube. "Take a deep breath and count backwards from ten, Ms. Bayley." Her voice was calming. And so I did, ten. And then my head started to spin, nine. The lights started to dim, eight. And I gasped, feeling an icy, painful chill stinging through my veins, seven, which made my body shake just as my head faded into complete darkness.

CHAPTER 10

"Ms. Bayley, can you hear me? Mumble if you can." Nearly seven hours later, a familiar voice was faint, sounding as though it was far, far away.

"Uh-huh." I was in extraloopy mode.

As he spoke, I felt his hand on my forearm. "It's Dr. Diamond. You're in recovery. You had your surgery and everything went super. We're going to keep an eye on you and make sure there's no rise in temperature for a few days, and of course monitor you to make sure that there's no sign of blood clots forming. There's always a chance of infection, so let us know if you're feeling an excessive amount of pain or if you have any bleeding."

"Uh-huh."

"Can you open your eyes?"

Through my supergroggy state, I obliged.

He said, "I'm going to raise you up and I want you to try and stay awake if you can, okay?"

"I'm so sleepy," was all I mumbled as he raised the head of my bed.

"I know. But please try and stay up if you can."

My head felt like I had on a helmet. And my chest felt like a dozen bricks lay upon it. I could see the edge of bandages across the bridge of my nose. I noticed the doctor suddenly walk away with my chart. My chin felt like someone had beaten it with a sledge hammer. All of a sudden, I began to shake like I was having chills. It was weird because I was not feeling cold at all. I was actually very warm. I just couldn't stop trembling from head to toe.

A nurse approached. "Here's a blanket, Ms. Bayley."

The heavy blanket did nothing to ease my case of the shivers. Maybe it was nerves, maybe a coming down from the anesthesia. But I felt like I was about to erupt.

"I hope this makes you feel better," she said, rubbing my legs and arms with her gentle hands, soothing my chills somewhat with a touch that seemed to work, if only for a little bit. "It'll be okay. You'll be just fine. Just think about what lies beneath."

Actually, that was all I could think about.

The navy- and cream-striped wallpaper of my large private hospital room was nerve-wracking. Actually, any movement was fairly nerve-wracking right about then. They wouldn't let my family up to see me. Not even Olympia.

The bouffant-wearing nurse with the flowered uniform talked just like Dolly Parton herself. "Your sister stopped by and wanted me to tell you that she left your things at the front desk. She's as cute as a button."

I had decided that I liked this lady and that was a good thing for her. I spoke a little more clearly, but still sounded groggy. And I was a little stuffed up. Even the sound of my own voice annoyed me. "Thanks. That was nice of her. No visitors, huh?"

"Not yet."

"I feel like the invisible woman all bandaged up like this."

She proceeded to check my blood pressure, looking down at her watch as she spoke. "Not for much longer. I know it's pretty darn uncomfortable."

My view of my feet was obstructed by my new, humongous chest. "And oh my God, I can see the mounds of my new breasts from here. They're huge."

"They'll go down. Everything's just swollen for now, that's all."

"They feel huge too. I guess Jabril doesn't know what he's missing."

"Who's Jabril?" She removed the cuff and took notes.

"He's my ex-boyfriend."

"Yeah, well he'll miss out because eventually those two puppies will need to be massaged daily."

Yes, she does soothe my nerves. "Sounds like fun." I laughed and coughed at the same time. "Oh, it hurts to laugh."

She washed her hands. "I know. Don't worry. You'll be just fine. So no hunk of a man to call and let him know how you're doing?"

"No, not right now."

"We'll keep an eye on you and you'll be spick and span in no time."

"Feels like I'm going to need some watchful eyes."

She grabbed the clipboard. "Are you in any pain other than your chest?"

"Yes, between my eyes, my cheeks, and my chin. Even my hair hurts."

She flashed her ultrawhite teeth. "Well we didn't touch that. We'll give you some pain medication in just a minute. You'll be swallowing more pills than you could ever shake a stick at."

"Has anybody else called me?" I asked, already knowing the answer.

"No, not yet. I hope you managed to get enough time off from work? This whole thing could take quite a while."

"Yes, I did." I squinted my eyes, cringing through a sensation that felt like my stomach muscles were fighting to contract. "Why does my tummy hurt?"

She flipped through the chart. "You signed the paper to have your cute little belly button worked on."

"Oh damn, that's right, I did. I forgot all about that."

"It makes more sense to get it all done at once. You did the right thing." She replaced the chart and grabbed a medicine cup.

"If you say so."

"Here's your medicine. Can you swallow these babies?"

My hand accepted them as I examined each one. "Yes. They're like horse pills though." She handed me a cup of water and I forced each one down.

"Good. Now rest up. I'll leave you alone for now. And, oh yeah, there's a bouquet of flowers over here for you." She pointed to the sink.

"Who are they from? Will you read the card to me, please?"

"Sure, darlin'." She removed the card from the tiny envelope. It says, "Happy fortieth birthday and makeover day. Love, your family—Dad, Corliss and Olympia." She set the vase next to my bed and replaced the card.

"That's sweet." I sniffed the air. "I surely can't smell them."

"Not for a few days anyway. Your nostrils are numb, missy."

"Do me another big favor if you can? What is your name anyway?"

"Carol Ann."

"Carol Ann, can you hook up my laptop? I think it's with all of my things my sister brought."

"Yes, but if you want to use the Internet, there's no modem or available phone line in these hospital rooms. You'll need to wait until you go to the hotel in a few days."

"I'll just wait. By the way, which hotel is that?"

"The best. Your recovery retreat will be at the lovely Beverly Hills Hotel."

"Now that I can't wait for."

A few days later, the elegance and splendor of the fancy, upscale Beverly Hills Hotel surrounded me. The room was tan and gold, and every ounce of décor was classy. The spacious bathroom even had a fireplace alongside the oval bathtub. My California King bed looked like an oasis with cushiony vanilla pillows. Propping up a few behind my back, I settled upon the feathery softness. The room was equipped with a modem, and so there I sat with bandages on my chin and nose, tape around my abdomen, and pads galore stuffed inside of my white size 42 bra with wide cups that unsnapped in a gazillion places. I was comfy cozy. Laptop city was all I needed.

LadyMB,
Where have you been?

Hey there, Jay Jay,
I've been here. Just resting up from a little surgery.

Surgery? Are you okay?

Yes, I'm fine.

I hope so. I don't want anything to happen to you before we even get a chance to meet.

Jay Jay, I think you're going to get your chance to see me.

I can't believe you're ready for that so soon.

Not actually meeting. I mean I'll be on BET next month.

What for? Do you act or sing? Oh, I get it. You're a newscaster, right?

No. Just tune in on April thirtieth, Sunday night at eight o'clock. You'll see me.

You've got me excited now. I won't ask you to tell me because I know you would if you could.

I just think it's better this way.

Now I can't wait.

So is everything going well with you?

Not bad. I just can't stop thinking about you. And now how am I going to hold out until then? That's over one month. I can't see you before then?

I'm afraid not.

How will I ever last that long?

You will.

We'll be watching.

You and your daughter?

Yes.

Jay Jay, my birthday was on March third.

What? Why didn't you tell me before?

I didn't want to announce it like it should mean something.

Well it does. Happy Birthday! You're full of surprises.

Yes, I am indeed.

Check your mail later. There just might be a little something in there for you. I wish I could do more.

Thanks, but you don't need to do anything. When is your birthday?

Coming up on March nineteenth. Your fellow Pisces. I'm going to have to check up on two fish getting together.

I forgot about that. What a heck of a coincidence. Now I just know you have a date or something planned, right?

No.

No more than I did, I guess.

I guess. But considering that you had some sort of surgery, that would have been a little difficult.

It would have been nice to have someone to care about me through this, you know?

I care. And maybe one day you'll get to see just how much I'm able to show that.

I'll check with you later this week.

Are you going already?

Yes, I need to rest up and shut down.

I'll bet. How about tomorrow evening? Can I meet you online at seven?

Yes.

Chat with you then. Have a great night. And take it easy.

I will.

Until next time, birthday girl, peace out.

Peace out.

Speaking of my big bra that snaps, a week later I had specific postop instructions to massage my breasts to prevent scar capsules from forming. I suppose massaging helps to keep the pockets open. As much as I would have loved to have had someone do it for me, I decided to do it myself.

The brassiere, which was the best word for this thing, had to come off for just a little while. It was way too big to be called a bra. It deserved at least two syllables. I stood in the mirror and admired my new, round breasts. They seemed to be hanging naturally, not like frozen cantaloupes that looked like rocks affixed under my chin, which had always been a nightmare of mine. Raising one

arm over my head, I used the opposite hand to squeeze underneath the breast. It really didn't feel like an implant. It was so soft.
That must be a double-D size there, I thought. How was I going to
live with these if the swelling didn't go down? After about two
minutes on each side, before I knew it I was flat on my back, lying
on the bed. The many down feather pillows supported my head.
Those hands of mine had a mind of their own sometimes. At least
they used to before I met Jabril. Tonight, they were headed down
south, and I'll be damned if one finger didn't find its way into me,
and then two, and then three.

Looking down toward my middle section and in between the
mountain-sized implants, I could see my womanness. My right
hand started to rub my right boob. The purpose right now was to
explore the new me. My nipples were not tender at all, but still, I
made sure to touch the tips ever so lightly. They immediately responded by hardening up like bugs on a headlight. Perhaps if I
closed my eyes and let my imagination run wild, I'd be onto something. Uh-oh, who was that? That man could have been Denzel
Washington's twin. Could it have been Jay Jay? I hoped he looked
half as good. Oh my goodness, what was he doing, leaning me
over a chair and hitting it from the back? Damn, he looked good
going to work. He was grabbing my queen-sized breasts from
underneath and giving a few good squeezes himself. I could feel
my juices starting to flow already. This wouldn't take long at all. It
seemed so real. I could actually feel the penetration and the
thrusting, deep and then shallow, but what was thrusting was really my own three middle fingers.

Suddenly, the hand that was giving attention to my breast traveled down to my most sensitive point. I was wet enough to bor-
row juices from just below. And so I slid my middle fingers from
side to side and up and down, and grinded to the sensation. And
within thirty seconds, my legs tightened up and I raised my butt
from the sheets. I was squeezing this pleasure right on up through
my soul, contracting all over and then subsiding. Another wave hit
and then subsided. I let out a loud moan and then collapsed. It
had been a while since I'd made myself feel good. I realized that
being suddenly single meant I needed to do that more often. Go

ahead, girl, get you some. Love yourself, okay? If there had been cameras in the room, they'd have gotten themselves an eyeful.

The next day there was a special-delivery envelope brought to my room. With semibaited breath, I tore open the manila-colored package before I could even take a moment to lock the hotel room door. It was a video from the radio station. It read, "We miss you—Your family."

Thank goodness. I was starting to get pretty lonely, molesting myself up in here. I knew the video was going to be great.

"Hi, Mom. I miss you. Can't wait to see the new you. I know everything is working out just fine. I thought I could handle not seeing you but it's hard already. I look forward to seeing you soon. Can't wait. Love you."

"Hey, Sis. Are you breaking hearts already? I know you are. You were breaking hearts before all of this. Just make sure you do what the doctor tells you and don't rush it. We can't wait to see you. I'm proud of you for being brave enough to go ahead with this. I pray that you achieved the results that you wanted. It was hard not being able to see you. But I hope that time flies fast, and before long, you'll be walking out onto that stage with a new look, a new attitude and a new sense of self. I support and love you."

"Girl, can't you have someone send me a bootleg photo so I can get a sneak peak? I thought that with me being the person who submitted you and all, I'd have carte blanche and stuff. Oh well, I guess not. Can't wait to see your face. More importantly, can't wait to have my girl back. I'm keeping an eye on things. Everyone's doing well. But we'll be doing a whole lot better when you come home. Take it easy, Morgan. 'Bye."

"Hey there, baby girl. Don't worry about anything. I've sorted through all of your mail and I'm taking care of all of the bills just the way you organized it for me. Some of your friends have called that heard about the makeover. I told them you'll be home in about a month. I see Corliss almost every day. Olympia comes by to check on me too. I'm doing fine. Well, play this video when you get lonely. We're all thinking about you so don't forget us. And don't stay longer than you need to. Make sure they don't talk you into getting too much done. See you. Good-bye."

Now that is what it life is all about, I assessed. Family and friends. They all looked so good. Looked like they taped Corliss's while she was at work. I couldn't wait to get all of the recovery time over with. Damn, the process would definitely take a whole lot of patience. *Yes, Dad, I'll play it over and over again for sure.* Actually, I rewound it and watched it again.

For weeks, I worked out like a mad woman. The radio station's video cameras were there every step of the way, catching me sweating and grunting and groaning and collapsing. But my goal was to go from a 30" waist to a 26" and lose about twenty pounds. I wanted to be leaner and stronger in every way.

"You have a great figure," the young, fine Italian trainer told me. "All you need to do is burn fat and build a little more muscle. We all lose muscle as we get older." Easy for him to say. He looks twenty-one. "But if you can keep up this routine, you'll be leaner and stronger in no time."

The two-hour routine consisted of thirty minutes of the treadmill or stepper, and then alternating upper and lower body parts every other day, so I was in the daggonned gym daily. And I was using free weights most of the time, not machines. My muscles burned like mad on the last few reps and after each workout my legs ached like crazy. I still couldn't really work my belly yet, but it needed the most attention. The routine was grueling, but I just had to go all the way.

Early one morning, a lady dentist made a special house call and came to my hotel room, along with an assistant and a production photographer. She did her thing by giving me a complete teeth-whitening treatment. My coffee-stained teeth looked like shiny pearls when she got through. I couldn't stop running my tongue across them.

A black stretch limo picked me up at ten the next morning and waited while I met a man at a glitzy store on fashionable Rodeo Drive for new outfits. The photographer was already there. People stared at my face bandages, which made me look like I'd been in a wreck. But I was used to being stared at. I was wearing my booty jeans, but it looked like I didn't have much booty left actually.

"This burnt-orange color looks great against your skin. I know, you always wear black, right?" the flamboyant stylist asked me.

"Yes, it brings less attention."

"But we want you to make a huge statement and for you to be the center of attention now. No more blending in with the crowd for you, Morgan Bayley. You are the star of the show of your life from now on. Now go on in there and try on that red evening dress. It's time to show off your new cleavage and major curves. Go." His hand was on my back as I walked away.

We decided on the daring red dress. It looked like it had been sewn onto my body. Along with a pair of red-satin Gucci heels, with a gold G hanging off the ankle, the look was hot.

My hair was done at the famous and chic Frédéric Fekkai salon. My usual, everyday look was a dull, drab brown color with a few strands of gray and long bangs. I was so used to doing my own hair that it felt weird to have someone else's hands digging through my head. And I could tell that this hairstylist was ready to work me to the bone.

He spoke with a lisp but with tons of enthusiasm. "I suggest we go with a bronze color with golden highlights. Or even a ma-hogany tone with chestnut streaks. Something other than what you're used to, girl." Brother Renay was a big bucket of gay and he made sure everyone knew it. He wore cornrows with major hang time and was tall and coffee-black with a whole lot of sugar.

"I don't know, that sounds a little radical," I admitted while staring at my mummified reflection in the enormous mirror.

"It will make you look ten years younger, I promise. Don't be scared. I think we should cut it into Oprah's hairstyle—you know, layered with the flip, or maybe even curly. Or we could do a blunt cut and add some height. But we definitely need to thin out these bangs, girl. Who you hidin' from? Either way, when I'm done it'll be full and bouncy and healthy looking, child. You're going to need to chase away all of those men after this makeover, girl. Send them right on over my way. Liars, baby mamma drama, stalkers, I don't care. I can handle all of the leftovers that all you picky straight kitty-cats let slip away."

"Renay." My hand found its way to my lips.

"You think I'm kidding. Try me."

"Did you get that?" I asked the videographer. He laughed and assured me that it would be cut.

Renay assured him, "I'm not afraid of who I am. Are you? Leave it in." He winked at the guy, who cracked a major smile.

We all laughed and Renay went to work. I didn't want extensions, but Renay got out his scissors and a big bag of hair, kind of an auburn color. That boy was ready to get busy.

The final stop was the nail salon for a set of acrylic nails and a pedicure. The Swedish manicurist used a shade called Devil's Food Frost and added a cute rose design on my toes along with a gold-star.

"Who in the heck am I?" I said to the camera. The camera guy grinned and turned off his equipment for the day.

"You are beautiful," he said warmly.

Words I was going to have to get used to, I hoped.

CHAPTER II

"Are you ready?" asked Dr. Diamond as I stared into his question-marked eyes. It was time for the big unveiling—the day the bandages would come off. The day I'd see my new nose, new chin and new tummy. Even though I no longer had a man, I did have a loving family and a wonderful friend who supported me. But right at that moment, I was on my own.

As I lay in a postop room, the camera guy hovered over us both. "I'm ready," I said with reservation.

"Here we go."

I held my breath.

First, Dr. Diamond peeled the round, Band-Aid-like pad from my navel. He raised the head of the bed so I could see. My navel was now an innie and was set to perfection. It was as though I was looking at Tyra Banks' belly in the third month of pregnancy. I still had crunches to do, but it was a thing of beauty.

He spoke first. "Nice, huh? What do you think?"

How could I possibly have formed my words if I couldn't close my mouth first? I willed my lips to meet. "Nice isn't the word. It's really very pretty. It looks . . . sexy."

"Glad you like it. Just clean the navel area with an alcohol swab every now and then for the next few days and it will be fine. As far as your breasts, you've seen those, right?"

As though he'd better not take them back, I covered my full

chest with my hands. "Yes, we're good friends," I said, slipping them in and out of my nursing bra and rubbing them for good luck. "They seem much bigger than a C cup."

"The swelling will go down and they'll get to their natural size in about two weeks. But they're proportioned, don't you think?"

"That they are. I feel like an hourglass with the size difference between my waist and breasts."

"It's probably more than eight inches and once you go through your workout routine a little longer, it could be an even greater difference. Now for your chin."

Eyeing the oval mirror, I felt as though I had to make a conscious effort to inhale. The thin bit of dressing was peeled away from my bottom lip, millimeter by millimeter, on down to my chin, and whatever he did, my entire jaw looked more pronounced. My chin also looked stronger and more pronounced. It was the one piece of work so far that I thought made me look younger. Inhale I did.

Squeezing the hand mirror, I glanced intently at my image. "It's barely noticeable but you can tell something has changed. It's subtle, almost as if I had had dental work or something."

He looked pleased. "That means mission accomplished. And now for the major change, your nose. Here we go. Ready?"

"As I'll ever be."

Taking in a deep, cleansing breath, I exhaled while pursing my lips, and waited for a minute before I saw who I was. Then I closed my eyes tight, squeezing them with all my might, willing the vision to be one that was not too extreme. *What if the tip of my nose curves up, or what if he removed too much of the hump and it dips, what if he couldn't straighten it out and they need to do it all over again, what if I look like one of those plastic surgery fiends—those rich women who just can't get enough, like that woman I met in the office when I first came in? Oh Lord, why did I do this?* As he pulled back the splint from the finished product, I felt the warmth from the florescent lights upon my face, my eyelids, and my nose.

His voice filled my ears. "Open your eyes, Morgan." He offered his hand to me.

I took it. "I can't."

He squeezed my hand tightly. "Morgan, open your eyes. You'll be very pleased."

He held the mirror for me since I was shaking and trembling so.

"I'm nervous, Doctor."

"I know, trust me. Open your eyes."

First with a tiny crack of my left eye, I peeked, and spied a face that was . . . that was . . . that was beautiful. My right eye joined in on the action and they both bugged in astonishment of the vision. My jaw dropped. I looked . . . new. I looked—changed. I looked—hard to recognize yet all too familiar. There were small bruises under my eyes and alongside one of my cheeks. My pronounced, deep-set eyes shone even brighter. My high cheekbones seemed even higher, framing each side of my nose as if saluting the finished product. I raised my wobbly hand from his grip and touched the bridge of my new nose ever so lightly. It felt normal to the touch. I could barely feel my own fingers because it was still a little numb, but it was probably half the size it was before. It was no longer crooked, no longer humped and no longer big. My nostrils were perfect. For the first time in my life, I looked like I felt: simply beautiful.

My voice began to crack. "Oh, Dr. Diamond, you're a miracle worker." A lone tear began to fall from my eye, right down into my mouth. I caught it with my lips, and savored the salty taste of joy as I swallowed, hard.

Dr. Diamond added his sentiments. "Your nose is straight and it's smaller. I think it really fits your face now."

Still, I gazed into the magic mirror, hand still shaking, forcing myself to focus through my tears.

He put his hand on my shoulder and informed me, "You can use bags of frozen peas to help speed up the healing of the bruises."

"Thank you, Doctor."

I wiped more tears from my cheek as he stood up and prepared to exit the room.

"You're welcome. Anything else you need?" he asked.

In spite of the massive lump in my throat, I couldn't help but speak. "No. I'll stop right here."

"Good. If you change your mind, I'll honor your requests for another few months or so. Just between you and me." He winked.

I sniffled. "Thanks, Doctor. That's nice of you. But I'm fine just the way I am."

The camera guy gave me an A–OK sign with his thumb and forefinger. I'd forgotten he was there. He exited the room too, leaving the new me to get dressed. But I still sat there, looking at myself. I was no longer ugly. I was beautiful indeed.

After two more weeks of calling the fancy hotel home, I was more than ready to be released. I talked on the phone for hours on end. I dared not mention what I thought of my new looks to anyone, and actually, no one asked. They knew the rules. I chatted online with Jay Jay almost every night. He was so excited about turning on the television the next night. But not as excited as I was. No word from Jabril. He was obviously history.

"Room service." A young gentleman stood at my door to bring my seafood dinner. I opened the door and the waiter smiled as he walked past me.

"Thanks. You can put it right there."

The young man couldn't seem to keep an eye on where he was walking. He only managed to look . . . at me. I felt his eyes owning my space. He stared me down from head to toe, even though I was wearing a bulky, white terrycloth hotel robe with a turbanlike towel over my head. He managed to mainly stare at my chest area, and then up at my face. He set down the tray without looking at what he was doing. I reached in my purse.

"Here, this is for you," I said, handing him a few bucks.

"No, problem, ma'am. It was my pleasure."

"Oh no. Please take this for your trouble."

"No, no trouble. The pleasure was all mine. Your husband is one lucky man, ma'am. Have a good evening."

"You too." I stood there with the money in my hand, actually blushing and stunned. As if in a trance, I slowly locked the door and turned to the side. I caught a glimpse of myself for the thousandth time that week. But still, even with the weeks that had gone by, I did a double take, even though it was the same face I'd seen first thing in the morning for a while now. It seemed that I still barely even knew my own reflection when I'd stumble in to use the bathroom half-asleep. This was the image that people would see—an attractive woman who was worth noticing. Like the taxi driver, and the lady at the front desk, and the waiter, and the man walking down the hall as I entered my room. This was what it felt like to be stared at not because you're odd, but because you're plain old cute. My nose was now simply centered above my lips and below my eyes. It was no longer the star of the show. *I could get used to this.*

A few hours before my big coming out, I took a soothing bath in the triple-sized Jacuzzi tub and dried off my toned and shapely body, patting and admiring my new boobs again. Proudly, I stepped up to the full-sized mirror, naked and damp, and looked at the rest of me. The muscle tone in my legs was again apparent after all these years. They actually looked sturdier. My skin looked healthy from all of those treatments with Corliss. Seemed like I didn't need Botox after all. I'd been using shea butter on my waist and breasts, so my tone had evened out. And my hair still looked relaxed and freshly cut. But I couldn't wait to remove those tracks.

Elated about showing my family and friends the new me, I was looking forward to enjoying the rest of my life, looking just like this.

The makeup artist from the MAC store stopped by, along with the cameraman, of course. This artist had already picked out his selections. I was almost starting to get used to being on camera every step of the way. I actually wondered where the camera guy was when he took a short bathroom break. He missed some good stuff.

The artist treated my face with a pumpkin pie-smelling moisturizer, and then used a cedar-chip pencil to play up my eyes along with a cinnamon eye shade and a maple-colored highlighter under my brow. He chose a frosted lipstick lined with a plum-colored pencil. Of course I made a mental note of each and every shade. All of the cocoa and copper tones made me look natural yet with a vibrant, wow look. It looked clean and elegant yet very intense. He even glued on some false eyelashes and plucked my eyebrows to perfection.

Next, my new buddy—fun and fabulous Renay—stopped by to touch up my do with a full wash, trim and blow-dry. He had my hair done to the nines. And of course he brought a little humor with him as usual.

He spoke when he was done. "Girl, you make a gay man want to go straight. I might ask you to sit on my face after looking at you but shit, I don't know if I'd kiss it or kick it." Strangely, he spoke as though he was serious as a heart attack. I hugged him, and then he walked out with the cameraman. Looked like they'd found new friends in each other.

After everyone left, I slipped on my cherry evening dress with the gold shoulder straps and put on my new heels. My heart-shaped ruby earrings, necklace and charm bracelet looked grand. I heard a knock at the door. "It's show time."

CHAPTER 12

"Tonight, we will unveil the major transformation of the lucky winner of the KJAZZ Soulful Renewal Beauty Makeover contest. She's a local who lives in Inglewood. Her name is Morgan Bayley. Let's check out her story."

As the five-minute video piece on my journey began, I stood behind a sheer black curtain, exposing my silhouette, fifteen pounds lighter, awaiting my cue to go onstage. The portion that got to me was the part where Tyra was interviewed, almost crying at the thought of seeing the finished product. My heart was fluttering like a hummingbird's wings, fast and furious. Quickly I found that inhaling through my nose and exhaling through my mouth was not helping. Within what seemed like twenty seconds, I heard the audience applaud as the tape ended. That only served to speed up my accelerating heartbeat. *Calm down, Morgan. Stay calm.*

"Ladies and gentleman, we present to you the new Morgan Bayley." The Diana Ross song *I'm Coming Out* began to play.

The curtains in the hotel's grand ballroom parted in slow motion as the applause and cheers and shouting began. The spotlights from above glared intensely. My forehead was covered with tiny beads of sweat from the heat. And then finally, the new me was exposed for the world to see. But all I could see were images of groups of people, rising from their seats. I stepped forward and suddenly their faces became clearer.

Dad was standing in the front row, with his jaw dropped. He was with Sierra, who looked a great deal like my mom. Olympia was standing with Kenyon, and she was actually crying at the sight of me. That caused a lump in my throat the size of Manhattan. Tyra was standing still, no applause, no emotion, just plain old frozen in place. She looked three shades lighter. And Corliss was clapping the loudest, actually whistling though her teeth, standing next to a gentleman who looked familiar. He was waving his left arm in the air, the other arm was around Corliss's waist. It was Marcus Coles, the one she tried to fix me up with. I remembered she said he was too old for her own auntie. Then why did he have his arm around her? His jaw was dropped farther than my dad's jaw. I took a few steps forward until I stopped on my mark—a piece of black tape, but the applause did not cease. I scanned the faces for Jabril, but he was nowhere to be found.

The music stopped and the host lowered his hands for the crowd to take their seats. He held the microphone under my new chin.

"Morgan, you look wonderful. Please tell us what this experience has been like for you."

My throat was dry. I tried to moisten it with a big gulp. I could hear the sound of my swallow in my head. I opened my mouth. "Wow, I'm so overwhelmed. I'm just at a loss for words. I must admit I was a little reluctant at first. You know my dear friend Tyra entered me in this contest." Tyra still wore a blank face. "I'm just so pleased with the work Dr. Diamond and the makeover team did. It far exceeded my expectations. I'm amazed each time I look in the mirror, which has been every five minutes for the past few days." I actually chuckled.

The host laughed along with me. "What exactly did you have done again?"

"My nose, chin, breasts, and my tummy." I could feel my belly button underneath doing the hula as though it was begging to be seen.

"He actually built you a belly button, right?"

"Yes, he did."

"That's amazing. I must say you are stunning to look at. You look like Angela Bassett."

"Now that's a real compliment. I feel stunning. I would recommend this surgery to anyone who can afford it. And I want to thank the radio station and Dr. Diamond for this generous contest. I'm extremely grateful and I'm very pleased."

"What do you say we get your family up here while we look at your Before-and-After again? Come on up, family members." He motioned for them to approach.

The video of the Before-and-After shots rolled on the large monitor overhead. My family and friends ran toward me and surrounded me with intense support and excitement.

"Mom, you look even more beautiful than I ever imagined. I might not have recognized you on the street if I didn't know you had this done," Corliss said.

Marcus stepped up in agreement. It was just that he had his eyes fixed on my new tits. "You do look great."

"Hello, Marcus. Thanks." He wouldn't let go of my hand, even though I tried to pull away.

"Hey, Sis. Aren't you just fine as hell? I'd better watch out for you."

Coyly, I snatched my hand from Marcus and embraced Olympia. "Hey, Sis."

"I might need surgery now myself. You look so good. I mean that."

"Thanks." I looked at her ex-boyfriend who I hadn't seen in a while. I called him the Kenny Lattimore look-alike. "Hello, Kenyon."

"Hello. Congratulations. Shoot, she was a fox before all of this," he told Olympia.

"That's nice of you to say."

Dad stood back, watching everyone else greet me. He looked like a new father in a nursery ward. He stood still with his hands hanging at his sides. Suddenly, he raised his arms toward me. I did the same.

"Hi, Daddy." We embraced for a long moment.

He broke away and spoke. "Hello, stranger. Nice to meet you." He looked me up and down.

A tear crept down from the corner of my eye. "Stranger, huh?"

Dad wiped it for me. "No, baby girl, you look so gorgeous. I just can't believe it's you."

"It's me," I replied, noticing Sierra standing behind him. "Hey, Sierra."

"Hello, Morgan." Sierra was sophisticated, short and pleasingly plump. She kissed me on my cheek and patted my back.

"What did you think when my dad told you?" I asked her.

"I was a little worried but they did a great job on you," she replied, looking at my features up close. Dad stayed quiet.

I simply replied. "Thanks."

Tyra said, "We're taking you to Lawry's restaurant, compliments of the station."

The closing credits rolled and we all said our good-byes to the staff.

We ate and drank ourselves into a fog. I mean we devoured everything under the sun from steamed clams to filet mignon to chocolate mousse. Corliss and Marcus seemed to be getting along swimmingly. Olympia and Kenyon seemed to be vibing. And Dad and Sierra were in their own little world. Tyra and I were each other's dates for the evening.

"You really do look great, baby doll," Tyra told me.

I grinned. "I feel great."

"And your teeth, woman. They're as white as snow. I thought you weren't going to have that done."

"Oh that was minor. It only took a minute."

"That's amazing," she said, glaring all into my mouth. "And your chin, at least I think it's the chin that makes you look ten years younger."

"I think it's both the chin and the nose."

She looked at my head. "And what did they do to your hair?"

"I'm un-be-weaveable, huh?"

"No way. That's a weave?"

"Yes, way."

"Damn." She just kept staring. "And you have to give me the name of that makeup you're using. You look like a chocolate porcelain doll. I mean it. You are looking good, girl."

After another hour or so, everyone started to leave and head home.

"Good to see you again," Sierra told me as Dad and I dropped her off.

She stepped out of Dad's Intrepid while I stepped out of the backseat and kissed her. "You too."

"If you need anything, I'm only a phone call away," she assured me, squeezing my hand.

"Thanks," I said, getting into the front seat, closing the door.

"Congratulations, again," she said, peering into the window.

"Okay, Sierra. We've got to get going." That's my dad.

"Excuse me, River," she said to him as if he was being rude. And he was. She gave me a look.

Giving back the type of look that only women understand, I said, "Good night." We pulled off. I confessed, "Dad, I like her."

"So do I," was all he could say.

In cavernous thought, I stared out the window. "I'll be so glad to get home and into my own bed. As nice as that huge Cinderella bed was."

"That house just hasn't been the same without you. Welcome home."

"It's good to be home." He took my hand while he drove. Reminded me of that ghost named Jabril.

While Dad took all of my luggage and new belongings out of the car, I headed straight upstairs just to sit at my own desk and check my e-mail. And I knew that my next stop was to get out of the restrictive dress and those uncomfortable, fancy shoes.

LadyMB,
Please call me right away. I need to talk to you. It's very, very important. Don't say no. Just do it, for me. My number is 555.0188.

Immediately, without hesitation, I dialed. "Hello," I said, as all I heard was silence.

"Morgan." His voice was that of a stranger, yet his one word gave a strange impression.

"So now you know my name I see."

"Yes, Morgan Bayley."

"Is everything okay? You sound like you just saw a ghost."

His voice was deep and he sounded personable yet concerned. "First of all, you're simply beautiful, Morgan. You look like a movie star."

The unfamiliar flattery resulted in flushed cheeks. That was a new one. "Thanks, Jay Jay."

"I watched you and I forgot about all that was going on around me. I was glued to my chair until the show ended. I'm so shocked."

"I know this was a heck of a way to spring this on you. I hope you don't mind that I did it this way."

"No, I'm fine with it. I totally understand. My daughter, Cameo, says you're very beautiful."

"Please tell Cameo I said thanks."

"And the girl in the blue jeans with the white top, was that your daughter?"

"Yes, that was Corliss."

"You have a nice-looking family. Morgan, don't you want to finally know my name?" he asked.

"That would be nice." I sat back.

"My name is Jamie. Jamie Jackson."

I sat up. "Jamie Jackson?"

"Jamie Jackson, from St. Jerome's school. We went to school together before I moved away to the valley."

My sentence was rushed. "Jamie, the fourteen-year-old with the friends who used to tease me every day, just for the hell of it?"

"Yes," he responded with the downtrodden sound of shame.

My heart pounded and my breath grew short. "Jamie, all I can say to you is, screw you."

"I know you're mad."

"You know I'm mad? The hell with being mad now. I went through torture at the hands of many cruel jokes and taunting. I was a young girl going through puberty, trying to find my own identity. You'd better know I'm mad. I'm so mad I'm fucked up. You owe the station fifty thousand dollars for my enhancements, you punk."

"I deserve all of that." He paused and waited for my next words.

I paused too. Putting my thumb to my temple, I continued to speak my mind. "You deserve to be castrated, Jamie. You took my virginity in my fucking kitchen and never even had the decency to look me up when you heard I was pregnant. How did it feel to get a glimpse of your grown daughter on television?"

The swallowing of his saliva was audible. "I thought she was mine. She looks just like my daughter, who I sat next to while she watched her own sister without knowing it. That was the hardest thing I've had to do in my life."

"Good, then that means I've had harder times than you. Like giving birth while all the other new moms had their baby's father holding their hands. My mom held my hand—did you know that? You cheated both of those girls out of years of love and sister-hood, all because you hid away like the coward you are."

"I want you to hear what happened, Morgan."

"I don't want to hear it, Jamie. And don't you ever contact me again. Here I am trying this damned Internet dating for the first time in my life and I hook up with you, of all people. And you tell me you show people you care about them by doing great things. I truly doubt it."

"Morgan, we were young. I've thought about you all the time."

"Like I said, I don't want to hear it. Just be glad I never had your ass tracked down for child support. Good fucking bye." I slammed the desk phone onto its base.

It was barely two months after my surgery, and I'd already re-sorted to cursing like a sailor. And after twenty-seven years, I'd been found by a man I wasn't even looking for . . . my daughter's deadbeat dad. *Why me, Lord? Why me?*

The next evening, my head was still reeling. Every other call was a distant family member or friend calling to offer congratulations. But through it all, even the drama with Jamie, all I could think about was the one man who didn't even have the decency to send a card or leave a nice message of well-being. Yes, all I could think about was how nice Jabril's touch would be right about now.

I dialed his number as if my hand had a mind of its own. He gave a faint greeting.

"Jabril, what are you doing?"

He waited to reply as if deciphering which answer to give. "I have company," he said as though he was trying to keep it down.

I just knew I had my ears checked last year. "Company? Did you see the show yesterday?"

"I saw it."

"And?"

"And what?" he asked as though it was life as usual.

"What did you think?"

"You already know what I think."

"You know what, what we had could not have been real after all these years if you let all of this happen to me and you're off sulking."

"I'm hardly sulking."

Suddenly a feminine voice spoke up in the background. "Jabril, the demo's about to start."

"Screw you, Jabril!" I yelled at the top of my lungs.

He hung up, leaving me to stew in my own anger.

CHAPTER 13

"What are you doing here?" Jabril asked me, wearing only plaid pajama bottoms as I stood at his door some four hours later.

Peeking around him I asked, "Did your company leave?"

"Back to my question, or should I rephrase it, who the heck are you anyway?" He stood firmly in the doorway.

"Funny. You didn't answer my question."

He still sounded smart-ass. "Yes, my company left."

"So, can your new company come in?"

"No problem, Morgan. Have at it." He turned and walked inside as I followed.

There were boxes and newspapers all around. And every table was covered with stuff, not to mention the junk all over the floor. It wasn't like his one bedroom unit had more than eight hundred square feet anyway. And he wasn't known for his decorating skills. He was a simple man who got by on the basics. "What's all this mess?"

"Boxes. Haven't you ever seen anyone pack?"

Damn he was sarcastic. "Pack for what?"

"I need to move."

"Why?" I stood amongst it all.

He almost teased me. "Full of questions, huh? I'd say my

goings-on should be the least of your worries, what with your new face and body and all."

"Jabril, why are you moving?"

He leaned his back against his bar, staring at me from head to toe. "You know, starving actors get paid funny money. Only I haven't seen a check in three weeks. We do what we've gotta do."

"Why didn't you tell me?"

"I saw no reason to. This is my concern, not yours." He cut his eyes.

"Jabril, I remember the day when your concerns were mine and vice versa. I would have given you rent money."

"Only punk-ass men take money from women. I've never done it before and I won't start now."

"Then call it a loan and pay it back if you want to."

"Hell no. Anyway, you're one to talk about not discussing things with someone first. What brings you here anyway? Trying to catch me doing something that I have every right to do?"

Stepping toward him, I stopped within an inch of his face. "Jabril, obviously we've broken up, right?"

"You made that decision." He crossed his arms, looking at me as though I was sucking up his air.

"No, you did. You're the one who ran off and became invisible."

"The only invisible one is you." He looked as if he didn't know me, staring right through me. "I'm looking dead in your face and Cookie is nowhere to be found."

I touched his forearm. "She's right here. I'm still the same person."

"No, you're not."

"How can you say that?"

"Once you made the decision to go against my wishes with something as drastic as changing your entire physical appearance, I knew you could never be my wife."

"Why, because that indicates to you that I'm not the dutiful woman who follows her man's lead?"

"Something like that," he admitted.

"I've followed your lead for more than five years, Jabril. I've been right behind you actually, not beside you, for the entire time I've known you. So now that I make one choice without your approval you bail on me? That's not fair."

"Look at you, Morgan. You stand here with your little nose and big tits, presenting yourself to me like a fancy gift to be unwrapped."

"Maybe that is what I'm doing, standing here for you to have again. But you already know what's inside. It's still the same old me."

My tight, zipped-down-to-cleavage level Baby Phat sweat jacket wasn't working, I noticed. He turned his head toward the muted television. "Morgan, excuse me but I don't want to open it. Good things come in small packages. I can see that there's a monster in you yearning to break loose and rear its ugly head." He looked back toward me, eyeing me up and down again. "The world is rubbing its hands together at the thought of you coming out into it with your naive self, trying to fit back into your regular life. Your life will never be regular again. That much I can guarantee you."

He definitely needed to be reminded of who I really was. "Jabril, will you make love to me?"

"What does that have to do with anything? That's not going to fix it."

Touching the side of his face with my fingertips, my voice went into sex-phone operator mode. "I just need you to touch me and accept me and make me feel like you used to. I'm still your same Cookie and I want you to feel that. Maybe once you're inside of me, you'll know I'm still the same person, on the inside." I did not blink, and neither did he.

Just then, I slowly unzipped my top, exposing my rose-colored underwire bra. Jabril was silent. His eyes grew a tad bit larger and his focus was definitely on my chest. I took his hand and placed it on my left breast. I felt his pulse race. I could see my own heartbeat through my skin, and I'm sure he could feel it. He removed his hand and began to scratch the back of his neck. He took a deep breath.

Taking a step all up against him on my tip-toes, I pressed my lips to his cheek, moving upward toward his deep-set eyes. He kept his eyes wide open and slowly put his arms to his side. I kissed the side of his perfect nose, and made my way to his perfect lips, inserting my tongue in between until he opened his mouth to accept me. As we kissed, his eyes were full on looking at me, and our stares were straight on. His chiseled face met my new face and strangely, we did not have to turn our heads much to the side to make room for my nose. He looked into my eyes, and I looked into his, as our tongues swirled about. Jabril stopped and backed me away just to stare.

"I love you," I said.

He replied by taking me by my hand and walking me into his bedroom. I slipped off my shoes, slipped out of my pants, and removed my bra.

Before I knew it, I was on my back in his unmade bed and he was on top of me. Jabril traced the path from my lips to my chest, and licked my nipples in a slower motion than usual. His eyes remained fully open while he licked under my breasts, along the top, and then he sucked my tips.

He spent a good ten minutes just playing with my breasts. He would squeeze them together, trying to lick both nipples at once, and then squeeze one with his hand, trying to pull on it with a sucking motion and then releasing it, watching it bounce back to its place. He looked like a kid in a candy store yet he had a tiny frown line between his eyes the entire time. After a while, Jabril continued to trace the path of my skin down lower, to my navel. He jerked his head back upon seeing the flatness of my belly, and the new belly button to match. He looked up at me, almost as if he wanted to shake his head in amazed disappointment, or simply say something preachy. But he didn't. He licked my abs and around my navel in a circular motion. He looked up at me again, and then kissed my stomach.

Jabril lifted me up to remove my pink V-string underwear. He traced my outer and inner thighs with his tongue, moving inward even more to outline the shape of my lower lips. My hips responded by grinding at the same time that I felt my center start to heat up. He kissed my opening as gently and as softly as he ever had. He slowly inserted the tip of his tongue, and then pressed the flatness of his full tongue all up and down my opening. He then moved upward to kiss my jewel, taking it into his mouth and flicking his tongue and sucking it ever so slightly. I could no longer take it. I watched him enjoy me, and watched that face that I thought I'd lost, once again pleasing me horizontally as he did so well. I closed my eyes, which forced a build up of tears down my cheeks, and let go, yelling his name as I contracted my muscles and then pulsated to my peak.

Jabril grabbed a condom from his nightstand drawer, put it on, moved my legs straight up, and joined me, realizing that I was fully ready for his entrance. He spread my legs upward along his chest and kissed my calves, moved to my ankles, and then he kissed my toes, each one in order on one foot and then the other. I could feel him inside of me, moving in and out with each stroke, but never missing a beat as he continued to please my feet with his mouth. Jabril found the arch of my right foot and began to bite it lightly. I cringed with pleasure, moaning and groaning, feeling myself getting more and more heated. He licked the bottom of my foot again and again, and then he stopped, shifting his mental focus quickly to his entry target, placing his hands under my behind.

"You lost weight," was his reply upon getting a handful of ass.

But he continued to grind deep into me, staring me down, eyeing every inch of my chest, and then lying upon me until his face was within one inch of mine. He kissed my lips just as he grunted his way deeper inside. Taking in the sensation of him pulsating within, he traveled all the way to the back of my depth, thrusting to one corner and then to the other corner. He hit a steady stream of in and out pumping and then he groaned, which led to a long exhale. His grinding ceased and he rested his head along my cheek for a moment. I kissed his sweaty ear. He then looked at me again, lifting his fingers to my chin and then to my nose, following the shape of my bridge with his index finger. Unlike he usually did, he didn't ask me if I came. And I didn't really care. I wanted him to really, really feel me.

With an afterglow whisper I admitted, "That felt great, baby. That's just what we needed."

He was speechless.

Trying to switch places with him to give him some serious deep-throat attention, he quickly moved to the side of the bed and sat straight up.

"Did they do a good job?" I just had to ask. I spoke to his massive back.

"Something's different," he replied, looking down at his feet.

Jabril got up, disposed of the condom, put on his underwear and went into his living room. He sat on his sofa playing channel change with his remote. I entered a few minutes later, standing in front of him in my birthday suit.

"Can I stay?" I so wanted him to say yes.

"I don't think it's a good idea. It's just not the same."

My feelings were crushed. "You're so negative, Jabril. I just can't figure it out. And by the way, who was over here today?"

"A friend," he replied, eyes stuck on the television screen.

"Jabril, why don't you just admit that you're seeing this Staples woman and stop trying to blame it on my nip and tuck."

"Whatever. You made the choice. Not me." His tone was nasty, especially considering our lovemaking session.

"Jabril, I feel great about my choice and I'm not going to let you ruin it for me."

He said nothing.

Headed back into his room to get dressed, I spoke as I re-entered the living room. "I don't believe you hate me. I just don't believe it."

Again, he said nothing.

Grabbing the cold doorknob, I slammed the door behind me.

Taking a moment to pause, thinking I needed to regroup, I leaned against the door and heard him at full volume. "Now that she has a new everything else, she needs to get a toe job." I never knew he didn't like my feet. I stood tall and walked down the hall, simply putting one foot in front of the other until I reached my car, and left.

Driving home I was really trying to work things through in my head. How dare he make love to me, and then decide he didn't know who I was? Or was he just curious? I mean after all, he's no fool. He wasn't going to refuse me when I all but molested him. Or maybe he just needed to do that as a symbol of his final good-bye.

Just as I took a moment to snap out of it, I remembered that I was driving a vehicle. I looked to my right to make a lane change and spied a handsome white man driving next to me. He rolled down his window and slowed down as I slowed down. He sped up as I sped up. I tried not to look over at the same time as he did. *What is he looking at? Oh my God, did he just whistle at me? What a day it's been.* He took off.

As I proceeded to make a few stops, it was obvious that I was consumed with thoughts of Jabril's rejection. I stopped at a local drugstore for some toiletries and left my credit card on the counter. Thank God the cashier put it aside by the time I returned. I stopped for a banana smoothie at Jamba Juice and spilled the dang thing in my car, all over the passenger seat. And then, while pulling into the garage, I pressed the remote to close the door and the sucker came down on top of the trash can. Now it's jammed and won't go back up.

"What are you doing here, Tyra?" I asked, walking into the house from the garage door.

"Just waiting on you," she told me, sitting on the loveseat in the den, right next to my dad, uncrossing her legs.

"Don't you think it's a little late?"

"I've been waiting for you for about three hours."

I asked, "Why didn't you call me on my cell?" I tossed my keys onto the bar.

"I was just talking to your father, girl. I lost track of time." The television station was airing an old episode of *Sex and the City*.

My dad scooted up as he asked, "Where have you been?"

"I went to see Jabril."

Tyra seemed concerned as usual. "Morgan, when are you going to stop chasing him down in hopes that he'll change? He's a true chauvinist with a macho soul."

"What were you two talking about for all of these many hours?" I inquired while slipping off my patent leather shoes. Her shoes were already off.

"Just things," she replied.

"Like?"

Dad asked, "Morgan, what is wrong with you?"

"I just asked. Who said anything was wrong?"

"You seem on edge," he told me.

"Yeah, well you two seem mighty cozy up here in my house barefoot, sitting in the dark with empty wine glasses resting on my coffee table without coasters." I walked over and picked up the glasses, and then headed toward the kitchen sink.

Tyra inquired, "Morgan, what are you trying to say?"

I yelled from the kitchen. "I'm saying that it's inappropriate for you to be sitting up here with my father this late at night. Since when did you two become such great friends anyway?"

Dad seemed defensive, yelling back. "In case you forgot, we've known each other since you two were little. I resent your accusation."

Approaching them, I stood still and crossed my arms at my waist. "And I resent your denial, Dad. You're the one who mentioned that she's changed a lot through the years. I saw you checking her out months ago."

Tyra finally slipped her shoes on. "Morgan, I think I'd better go."

Stepping back, I made room for her exit. "I think you'd better."

"I just hoped you knew me better than that." She stood up and straightened out her short skirt.

"I'd hoped I did too."

She pointed toward an envelope on the coffee table. "I brought you something. I'll leave it right there."

"I'll walk you to the door, Tyra," Dad offered.

"Yeah, you do that, Dad." Rushing off to my sanctuary upstairs, I plopped down on my bed.

I lay on my back, resting the base of my neck inside the palms of my hands. I knew it was not my imagination. I just knew it.

CHAPTER 14

Thankfully, after a lot of praying and a few good nights of sleep, I felt better. I changed into one of my new, slimmer pantsuits, applied my new makeup, and bumped my new-behaving hair. Thank God I'd already had that bothersome weave taken out.

My boss's assistant faxed over an assignment sheet, along with a welcome-back note from the office. As I pulled out of the driveway I noticed that the day was absolutely gorgeous. It was extra-gorgeous actually. More gorgeous than I'd ever noticed before. The sun's honey-colored rays greeted my golden face as I pulled down the street to make my way back to the bump and grind of doing what I did for a living. My first appointment since my eight-week hiatus was at a youth center that my company built years ago. My boss thought it was in need of a few upgrades.

"Can I help you?" Audrey asked me.

"Hey, Audrey, it's me, Morgan."

She stuck her neck out to check me out. "Mrs. Bayley? It is you."

"Yes, it is."

She stood up from behind her desk. "Wow. I heard about your big contest win but didn't get to see the show on TV. You look so beautiful, Mrs. Bayley. But you always did anyway."

"Well, thanks, but it's *Miss* Bayley. But since when did you stop calling me Morgan?"

"I don't know. I'm sorry, Morgan." She yelled to her coworkers. "Chelsea, Deirdre, come and see Morgan from the head office."

"Oh my word, you look spectacular," Chelsea commented as she advanced with caution.

Walking behind her, Deirdre added, "You look ten years younger. What a difference that surgery made. And your figure, you're making me want to go out and get me some work done."

Giggling with them, I said, "Well, thank you ladies. I'm very happy with the way it turned out." I looked around. "So where's the decorator?"

"He's in the back room. I'll show you to him."

"Okay, thanks." I followed Audrey as she looked back at me most of the way. We arrived in the back room of the lower level.

A short, designer-suit-wearing man stood near the back wall with his briefcase in hand. "Mr. Mitchell, this is Morgan Bayley. She heads up all of the project locations."

I extended my hand to greet him. "Nice to meet you, Mr. Mitchell."

He bowed his head and extended his hand too. "Call me Paul, if you don't mind."

"Okay, Paul. That's easy to remember. Like the hair-care guy, Paul Mitchell?"

He looked at Audrey, and then looked at me and chuckled. "I get that all the time."

Audrey excused herself. "Well, I'll be at the front desk if you need me."

"Thanks," I replied to her. "So, were you able to look around?" I asked Paul.

"I was."

"And did you come up with any ideas for sprucing up this place?"

"Ahh, yes, I made some notes here. Excuse me." He wanted to put his briefcase on a nearby desk but he dropped his pencil at my feet at the same time. We both bent down to pick it up.

"Oh I've got it. Thanks anyway," he said, leaning down.

Upon his words, I immediately resumed a standing position.

He stood back up with pencil in hand. "A lady like you shouldn't be picking up anything that a klutz like me drops anyway."

"It's just a habit, I suppose."

"Queens don't need to do that."

"Oh, queens, huh?" I asked as though I'd heard incorrectly.

He caught my glance and held on to it. "You are that. If you don't mind me saying, you have the most beautiful eyes I've ever seen."

Blinking, I looked down toward my feet, and then back at his face. "Oh my God, I've never heard that before." I wondered why his glance was quickly moving down to my waist area. "Thank you."

"I just totally forgot what I was . . . oh yes, the notes I made." He opened his case.

"Yes, your notes."

"Miss Bayley is it?"

"Yes."

He turned toward me and shifted his weight onto his right leg. "Are you married?"

Flashing a warm smile, I spoke. "Mr. Mitchell, I don't see what difference that makes."

"I apologize if I appear out of line, it's just that I don't see a ring on your finger and I'm about to ask you something that might not be an appropriate question to ask someone's wife."

"What's that?"

He looked as serious as a heart attack. "Would you like to go out with me sometime? I mean for lunch or even dinner?"

"Mr. Mitchell, I'm flattered."

He went on to explain, "This is not the norm for me, to just preface any business with such a question. But for some reason, I can't think straight. You are the most beautiful woman I have ever seen."

"Ever seen?" I'm sure I sounded insecure.

"Yes. I just have to know what the rest of you is like, on the inside, I mean."

Instantaneously, I ran my fingers alongside the back of my up-flipped hair. "Mr. Mitchell, I don't even know what the rest of me is like these days."

"Meaning?"

"Meaning, I'm going through a sort of transitional period in my life. Kind of a me period. A lot has happened lately and I just don't think I need to get to know anyone else until I get to know myself."

"Sounds like you're doing some real soul-searching."

"I am."

"I've done a lot of that myself. I understand. But will you think of me just in case you're ever in need of a coffee buddy?" He raised his eyes.

"Mr. Mitchell, those notes," I reminded him.

"Oh yes, those notes."

We proceeded to walk along through the rest of the premises, discussing ways to upgrade the center. I watched him talk and gesture and do his work. He knew his stuff and his ideas made sense. But all I could think about was why all of a sudden, this was happening to me. Why was I getting hit on so quickly, so straight on, so hard, by a man who, for the first time in my life, noticed . . . my eyes?

Later that day I decided to stop by my home office in downtown Los Angeles, just to show my face. It was an older building with a not-so-reliable elevator and out-of-date furnishings. I tried not to come in to the office too often. I was actually kind of glad that most of the employees had already gone home for the day. I just didn't want any commotion about my new looks.

My grand executive office was actually a small cubicle on the first floor. As usual, my desk was cluttered with tons of papers and files. To my surprise, on top of my computer there was a box of chocolates. The card read that it was from the staff, congratulating me on winning the makeover.

"Ms. Bayley, hello there. I saw you on television so I know it's you." The thick brunette receptionist walked up holding an empty coffeepot. Girlfriend always wears a muumuu and tennis shoes.

"Otherwise you wouldn't have, huh?"

"Probably not. You do look pretty different."

"I guess so. How are things with you?"

"Fine." She looked around before she spoke. "You know, I actually thought about having a little work done myself."

"Oh really, what would you ever need done?"

"Liposuction. You know, on my arms and thighs." She shook her arm and it jiggled back.

"But you look like you're a nice weight."

"I hide it well. I'm very overweight actually. And I just can't seem to stick to any diet."

"Dieting is not my thing either. And I can't say that I would talk you out liposuction if that's what you want to do. If you think it will help, then I say go for it."

She put her hand near her chest. "You really think I should?"

"If you really want to, absolutely."

"Wow, you're one of the few people who thinks I should. My family thinks I'm absolutely crazy. They tell me all the horror stories."

"But there are a lot of success stories too. Just make sure you have a good doctor."

"Oh, okay." She glanced at the clock on the wall. "I need to get ready to leave for the day. My boyfriend is about to pick me up. It's good to see you though."

It was good to know that somebody cared for her. She seemed sweet. "You too. Is Mr. Johnson still in?"

"No. He hasn't been in today. He had an executive meeting in San Francisco."

"I'll leave him a voice mail. You have a good evening." I flipped through the stack of daily log sheets.

She stood for a second, eyeing me from behind. "You too." She headed off, looked back at me and smiled shyly as she turned the corner.

Standing over my desk, I checked my voice mail and cleared out my message box. Corliss had called three times.

"Is Corliss there? I must have the wrong number," I asked with caution.

"No, this is Corliss's residence," a deep voice replied.

"Who is this?"

"This is Marcus," he said.

"Marcus, this is her mother, Morgan."

His voice perked up. "Oh, hey. How are you?"

"I'm just fine."

"It's good to hear your voice."

"Hear my voice? That's funny because I must say I wasn't expecting to hear your voice, at least not on the other end of Corliss's phone."

He quickly seemed to pick up on my irritation. "Here, I'll put her on."

"Thanks. You do that." I heard him mumble something.

"Hi, Mom," Corliss said matter-of-factly.

"Corliss, what's up with that?"

She spoke casually. "Mom, how are you?"

"You're not even going to answer my question?"

"I heard you. I think that's my business and not yours."

I finally took a seat. "Corliss, that man is old enough to be your father."

"No, he's not. But if he were, that might be good in some ways, huh?"

"Meaning?"

"Meaning at least I'll get to know what it feels like to be loved by someone who's like a father figure, huh?" She sounded like she had nothing to lose by tossing those words into my ear.

"You're not serious. When you brought him to my unveiling I thought you two were just good friends. Now you're talking love?"

"Mom, why don't you calm down and take a minute to ask me what's going on?"

"I just did. Besides, I think it's pretty obvious. Is he living there?" I inquired, almost expecting her to not answer me.

"No, he was just using the phone and he told me I had another call. I asked him to click over and answer it. Satisfied?"

"No." I grabbed a pen and started to doodle on the back of an old pink message pad.

"What's gotten into you? Why are you so, so, emotional about this? Is it because I tried to hook you two up?"

Circles, triangles, squares and flowers, all connected inside of a square with fancy leaves all around the corners of the sheet. "No, are you kidding? I could care less about that."

"Then what is it?"

"I just didn't like the way he looked at me at my coming-out party, that's all. It was like he'd never met me before." Diamonds and zigzags.

"I think we all looked at you in that way, Mom."

"Corliss, I think I'm old enough to know when a man looks at me in that way." I tossed that page and started to doodle on another one.

"Oh, are you old enough to know? Listening to you before, I didn't know it even happened to you that much."

I paused from my scribble. "And what does that mean?"

"Mom, can we start this conversation over? Unless you want to share with me what's really going on with you."

"Never mind. You and Marcus enjoy your evening."

"Aren't you cooking this weekend?"

"No, I don't think so. I'll talk to you later."

"Good—"

Before she could release the second syllable of her farewell, I hung up, resuming the second page of doodling. It turned out to be mother-and-daughter stick figures, holding hands, walking in the park, with the sun shining, the birds flying overhead, and the plush grass under their feet. It was a beautiful scene. There was nothing like a mother and daughter, even when one could choke the other. I tucked the sketch into my purse and headed out of the office. All I could recall was Corliss's question, *What's gotten into you?* Damn if I knew.

"How are you?" asked the man in the grocery store.

"I'm fine." I replied, paying for the few items. I made way too many trips to the store.

"You sure are. You are truly blessed."

"Thank you." I took my bag from the box boy and walked away. The man followed.

"Can I help you to your car with that?"

I didn't even turn back toward him. "It's just a carton of eggs and some paper towels."

"I know, but I wouldn't want you to strain yourself."

"Oh really? No thanks." He gave up and walked in the other direction. *Oh please. Where was he before I increased my breast size by three inches and decreased my nose by the same? Men.*

Dad parked his car in the middle of the driveway so I parked in front of the house. He had the front door open, playing the role of handyman.

"Dad, what are you doing?"

"Just trying to fix the lock on this door. It looks like the bottom lock was tripped, or just stripped."

"From what?" I stopped and took a peek.

"I don't know. Maybe from normal wear and tear," he replied with screwdriver in hand.

"When did you notice that?"

He glanced up at me. "I don't know, child. It's no big deal. You know something, you really do look a whole lot different."

After walking over to the refrigerator to put the eggs inside, I went back to the sofa to put my things down. "Tell me about it."

"Are you happy with the results?"

"Yes." I started to go upstairs, and then stopped to follow up with him. "But what about you, Dad? What do you think about your new daughter?"

He kept his sights on the lock. "I don't see you as a new daughter. I still see you as my oldest girl, Morgan. But you're just top heavy and a little cockier now."

I wasn't amused. "Ha ha. And my face?"

He stood up straight and stared at my face, squinting his eyes. "Honestly, if you ask me I think he did too much. Your nose from the side looks like a white girl's nose. No black woman's nose is like that. And from the front, it almost looks too perfect to be real."

Raising my eyebrows, my mouth opened on its own. "Dad, you're kidding me, right? That's how you see me now? Are you saying I'm still not good enough for you?"

He looked back down at his work. "I didn't say that."

My hands cinched my waist. "All of this surgery I had in order to get more normal and more like Olympia, and now I'm your oldest daughter with the too-perfect nose and the fake titties."

He actually pointed the screwdriver in my direction, speaking in a fatherly tone. "Morgan, child, you'd better calm your ass down and remember who you're talking to here. What the hell has gotten into you?"

I could hardly catch my breath. "You just insulted me. It's hard enough for me to deal with the changes myself. I made a radical decision and the least you could do would be to make me feel good about it."

"I thought that was the whole purpose of your surgery, to make you feel better about yourself. If the surgery alone didn't do it, I can't boost your self-esteem all by myself. You've got to do that on your own. That's why they call it 'self' esteem."

"No, you've got to be a little more sensitive for once. After all, you're the one who damaged it in the first place." My head rolled even after I spoke.

"Okay, now you're really talking crazy, Morgan. Make me the bad guy because it was my genes that contributed to your looks. Then blame your mom too."

I pointed at him this time. "It was you who didn't help me through it from day one. Dad, I've always tried to please you. To do better, to be better, to be sweeter, to try to get you to stay here with me so that you'll give me extra points, hoping I'd equal the image that Olympia has in your mind. You'd always show up for her piano recitals. I don't think you ever missed even one. But when it came to my ballet recitals I think you might have made only one. And now I try to please you by getting all of these enhancements, and it's still not enough for you. I'll never be as special to you as she is."

"First of all, I know you didn't get the surgery done for me. And secondly, both of my daughters are different. I love you both equally, but differently."

It was impossible to speak anything but the truth. "Then how come you never used to beat the shit out of Olympia? Why were you always bragging about her?"

Dad looked as though he had been stabbed. He held his breath, and then closed his eyes for a long two seconds. He walked over to place the screwdriver in his toolbox, closed it, and then walked back to the door to test the lock. He then closed the door and walked right up to me. "Maybe because you were the oldest and I was just learning to be a father. Maybe I sort of experimented my way through the anger I felt at times by striking you when I should have hugged you. Maybe I learned my lesson by the time Olympia was born. Maybe there were other reasons." He silenced himself for a moment. "One thing is for sure. I would never lie to you. I love you and I want you to be happy. But I can tell you one thing, you were a hell of a lot happier before you went under the knife, I know that much. Now you have to face the consequences as part of God's evolution for your life and your choices, not mine."

"Consequences?"

He turned his back as he spoke, heading toward his toolbox again. "Good night, Morgan." He grabbed it and went back toward the porch, throwing in one last jab, "You need a new attitude to go along with that new body."

Walking away, I bolted upstairs and slammed my bedroom door in response to another man who I just couldn't seem to get along with.

CHAPTER 15

"How are you, Morgan?"

Stopping at a local coffeehouse, I removed my leopard-patterned shades and stood in line for a Chai Iced Tea. I guess my best friend had the same idea.

"I'm fine, Tyra." She wore a formfitting, caramel-colored velour jogging suit. The letters JUICY spanned her butt. I was in my usual business attire: a dark blue pin-striped suit, but with a pink semi-unbuttoned blouse.

She said, "I haven't talked to you in a few days."

"I've been busy." My distance was obvious.

"Have you?" she asked, standing behind me.

"Yes."

"I haven't been too busy to miss you."

I twisted back toward her. "Tyra, you can't come to my home and flirt with my father and expect me to not say anything."

"I do admit that I like your father, Morgan. But I would never do anything like that to you. He's like a dad to me. I just don't see him in the way you're suggesting."

"Well he sure does."

A guy walked by and slowed down. "Hey, baby, how are you?"

It took me a minute to get the fact that he was talking to me. "I'm good," I replied.

"Tell me, is your husband married?"

"Very funny."

He commented again. "Looking all good all early in the morning."

"Thanks."

Tyra looked at him, dismissed him with her eyes, looked at me, and then looked at him as he walked away looking at me. "Dang, girl, look at you getting all the attention."

"It's been happening a lot lately," I admitted. I tried not to sound cocky, but sort of didn't care what girlfriend thought of me.

We got our drinks, two of the same, and then glanced over the crowded room to find a couple of seats.

A man spoke up as he and his friend stood. "You two can have this table, we were just leaving."

"Are you sure?" I asked.

"I'm sure."

His friend spoke too. "Yes, please go right ahead. Especially since you walked in here and brought all of that sunshine with you."

I grinned at his corny rap. "Thanks."

Tyra broke the connection. "Oh Lord." She shook her head at him and looked at her wristwatch. "You know what, I've got to get into the gym to meet a client." I took a seat but she did not. "Unlike you, I have a boss who expects to see my ass every day like clockwork."

I barely looked up at her. "Okay. I just need to sit here for a minute until my next appointment. You have a nice day."

"Yeah, you too." I did watch her step away. She looked around the room, and noticed a couple of eyes, just as I did, looking over at me. She proceeded with a shimmy in her walk, but then turned again to find that she did not have an audience. For the first time since I'd known her and had been around her, I did. Tyra walked out.

"Do you mind if I join you?" a man asked as I glanced down at my organizer.

Looking up unfazed, I found that it was Mr. Watson, the investor I'd met a while back.

"Come here often?" he asked.

"Yes, I do as a matter-of-fact. I was just here not long ago, with you."

"With me?"

He looked at me and turned his head slightly askance. "Morgan Bayley, is that you?" he asked as if I was hiding under a mask.

"It's me," I sipped my drink.

"My goodness, you look so different, what did you do?"

"I went on vacation." *Or should I have said I had a little work done?*

"I'll say. Rest never looked so good on me."

"How have you been?"

"Good," he responded, moving his head up and down.

"And you wanted to join me, you asked."

"Oh, yes. I'm sorry for coming up to you like that. I just really liked what I saw from across the room. I didn't mean to be disrespectful."

"Not at all. Have a seat." I waved my hand toward the vacant chair.

He scooted the seat in closer to me and sat down, placing his cell phone and keys on the table. "Have you made an offer on that property yet?"

"No, not yet. We're still trying to get the backing together."

"That's right. I didn't hear back from you, Morgan."

"You gave me that don't-call-us, we'll-call-you closing."

"Did I? I'm sorry about that." He leaned in closer. "Tell you what, have dinner with me this weekend and we can talk about it some more. I still have a few questions to ask you."

"Like what?"

He spoke slowly as though trying to sound sexy. "If I ask you now there'd be no need to use that as an excuse to have dinner with you."

"Exactly."

He backed up a bit. "So you don't mix business with pleasure?"

"Just recently, I have made it my new rule."

"New rule respected. My first question is, who do I make the check out to?"

"To our escrow company, First American Title."

"Oh yes, FATCOLA?"

"That's the one."

He grabbed his keys and cell. "I'll have my business partner call you later this afternoon. Can I have your card again?"

"Lost the other one, huh?" I teased as I reached in my pocket and then handed him another.

"Just don't want to look for it. Thanks. This way I can call him from the car and give him your information."

"I really appreciate it, Mr. Watson."

"My pleasure. I was going to do it anyway, you know, it just slipped my mind what with all of this crazy economy. I'm fighting to keep my head above water right now. But offers like these are just too good of an investment to pass up."

"I think it'll prove to be beneficial to you, Mr. Watson. Thanks so much."

He stood up. "Thanks for the opportunity. And I'll talk to you later. Can I reach you at this number after hours?"

"No."

"Well, I would give you my numbers but I'm about to move and . . ."

"And you're married anyway, right?"

"You're good." He gave me a devilish grin.

"I'll look forward to that call."

He reached out for my right hand, pulled my fingers to his lips and then kissed my knuckles. "Well, I've got to get going. You have a blessed day." He pimp-walked his way toward the exit.

After a long day, I sat at my desk at home, devouring Chinese food. I had days' worth of unopened e-mails, including a reminder from the dating service that I needed to add my picture to the site to increase my number of contacts. At this point, that didn't even sound inviting. I had a few bland messages from a couple of men whose profiles did nothing for me. And I had a Yahoo greeting card.

Morgan,

 *I send you this card as an extremely belated cele-
bration of your fortieth birthday. Even though it's late
in the day, I pray that your day is special and beautiful, just like you are and always have been.*

The attachment was an e-card with a big bouquet of vivid yellow flowers. Stevie Wonder's *You Are the Sunshine of My Life*
echoed through my speakers.

 *The thought of you has brought bright sunny days
my way. May I make a wish on your birthday? I wish
for an opportunity to share a few sunny days with you,
as well as many warm nights with you, too.*
     Always, Jamie.

That man had sent e-mails every day since we last spoke. His
last one read:

*Morgan, it's Jamie. I've decided to no longer refer to myself
as Jay Jay. I haven't heard from you so I can understand
that you are still angry with me. And I don't blame you.
There you are hitting the big 4-0 in your life and here I come
springing some new stuff on you from out of the past. I don't
know how things happened like this, but they did.*
 *I was young and so were you. You were my first, Morgan.
I was hormonal and I didn't know how to really charm you
or make you feel courted. I didn't know what courted meant
back then. We never went to the movies or sat in the park
just talking. I was a dumb fourteen-year-old. But being with
you was never on a dare. I noticed you when all of the other
boys talked about you for looking different. I noticed the
way you walked, and those big brown eyes of yours.*
 *I walked you home from school that day, totally prepared
to ask if you would go with me. But the words never came.*

I'm sure, to you, I was just a boy coming around to use you. To me, though, you were a girl that I was hot and bothered over who I really, really liked. I was ashamed of myself, Morgan. I had you up against the refrigerator and it felt good. I can recall you feeling me with your body, and even though words were not spoken, you seemed to be responding to me, so I kept going. And the next thing I knew, I'd barely penetrated you and I lost it. When you ran out of the kitchen, I was so scared. I stood there for a moment and then just ran out of the door. I ran all of the way home and never told a soul about it. Not even my best friend. Right after that my mother and I got evicted from our place and we moved away. I remember seeing you the last week I was at school, but I hid from you in shame. I didn't know what to say.

As the years went by, I heard about your mother dying. It wasn't until at my wedding, when a fellow classmate mentioned that he went to a reunion and your profile listed that you had a daughter.

I'm sorry, so sorry for letting all of these years go by and not reaching out to find you. Every time I look at my eighteen-year-old daughter, Cameo, I now know in my mind that she is not my one and only, as I've always told her she is. It pains me so deeply. I just pray that one day I will be able to make things come together.

And so, for some reason, God brought us together in this way, via e-mail. Here I am, and there you are. Cameo and Corliss are sisters. So what do we do now? Don't you think they deserve the years we denied ourselves? I wish I'd met you again before your surgery, Morgan. I know you don't believe it but I'd have said the same thing I'm about to say now. I want to see you again. I want a chance to see if there's something there, in person. No longer through the computer, or over the phone, but face-to-face. As I said, I'm single and available. I ask you with all my heart to forgive me and understand. I want to see you. And most of all, I want an opportunity to explain myself to Corliss, if only you would let me. Longingly, Jamie.

While digesting his message, the ring of the phone interrupted my thoughts. The third ring ended and I knew voice mail would kick in, but I heard, "Mom, can you meet me at Houston's in Century City? I want to talk to you."

All I could focus on was Jamie's words. I forced myself to snap out of it. "Why, Corliss?" If only she knew I was just reading an e-mail from her birth father.

"I just need to talk to you."

Perfect timing. "I need to talk to you too actually. When?"

"Tomorrow night."

"What time?" I asked while shutting down my e-mail account.

"Eight."

"Okay."

We met at the meat-market-like, crowded restaurant on the upper level. We both walked up at the same time and surprisingly, after being handed the vibrating beepers, we were seated within just a few minutes.

"Mom, I have to ask you what the deal is with you. To be honest with you, I've talked to Grandpa, Aunt Olympia and Tyra, and they all say they're worried about you too."

While looking around for the waiter, I replied. "Oh, did you ask Jabril too, to see what he thinks? Maybe he'll join your little Morgan-hater team."

"Mom, no one is against you. I just know that there's something inside of you that has changed and I have to know what it is. It pains me to see you so agitated and emotional and opinionated. It's so not you."

"Maybe it has been me all along and I just needed a boost of confidence."

"I know that's not it," she replied.

The waiter walked up. I looked toward Corliss. "Do you know what you want to order? Because I do."

"Our usual garlic chicken and black beans is fine," she replied.

"Make that two," I told the waiter and then spoke to her. "Baby, you have to understand, I am a new Morgan, much different from the old Morgan. I hope that you and everyone else can handle that. I'm awake again."

"I know that. But it's like once you took the focus off your nose, you started focusing on everything else. I don't understand— how does surgery cause all of this? I was totally unprepared."

"Me too, believe me. And it's not just the surgery. I've had a lot of other things on my mind too, Corliss," I admitted.

"Okay." She didn't look convinced.

"And aside from whatever you think I'm doing or saying that's different, there's something else on my mind that I just cannot keep from you any longer."

"What's that, Mom? What's up?" She looked truly concerned.

After a forceful exhale, my shoulders dropped. "You know how I told you that your father was just a one-time fling I had when I was very, very young?"

"Yes. Was he?"

"Yes. Wait a minute. And then I told you that I met this guy named Jay Jay on the Internet?"

"Yes."

"Well, Corliss, it turns out that . . . he's your father."

She blurted out her response. "He's my father?"

Out of guilt, I suppose, I looked around the restaurant but no one even looked our way. "Yes."

She still spoke loudly. "Mom, what are you talking about? How did you hook up with him like that?"

"I didn't know it was him. I was talking to him for a little while, and then when he saw me on TV, he asked me to call him. He told me who he was and I all but flipped."

"This same guy you've been talking to is the very one who you went to junior high school with?"

"Yes."

"He is Jamie Jackson?" she asked as though holding her breath.

I replied with the truth. "Yes, dear, he is."

She leaned in across the table, seemingly trying to bite her lip. "Mom, you have got to be kidding me. There's no way this could be true. It's far too much of a trip to be real. Why would he just show up after all these years?"

"He has his own story to tell."

"And what is it? What could his story possibly be?" She sat back and picked up her spoon, tapping it on the table.

"That he wasn't sure if you were his when he heard I had a daughter."

She banged the spoon down and it flipped onto the floor. She didn't even look to see where it landed. "Bullshit, Mom, excuse my language, but I'm not even buying that."

There was nothing left to do but unload the whole ball of wax. "Well, here's some more news. You also have an eighteen-year-old sister named Cameo."

"I have a sister? Does she know about me?"

"I don't know."

"Mom, hold on a minute." She took a deep breath and started blinking a mile a minute. She paused and shook her head. "So now what?"

"He wants to meet me. He wants to meet you. He wants Cameo to meet you."

This time she picked up the knife and started tapping it. "After all these years of coming to terms with not having a father who cared, knowing that the only real father image I'd be able to learn from was Grandpa, who was just nowhere near able to nurture me like I wanted, I'm finally being told that I can meet my own father who has never seen me in my entire life?"

"I know." My heart bled for my child.

"Mom, you never even really told me a lot about him other than his name and the fact that you were young and he moved away. I never asked you to look him up and you never offered. I've gone all these years coming to terms with the fact that my father didn't exist. That's the only way I've been able to get past not being wanted by him."

"Corliss, please don't feel as though he didn't want you. He never knew about you until now. He saw you on TV and just knew it."

"What do you want me to say, Mom? I have a new dad I've never met. And to be honest with you, a new mother too, who I thought I knew. All of this because you had to go mess with Mother Nature in search of a prettier face." She aimed the knife my way. "Mom, I didn't ask for this."

This was a good time to pray that she put the sharp object down. And she did. "I know you didn't. And I'm sorry. I haven't thought about what you would say or do. I'm still dealing with it myself."

"Mom, is this why you've been so on edge?"

"I don't know." The waiter brought our plates, bent down to pick up her spoon and walked away.

Corliss peered at me. "Could your edginess be because of this, along with, don't tell me, the fact that you miss Jabril, right?" Sarcasm was in the air.

I picked up my fork. "Like I said, I don't know." I closed my eyes to say my blessing. When I opened my eyes, Corliss was saying hers.

She opened her eyes and picked up her fork too. "Mom, do you mind if I order a drink?"

"Let's make it two." I motioned for the waiter to come back over.

CHAPTER 16

"Morgan, you're in sort of a mourning period. Give yourself time." Dr. Grace spoke with patience.

I'd come to the conclusion that I couldn't go another day without sizing up my chaotic life. I decided there was no other person to talk to, other than the counselor who screened me before my surgery. She agreed to see me right away. We faced each other, both sitting in the paisley-cloth chairs in her office. "I know, but I'm dealing with a lot of emotional issues. It's a new life for me." I rubbed my forehead. "With all of the education I have, why can't I get my own life together? I had no idea that when I came face-to-face with the new me, it would be this mind-blowing."

Her words were calming. "This was much different than having a degree. We all need someone to give us feedback from the outside in. So don't blame yourself because you've been schooled. This is real-life school."

"Yes, but Doctor, I'm different."

"Well, it is a life-changing event. But in what ways do you think you've changed?"

"I think I'm angry, whereas before I wasn't."

"Why do you think that is?"

"I'm much more sensitive to criticism and rejection than ever before."

"How have you been criticized or rejected?"

"For one, my own father basically told me he doesn't think the surgery on my face turned out that well. He said it's too perfect."

She put the old quote move on me. "As Eleanor Roosevelt said, 'No one can make you feel inferior, without your consent.' Did you perceive that as an insult?"

"Wasn't it?"

"I can't answer that. But it does sound like he's been a pivotal person in your life. What else?"

"And my boyfriend, well, ex-boyfriend, no longer wants to be with me."

"When did you find this out?"

"He gave me an ultimatum before the surgery."

"And you made your decision anyway?"

"Yes."

She continued to dig. "So you knew there was a possibility that he would leave you?"

"Yes, I knew it."

"So you must have accepted it."

"No, to be honest, I never thought it would really happen."

"Are you mad at him?"

I took a moment, and then another, and then realized that perhaps it was anger. "Yes."

"Why?"

"Why?" I looked up at the ceiling. "Because I used to be able to make him come back. Originally, I think I tried to get back at him for chatting with other women on the Internet. But it looks like I'm not getting him back after all. He always said he would never leave me. But nothing I do changes his mind. I even had sex with him the other night but all he said afterwards was, 'It's just not the same.' But it's not just him. I feel like the whole world perceives me as different. I can't be mad at him. He's right, it's not the same."

"What did you expect after your surgery?"

My hands assisted my explanation. "I expected life to go on as it had been, same man, same job, same relationship with my best friend and daughter, just a prettier face to smile from. Now I don't know who I am. I have to ask you, is it normal to be abnormal?"

She broke it down. "Yes, only because we put those standards out there as a society, based on our own perceptions. We're all guilty of that. The Father Time-type things can be diminished. But you have to deal with the fact that you wanted major features altered. That's not easy to adjust to no matter how much people on the outside might envy you. You are justified in your feelings. But I want you to think back to what you said when we first met the day before your surgery. You told me that you had been excluded and treated differently because of your looks your entire life and that you wanted to look less abnormal. Remember that?"

"Yes."

"Well? Do you think you look less abnormal?"

"Yes."

She uncrossed her legs and leaned forward. "So, mission accomplished. Yet here you are still being treated differently even after your physical changes. It's just a different type of treatment, from a new place and position. You have to give it time. You lived with the old face for forty years. You must give the new face a chance. Rejection is rejection, whether you're Halle Berry or Attila the Hun. We all deal with our internal being as well and it tends to hold more weight. Looks won't make you happier any more than money will, Morgan. I told you that before. This is a process. All I can ask you to do is ask yourself if people are still not getting past the outside."

"No, they're not."

She removed her eyeglasses. "Then you've got to get past it yourself. You've got some serious thinking to do."

We both sat back in silence.

"Jamie, can you meet me tomorrow?" I asked while driving home.

"I'd be honored to, Morgan. Just name the place and time."

His excitement and certainty pleased me. "I'll think of a place and let you know."

"Sounds good to me. Just send me an e-mail if you need to."

"I'll do that. So I'll see you tomorrow."

"I promise, I'll be there, no matter where. Nothing could get in the way of seeing you after all these years."

It was four o'clock on a beautiful Saturday afternoon. I'd chosen the gardenlike meditation center in the Palisades. It was very serene, peaceful, scenic and spiritual. Picture cherry blossoms, bonsai trees, flowing waterfalls, and birds singing. That was the tranquil meditation center.

A baldheaded man with a light complexion and a finely trimmed goatee walked up.

"Morgan," he called with a peaceful glow to his face. He was nowhere near as tall as I'd remembered him.

"Hi, Jamie." I never would have picked him out of a lineup. He looked completely different.

"Stand up, please."

And so I did. He immediately hugged me, his arms around my waist as mine were to my side. He smelled of the fragrance Angel. His bulging belly met my abdomen before anything else did. He was a lot heavier now, and a lot older looking. He had abrasive-looking shaving bumps on his chin and his facial hair was lightly graying. I could see the shadow of his hairline that had started to recede. He pulled me closer and closer, tighter and tighter, without stopping for a minute to get a second glance at my face. He was still for a couple of minutes, and then his right hand patted my back in a way that felt welcoming and warm. I reached around his waist and hugged him as well. He rocked back and forth and to the side with a rotating swivel. He said nothing. And I followed his lead. It was a sweet exchange. Long moments went by.

"Beautiful blouse you're wearing. Your favorite color, huh? Yellow."

"Yes." I cracked a smile at his desire to make note of my likes.

He took my hand, and we started to walk.

"Nice place," he said, looking all around.

I replied, "It is beautiful here."

He glanced at me to draw my eyes. "You have no idea how much this means to me, Morgan. Thank you."

"I'm doing this for Corliss . . . and for me." I gave a long blink.

"I really did accept you back in those early years. I really did like you." He looked humble.

"You had a strange way of showing it."

"I know, you're right about that."

"But somehow, I think deep down I knew you were different," I confessed. We exacted each other's steps like back in the day.

"I was not one of the boys who taunted you back then. You know that."

"Oh, I know them all. Their faces are etched in my mind forever. You would not have been in my home if you'd been one of them."

"Morgan, I have to ask, why is it that you never tried to find me?"

That was the very question I expected him to ask. "I guess I was angry for so long. I blamed myself for letting that afternoon happen. I dealt with the guilt for years. When I brought Corliss into the world, I told myself I had to be okay with the fact that she may never meet her father. I got used to the idea just like she did. And my mom helped me keep my head on straight. She told me to look past whether or not I thought I needed you, but think about whether I thought Corliss would ever need you. My agreement with my mother was that I'd leave it up to Corliss if and when she became curious enough to want to find you. It's just that it never came up. My mother prepared me for the realities of raising Corliss all alone, all my life."

He stopped in his tracks, and so did I. "Thanks for that explanation, Morgan. I respect your honesty."

"No problem."

"Your mother and you were obviously very close. I'm sorry she died."

"It was tough. So how is your mother?"

"She's fine. Back when I was in college she married a man who is pretty well off. They live in Virginia now. He'd worked for the Pentagon as a defense executive. They're retired so they travel all around. They come and see Cameo twice a year."

"I'll bet she's beautiful."

"Can I show you her picture?" he asked.

"I'd love to see it." He handed me his wallet and flipped it open to Cameo's photo. "She has such a sweet look about her. And look at all of that hair on her head."

"Yeah, it's pretty long."

"Does it go all the way down her back?"

"Yes," he said proudly.

"I'll bet you'd go wild of she ever cut it."

"You know it."

I handed him back his wallet. "Here you go."

He fixed his gaze upon my face. "I still can't believe I'm standing here talking to you." I looked down without knowing how to respond. He continued, "How about Corliss? Do you have a picture of her? I saw her on television but I'd love to see her face up close."

"Yes, actually, I have one." I reached into my bag and pulled out a picture I brought just to show him.

He took the picture and then put on his reading glasses before turning it right side up for a close-up view. "Oh my God. She looks so much like Cameo. Don't you think?"

"A little bit."

"She's beautiful, Morgan. You did a great job."

"Yeah, I guess so. Raising her by myself and all. Where's Cameo's mother anyway?"

"She's around. We divorced years ago. We have joint custody but now that Cameo's eighteen, she's on her own."

"And you never had any other kids?"

"No, and you?"

"No. I never wanted to have any more, to be honest with you. I don't think I would have had even one if I hadn't conceived the way I did. I just never wanted to take a chance that they would . . . look like me."

"Morgan, what are you talking about? Just look at Corliss, she looks just like you and she's beautiful."

"Easy for you to say that now. You know what I used to look

like, Jamie. Anyway, I never got married and never wanted any more kids."

"Even now?"

"Oh please, my eggs are probably all dried up like prunes by now. What would I look like with a baby as young as my future grandbaby?"

"Like one pretty grandma, that's how."

That deserved a grin. "You're a lot sweeter than I remember you being."

"Yeah, well we didn't take the time to get to know anything about each other back then."

"I know that's right."

"Did Corliss ever get married?"

"No, but she does have a new boyfriend. I think he's right about your age."

His frown spoke volumes. "What? What's he like? Is he nice?"

"He seems okay. She's a good judge of character so I should just trust in the Lord on that one."

"Do you do that a lot? Trust in the Lord?"

"I probably don't do it as much as I should."

"Do you still go to Catholic church?"

"Not often enough."

"We should go together sometime," he recommended.

"Maybe so," I replied.

"Will you promise me something?"

"What?"

"Trust in Him now. He brought us together, Morgan. We wouldn't be here right now if it wasn't part of His plan. And another thing, you are to be honored for not having an abortion. You are quite a woman."

"Thanks for the praise, but I can't take all the credit. My mother talked me out of that." We walked again. "You know, for some reason, I'm not mad at you, Jamie. I'm just sort of stunned that we've come together after all this time the way we have."

"I'm glad we did. Thank God for the Internet."

"Have you made any other connections online? Or should I say reconnections."

"No, not at all. I stopped responding after I started talking to you, even before I saw you on TV. But that just solidified my feelings. See, Morgan, I believe you and I are supposed to try this thing out. I see no reason not to, unless you've gotten back with that guy you mentioned before."

I waited for a second. "So, what do you do for a living again?"

"Okay, I give. I'm the head chef at Escala."

"Oh, that's right." *Not good that you forgot, Morgan.* "I'm impressed. You prepare cuisine, not food, huh?"

He gave a short chuckle. "You could say that. I'll have to cook for you and Corliss one day. Or am I being too presumptuous?"

"Perhaps you could. I've never met a man who could cook," I confessed.

"Well now you have. My mom made me cook. We'd practice making recipes from her many cookbooks. She owned a soul food place years ago."

"Oh really? Where was that?"

"Back before I was born when she lived in Chicago."

"You know, my sister, Olympia, works as a caterer. I'll bet the two of you would have a lot in common."

Suddenly, my cell phone rang. It was my home number so I let it go at first, and then it rang again.

"Dad, what's up?"

Dad spoke fast. "Morgan, you need to talk to your crazy friend, Jabril. He's here and he's about to get his ass kicked, by me."

I immediately stopped walking. "What's he doing?"

"Apparently he intercepted your e-mail password and he's threatening to head up to wherever you are, at some place in the Pacific Palisades and confront your new man, or so he says. I'm about to call the police on his crazy ass."

"Dad, is he still there?"

"Yes, can't you hear him? He's at the door. I think he's drunk as hell. But I took his keys."

"He doesn't drink and drive, Dad. Let me talk to him, please." I touched Jamie's arm. "Please excuse me for a second."

"Sure." Jamie looked worried for me, but stepped away.

Jabril yelled into the phone. "Where are you, Morgan?"

"I'm out." I turned my back away from Jamie.

"At the same damned place we used to go to talk? With Jamie Jackson. He's Corliss's father or some bullshit. Have you lost your mind?"

"How dare you violate my privacy like that, Jabril? You wrote me off and you have no right to intercept my e-mails and threaten to confront anyone. You need to go get with your new friend." Jamie was getting an earful.

"Listen to you. You talk a lot of trash lately, don't you? Who are you?"

"Who are *you*? Well, actually I know who you are. You are one controlling, spoiled brat who rants and raves when he doesn't get his way. Well, you're not getting it anymore so just go home, wherever that is."

"I'll be there in twenty minutes. Don't let me find your asses together. He'll be one dead motherfucker."

I heard a muffled sound over the phone, and then it was as if the phone dropped. "Jabril?" I shrieked.

"You get the hell out of here," my father hollered. "No one talks to my daughter like that. I told you that before. Now take your keys and your crazy ass and get out of this house. And don't come back."

The phone disconnected abruptly. I called back but there was no answer. I called Jabril's cell phone, but his voice mail came on.

Jamie sounded alarmed. "Are you okay?"

"Yes. And to respond to your other comment, no, I'm not back with him and never will be. That was the last straw." I put my phone back into my bag. "I hope you don't mind but I need to get home right away."

"I understand." He tried to draw my eyes to his but it didn't work. "Are you sure you'll be okay? I can follow you if you need me to."

I walked back toward the parking lot. "I'll be fine. It's just my ex on one of his tirades. I'll call you later."

"Okay, but be safe. If I don't hear from you I'm going to worry."

"No, I'll call."

"Deal. Good-bye, Morgan." He reached out for a hug.

"Good-bye, Jamie." I hugged him back.

We broke from our embrace as I turned and stepped away at a fast pace, wondering if Jabril would indeed show up in a crazed rage. Approaching my car, we turned back for a quick peek at the same time and smiled. *So that's my baby's daddy?*

The sun was just starting to set. Dad sat on the living room sofa with only the reflection of the television bouncing off his face. This time, he did not have a beer in hand. A half-empty, tiny bottle of Wild Turkey sat on the coffee table. I'd just hung up from calling Jamie to let him know I was home.

"Dad, what ended up happening?" I asked, rushing in to sit next to him.

"He went home."

"How did you get him to do that?"

He started to ramble on. "I'm still stunned that I did it at all, baby. I had an epiphany of sorts. It was like an out-of-body experience. He stormed out like a madman on a mission and stepped into his car. Once he started the engine, I snapped. I ran toward him as he was backing up and opened the car door. I dragged his long, lanky body out of that car like I was half my age. He fell onto the concrete, and then I jumped in his car, placing the gearshift in park while taking the keys. Jabril ran toward the street, almost like he was going to run all the way to you. I tackled him to the ground and forced him to calm down. Jabril started crying. He sobbed like a newborn baby, Morgan. That boy was hurting. I begged him to sit on the curb with me and just listen. He was stubborn but he gave in, and then I told him."

I then noticed that Dad's wrist was scraped up and scratched. "Told him what?" He continued to speak but it was as though he was still talking to Jabril. "Twenty-three years ago I followed my wife when she went to meet who I thought was her lover. I was just like you, macho and always the boss. I could always make her do whatever I wanted her to, except this time. In her mind, she was going out no matter what I said. And so, I followed her when she got off work late, but she didn't know it. She pulled up at a parking lot of a major supermarket, and she sat for a little while. I parked to the side of a building and turned off my headlights. And then a big car pulled up. It was nighttime and I could barely make out who it was, but it was a man for sure. He had an Afro, and he appeared to be a big man, almost stocky enough to be considered overweight. My wife got out of her car, and opened the passenger door to his car. She got inside, leaned over, and to me, it looked like she kissed him on the lips. I felt a burning inside of my gut. My soul was an inferno and my heart cracked like an egg from the pain that shot through my insides. All I could do was start my car and floor it, but they had already started to pull out onto the boulevard, signaling to make a right as I approached, and then, all of a sudden, as if out of nowhere, they were broadsided by a new pickup truck. Their car spun around and around. It was as if my eyes were deceiving me, but they weren't. I was paralyzed. The right side of the car slammed into a light pole and my wife was crushed. Her friend was ejected from his open widow. They both died instantly."

"Daddy, oh my God." My gut was panging.

"I stood in the street, yelling to the Lord, asking why, just as the police came up and tried to calm me down. I told them what I saw and who she was to me—my wife of many years. They held me at the station for a while until they were convinced that the man she was with was not trying to escape from me. But I've never been so convinced."

"Dad, they didn't see you, I'm sure they didn't."

He seemed to snap back to the present. "If I could only live that night over again. If I could have just went up to the car to claim my wife instead of letting them pull off."

I put my hand on his knee. "Don't let this whole thing kill you, please. It was supposed to be. Mom died exactly when she was supposed to."

He went on, still staring straight ahead. "And there I stood, wondering if Jabril was going to run you down, causing a tragedy like I did. I really felt like I had a chance to do something good by saving him from himself."

"Dad, you not only saved him, you saved my friend and me, and it seems as if you possibly saved yourself too."

"How's that?" He looked dazed.

"After all these years, you've finally let it be said. You spoke the words that will set you free, Dad. You've suffered enough. Let it go."

"But, Morgan. Hold on."

"Dad, you saved my life tonight. How can you possibly second-guess yourself?"

"I have second-guessed myself for many years now. And so did your mom."

"Why?"

"Morgan, I told you I'd never lie to you, but that was a lie." I could hear him inhale and exhale. "That man who died with your mother . . . was your real father."

There was a thud in my chest. "My real what?" I snatched my hand from his knee.

"He is your birth father. Not me."

My breathing was uneven. "Dad. What are you talking about?"

"Your mom didn't believe in abortion any more than you did. You were conceived before I met your mother. I loved you like my own."

Without a second thought, I rose to my feet and yelled. "Oh the hell you did. Now I see. You loved me like the wicked step-daughter. Get the hell out of my face. Now."

Without saying another word, Dad walked toward the stairs, went up to his room and closed the door.

Stepping through the sliding glass door, I plopped down on a lounge chair by the pool, glancing up at the stars.

What a crock of bull! How dare this man—this judgmental, criticizing, chauvinistic asshole—spring this on me now. First he told me that I now look too perfect. Still not good enough to meet his standards. And now this. But damn, if I'd only known that his vision of me had nothing to do with my anatomical makeup, but rather with my DNA, I'd have been a whole lot more accepting of his harshness and insults. He'd always seen me as this man's daughter, always knowing that I was not his, that I was conceived out of wedlock, that I was another man's child. But who was this other man? And who in the hell was I?

I allowed my inherited features to be chipped away, grinded down to who I thought I should be: more like this man who I called father, more like my mother. And what in the hell was in her head to make her stray? Oh hell, I know why she would stray. Because River Bayley was a controlling fool, that's why. Why she never left this man is the real question. For her to keep my birth father on the side all of those years, to plan a rendezvous with him, and then lose her life with him, is unreal. She died with the man she probably really loved enough to not give up. Who the hell was he?

Heading back into the house, I was compelled to stop in front of my fireplace. My mom's sketch met me face-to-face. This is how she saw me in her mind, knowing that she chose a man who I'd probably never get a chance to know more about if Dad hadn't told me. Maybe she would have told me if she hadn't died. But for now, Dad has to hear my mouth. I marched straight up to his room. I entered without knocking.

"Dad, oh I'm sorry, you're not my dad. So what do I call you now?"

He sat at the end of his bed. "I will always be your dad."

"No. I don't think so." I stood over by the window and crossed my arms in his direction.

"I should have never told you."

"No, both of you should have told me years ago. But you didn't, for whatever reason. Is Olympia your real daughter, or does she have to come to terms with having a mystery father too? Or maybe a mystery mother."

He answered without hesitation. "Yes, she's my daughter."

"So Mom tried to run away with him after umpteen years of being married?"

"They knew each other through a friend of hers, but worked together years ago from what I hear."

"I thought Mom didn't start working until after I attended high school."

"It was only a temp job that lasted a few weeks, a year or so before we met."

"And what do you know about him?" I looked at him, anxiously awaiting full details.

"So now I guess you're going to run off and bond with your father's side of the family?"

How dare he? "That's my business. I think I have every right to do what I want considering that you two lied to me from day one."

"We thought we were doing the right thing."

"You're not my father. I was told that you were. How can that be right?"

"I'm sorry that you learned to call me Dad." His frown was deep.

My heart felt like it was cracking bit by bit as I spoke. "I wondered why . . . why you were so cold, so unloving."

"It wasn't that bad, Morgan."

"Speak for yourself. Now I need to know everything, every answer, every name, and every bit of information. Now."

"What do you need to know?" He looked at me, knowing he would not get an answer. He continued, "Your dad's name was Gary Washington. That's all I can tell you."

Cutting my eyes, I watched him sit with his face buried in his hands. I knew that name, Gary Washington, from when I read the police report the day after my mom's death. I knew the man's name that she died with but paid it no mind as being anyone who was biologically significant. I knew he was a friend, I actually thought that possibly he was more. Deep down, I didn't want to know.

He grabbed his backpack in silence. I watched his every move with darting eyes, thinking maybe he was the real one to blame for my mother's death after all.

"I'm Gary Washington's daughter. What do I do now?" I asked him and the heavens above.

Dad, River Bayley, simply packed a few of his things and left.

CHAPTER 17

Corliss spent the entire day getting her precision hairdo trimmed up, spoiling herself with a manicure and pedicure, and buying a new outfit. And then we actually went to the mall together. For the first time in our lives, we were actually wearing the same damned size . . . a size eight. We even stopped at The Limited and bought matching outfits: a khaki-colored pair of stretch jeans and an olive-colored top. Her top was long-sleeved and mine was short-sleeved.

We walked hand in hand through the Northridge Mall, taking a moment to enjoy a Hotdog-on-a-Stick and a cold cherry lemonade. For the first time, even with only fourteen years between us, it was like we were girlfriends instead of mother and daughter.

As we headed to my car, I reached in my purse for my keys. The piece of pale pink paper I'd scribbled on in my office fell to the ground. Corliss chased it as the light wind carried it and she picked it up.

She kind of snickered. "This is cute. Who's this?" she asked, almost as if to tease.

"It's us, actually."

"You did this? When did you learn that?"

"Your grandma used to do that. I got it from watching her."

"You'll have to teach me one day."

I started to zip up my purse, but put my hand out for her to return the paper. "Corliss, there are a whole lot of other things you need to be putting your energy into. And doodling is not one of them."

"Okay," she replied, giving me a look like I was being way too serious. "Can I have it?" she asked.

"Why would you want that?"

"Because you drew it with us in mind, that's why."

"Have at it," I said as she laughed, folding it into fours and tucking it into her pants pocket. I dared not burst her bubble.

For her, this was the day she had a chance to meet her own father for the first time in her life. Something I'd never get a chance to do. I dared not tell her that to top it off, her grandfather was not her real grandfather. That would surely negate the good feelings. Oh yes, and she'd also get a chance to meet her half sister.

For me, it was a chance to sit back and watch her make the connection. To watch her meet the other half of who she was, in Jamie Jackson. And I wanted to see how he'd handle himself.

Running about fifteen minutes early, Corliss and I arrived at the Italian restaurant where Jamie worked. We stepped inside the dark, swanky place, with the rich green color scheme, and stepped up to the greeter at the reservation podium. Corliss grabbed my hand. We interlocked fingers. She gave me a squeeze. I squeezed her hand back. The youthful greeter said, "Oh yes, right this way," after we gave him our names. "We've been expecting you."

We were escorted to a small, cozy booth in the back room. It was very private. With bated breath, we came within a few feet of the booth. Jamie stood up, eyes fixed on Corliss. She squeezed my hand even tighter. He reached out his arms. She released her grip and took one giant step right up to her father, embracing him tightly with her head to his chest. He secured his embrace by closing his arms around her back. I could hear her internal buildup of an emotional heave. Corliss let it out, even before words were said, she simply released her joy and pain in the form of tears. I stood back, almost afraid to make a move. I had a fluttering feeling in my stomach that rose to my throat. The greeter walked away with a look like he felt we needed some privacy. And seated at the table, chasing away a tear that traveled from the corner of her eye to the tip of her nose, was Cameo Jackson, young, pretty, and wide-eyed. I scooted in to sit next to her. We hugged as well.

"Hello, Cameo. It's nice to meet you," I said.

"You too." Her voice was high-pitched and soft.

Jamie and Corliss broke away from their embrace and he kissed her cheek, still queezing her close with a one-armed hug. He looked down at her face as she sniffled. "Well hello, Corliss. You are so very beautiful. I'm happy to finally meet you."

"Me too," she replied, wiping her nose with the back of her hand.

Jamie took a napkin from the table and handed it to her. He pointed toward his younger daughter. "And this is Cameo." He handed Cameo one as well.

After dabbing her eyes, Corliss tried to compose herself, and then slid in next to her sister. I watched them hug too. They had very similar features. Especially their noses—they were identical. Their wavy grade of hair seemed to be the same too. Corliss wore her hair extremely short, and Cameo's was extremely long, almost so long that she could probably sit on it. They had the same round faces and thin lips. Jamie had some strong-ass genes.

"Hello," Cameo said.

"You look just like me," Corliss told her.

"I know, we do look alike," Cameo agreed.

"You're both beautiful. All three of you," Jamie said, while looking my way. He leaned over to kiss me lightly on my cheek, and then sat down on the other side next to Corliss.

He spoke as he enjoyed the view. "Wow. Well, here we are."

I spoke up too. "Yes, here we are."

"How old are you?" Cameo asked Corliss.

"I just turned twenty-six."

"Wow, you look a lot younger."

"I like her already," Corliss joked to her dad.

Jamie told Cameo, "Corliss is an esthetician."

"What's that?"

"Non-medical care of the skin."

"Cool. You must be really smart."

"I wouldn't say that." Corliss looked humble.

"Ladies, I'm sorry it's taken so long for this to happen. But I'm also so blessed that it happened at all. This is a very happy day for me. It feels like a dream come true."

"It feels like a dream to me too," said Corliss.

"Corliss, I don't know what your mother's told you, but I want to put this out there for all of you to hear. I can understand why your mother didn't try to find me. None of this is her fault. I can't give us back the lost time, but I'd like for us to get to know each other. All of us."

"I'd like that too. How about you, Cameo?" Corliss asked her sister.

"I think that's fine."

"You don't mind sharing your dad with me?"

She shook her head. "No."

"Are you happy, dear?" Jamie asked his baby girl, sensing a little reservation in her voice.

She then seemed a little more enthusiastic. "Who wouldn't be happy? I have a new sister." She flashed her braces and leaned in to hug Corliss.

"I have a new sister. I can't believe it," Corliss said to her dad.

He replied, "I have a new daughter."

They looked at me.

"I have a new family member too. Cameo, I look forward to getting to know you," I said.

Jamie seemed assured. "If I have my way, we'll all be just fine. Together."

The tux-with-tails-wearing waiter approached. "Are you ready to order?"

Jamie responded, "Not even. I haven't given them a chance to take one single look at the menu. I had the chef prepare some special selections for you all. I hope you like it."

"I'm sure we will," I said.

We all picked up the leather-bound menu and made our choices. We all agreed on his meat lasagna.

For the next two hours, more laughter, smiles, stories and good old-fashioned fun were had than I'd experienced in many, many years. I'd never seen Corliss look so radiant. It was like she and Jamie had known each other her whole life. And teenaged Cameo was the most respectful, loving young lady. I was looking forward to being in her life.

As the evening wound down, Jamie wanted to order yet another round of refreshments or coffee. Corliss and I chose the coffee. Cameo ordered iced tea. Jamie ordered hot chocolate. After a while, we were the only customers left. We stayed until the restaurant closed.

Later, Jamie called me to make sure I had made it home.

"Morgan, you did a great job. That young lady could have had hostility and hatred for me. But she did not."

"A lot of the credit goes to you. You were up-front and warm. And you seemed sincere."

"Thanks."

"I think you two will be just fine."

"I agree. Thanks for logging on to the Internet that day."

"I suppose it was meant to be, as you said."

"All I can say is I've never been happier."

"Yes, it looks like Corliss is yours for the taking."

"Now if I can only work on her mother," he commented and then paused.

I paused too. "Good night, Jamie. Thanks for dinner. Talk to you tomorrow."

My house was quiet that evening. It was a kind of silence that I was not used to. No more Corliss living at home. No more Jabril hanging out, giving off his testosterone scent at a moment's notice. No more Dad to cook for, who fixed things around the house and who always seems to be attached to the couch, brewskis and all, watching ESPN. I really didn't even watch television anymore. I didn't feel like surfing the net. I didn't feel like sleeping yet either. I walked from room to room, eyeing my surroundings and taking mental notes of what I could do to spruce up the place.

I entered Dad's room, which was always cluttered, but for sure, his bed was always made. What if he didn't come back? Could I turn his room into a gym? I supposed that would work out nicely. Or maybe a nice meditation room. I looked over next to his television. Dinner receipts, his check stub from his Social Security payments, some old lottery tickets and ATM receipts were on top of his dresser, and a small orange card that looked familiar to me. It looked like the type of card they put on my windshield when I visited . . . Tyra.

Without even knowing how I got in my car and which traffic lights I ran, I ended up standing at Tyra's door, knocking hard, blinking like the wind was in my face.

She opened the door as if startled. She was barefoot, and wearing a cheetah-print short robe. "I was surprised when they announced that you were here. What's up?" She rubbed her eyelids.

As soon as her mouth closed, I spoke. "Tyra, are you uncomfortable with my new looks?" I stepped inside and walked past her.

She left the door open as she turned toward me. "What the—? No, not at all. I'm happy for you."

"Then why are you sleeping with my father?"

"What?" She actually had the nerve to look offended.

"You need to stop denying it, Tyra. I already know."

She closed the door and waved a dismissal hand back at me, heading toward her tan recliner. She plopped down. "You don't know a damned thing. I thought you'd gotten over your paranoia."

I traced her every step. "I thought you'd gotten over being a hoochie."

She looked up at me and fired back. "Oh please. Just because of the stories I told you before, you actually think I'd sleep with a sixty-year-old man who's my best friend's father."

"Older men are right up your alley. And I hardly consider what you did as the act of being a friend."

"Well that's news to me. You've known me since elementary school. You need to come back to reality on this one."

"You need to stop your little lying game and come back to earth yourself."

"Morgan."

"Whatever." I made that one word sound like ten.

She reached back and fidgeted with her ponytail. "Morgan. I don't know why you're so damned angry."

"I'm angry because I don't have my man anymore, my daughter is dating someone old enough to be my man, my dad is not my real dad, my birth parents are dead, and someone who I thought I could trust is sleeping with the man I thought was my father my whole life. How's that?"

Her voice got loud. "I would never sleep with your father."

I spoke in a civil tone, but was adamant. "He's not my father, and you're not my friend."

She didn't blink. "Morgan, please believe me." Frustration coated her sentence.

"Tyra, cut it. I just saw the parking pass to your condominium on his dresser. I guess we're even now, huh?"

"Morgan, I'll say it again, I am not seeing your father. You've got to believe me." She continued to sit. "And what do you mean your birth parents are dead?"

Heading back toward the door, I added, "You know what? You two deserve each other. I'll be fine. But you need to go to the Hollywood Hills cemetery and get on your knees and apologize to my mother who had you in our home and treated you like a third daughter all those years. I don't know how you sleep at night."

Poker-faced Tyra did not say a word.

I continued. "I knew I'd be unrecognizable to my own friends, I just never knew my own friends would be unrecognizable to me. So to answer my own question, I guess you are uncomfortable with my new looks after all."

She spoke to my back. "Just like I told you after dinner the day of your debut, I think you look simply beautiful."

"And why did you befriend me when we were young? Why me? Did I make you look better? Was that it?"

"No. I've always seen you as beautiful."

Turning back toward her, I noticed she was playing rub and squeeze with her hand. "Well, suddenly, you look just as ugly on the outside as you do on the inside. Suddenly you're very ugly, Tyra."

She bit her lip. "I'm sorry you feel that way, Morgan. Actually, your dad did tell me about the man who died with your mother. But he told me over the phone, not in person. He chose to talk to me about it because he was worried about you and he knew me to be the one person, aside from Olympia, that you'd talk to about it. I didn't know he told you, but I'm glad he did. And the only time your dad ever came over here was when you were away getting your makeover. He was kind enough to come by one morning to take me to pick up my car from the shop and I appreciated that. He didn't even come up. I never had a man to call Dad like you've had. Morgan, you, of all people, know my history. My mother and father live in New Jersey and we don't speak. They've always been mad at me for accusing my uncle of abusing me when I was ten years old. Once I graduated from high school, they moved away and pretty much left me. I've had to make it on my own ever since then. You and your family have been much more of a family than they were. But, Morgan, birth father or not, I'd give anything to have a father like you have in Mr. Bayley. He plain old cares. We all make mistakes. But don't think he hasn't been going through a living hell since witnessing what he saw the night your mother died."

"I see you know all my business, Tyra, but with all due respect, I don't need you to run things down for me. I know you've been through a lot. But dammit, so have I. My life has turned upside down lately and you're the last person I thought I'd have to worry about."

"That's just it. I am the one person you don't have to worry about. I'll always be here for you. I love you, Morgan." She stood up and approached me as I turned the doorknob.

All I could do was think about how badly I wanted to go home. "I'll talk to you later." I looked at her standing there. Her shoulders were hung low. Her eyes were red. Her face was flushed. She looked spent.

"Morgan, please open your heart and remember who I am."

I paused, forcing myself to clamp my lips. I looked around her cozy place, noticing the scented candles she loved that I'd given her, the African mask we got from a marketplace, the wrought iron mirror we picked out together at Pier 1, and the ceramic statue of two little pigtailed black girls hugging that we each bought while on vacation in the Bahamas. "And one more thing,

I'm having dinner at my house on Saturday night at eight so everyone can meet Jamie."

She spoke without hesitation. "I'll be there."

Jabril was blowing up my phone as soon as I stepped into the house. It was damned near midnight. I eyed the caller ID and wanted to pick it up, but just wasn't in the mood for any more drama. However, drama seemed to be my middle name lately. "Hello."

"Hey there. Do you have a minute?" he asked, talking low. I heard Frankie Beverly and Maze in the background.

"Yes."

"I want to apologize for showing up there and causing a scene. I wasn't going to hurt anybody."

"It didn't sound like you were thinking straight. I didn't want to take bets on what you would do."

"I know."

"And I changed my e-mail code so you can just forget about trying that again. I've never done that to you, Jabril."

"I was wrong. I hope you forgive me."

"Okay." My reply was tainted with distance.

"Are you seeing anyone?"

"Why? Aren't you the one who was threatening to hunt me down?"

He tried to sound believable. "I just don't want to intrude if you are."

"Let's not go there. How's your apartment search going anyway?"

"It's not. I'm trying to put the manager off until my agent pays me all the money they owe me. It should be around eight thousand dollars."

"So, is your manager trying to evict you?" I asked.

"No, they're working with me."

"Then why are you all packed like you're ready to go?"

He took a breath before replying. "Because I'll be moving when I get the money."

"Well, if you don't pay them they'll put you on record as being evicted and it'll be harder to rent somewhere else."

His voice grew louder. "I know that. Who said I wasn't going to pay them?"

"Oh, sorry. Forgive me for giving you advice. I forgot my place."

Surely he wanted to react to my cynicism but the track changed on his CD. He started to sing along with the *Before I Let Go* cut and then stopped. "Sorry about raising my voice. But I've got it all covered. To change the subject to something much more serious, I think you already know that your dad saved my life."

"I heard."

"He's been to hell and back. He finally made me realize that being stupid is a waste of time."

"I really don't want to talk about him."

"Cookie, I'm miserable without you. I need to see you."

"No, Jabril."

"Please."

"No." I sounded certain.

"I was just afraid of how I would handle the competition. I wasn't being fair to you. Baby, we belong together. We fit like a glove and you know it. I know you're not feeling this dude who treated you like that back then. And then he didn't even try to find you."

"You treated me pretty bad a lot more recently than he did. You can't intimidate and threaten people into doing what you want them to do, you know."

"I know what you're saying. I've changed. I'm not that man anymore."

"I'm not that woman anymore, Jabril. I've changed too."

"Cookie, I loved you just the way you were. You had to go and ruin what we had by trying to be someone you thought you wanted to be. Someone you thought I'd want you to be. You fell victim to the enemy of good. You kept trying to get better when you needed to leave well enough alone."

In no mood to hear his opinions, I spewed, "You were never totally happy with me and you know it. We were far from perfect."

He explained, "Then we should have worked on us and gone

into therapy or something. What would you have done i̇
ahead and had my nose changed, my complexion lightene͘
head tatted up with symbols?"

"You know I wouldn't have had a problem with whatever yoṳ
decided to do. That's called unconditional love. But you don't
know about that."

"I know all about that unconditional love. I also know that it's
easy for you to say what would have happened if the shoe were
on the other foot. You'll never have to deal with it though."

"You're right. I never will."

"So you're happy?" he asked.

"Yes, I am."

He gave a single chuckle. "I don't believe you. I think you're
more of what you wanted to be on the outside and less of who
you were on the inside." There's the old Jabril.

"That's your opinion. I'm not perfect inside or out. But I'm
working on being the best person I can be."

"You should have done that before you were sculpted into
whoever you are."

Ouch. "Listen to you. You really don't get it, do you? I'm still
the woman who loved you, Jabril. The woman who tried to get
you to love me in spite of my personal decision."

"We'd been together long enough for it to be a *we* decision.
You were very selfish."

"What makes you say I'm selfish—because I put myself before
you for once? Jabril, I went dumb for you for too long. You need to
know that you're not necessary for my existence."

His long exhale was loud. "Cookie, look. Let's stop this. I want
another chance with you. I love you like nothing else ever in my
life. You were the best."

"Whatever. You probably wouldn't like me now anyway. I'd
probably kick you out if you questioned me in my home or made
sly comments today or chatted with Platinum Babe. You can no
longer make a part-time job out of making me feel bad."

"You could have done all that 'I'm everywoman' stuff before."

His derision turned my stomach. "You were with me because

you knew I wasn't the type to check you. That's precisely why you liked me."

"So, tell me then, do you check your baby's father?"

"He doesn't give me a reason to check him. Jabril, I've been through a whole lot more than what a scalpel and saline can be responsible for. I am a new woman. I'm stronger and more proud. I can't go backward."

"Cookie, I need you to move forward with me."

"I can't."

"Cookie, don't do this."

"Jabril, I'm happy. Please accept that."

"I can't."

"Well, you're going to have to, especially if you love me. And I want my house key back too. I haven't forgotten about that."

"Cookie, please."

"Jabril, good-bye. I'm hanging up now, whether you respond or not. And I changed my alarm code and every other code too. Now good-bye."

Silence. It was obvious that the whole aspect of loving myself more than I loved him was eating him alive.

I hung up. But within one minute, Jabril called back, again, and again, and again, no longer in control. No longer able to make me be the way he wanted me to be. He ended up leaving a message. The tone was as if his heart was heavy.

> *Cookie,*
>
> *You've seen pictures of my mother, right? And you commented on how beautiful she was, remember? Well, my mother entered a ton of beauty competitions before she got married, even as a child, and she won every one of them. Later, after she married my dad, she even won the Mrs. California contest. She was looked upon for her beauty all of her life, and no one ever took the time to look past that. Morgan, my mom was raped in high school. And then a man, who just took*

her as his own for hours and violated her for his own
sick satisfaction, raped her when I was sixteen years
old. He tortured her so badly that she died from her
wounds. I swore if I ever met the man who did that to
her, I'd kill him. But before I could, my dad did. I told
you they both died together, but that was a lie. My dad
was serving a life sentence for murdering the creep
who went too far, and killed her. A year later, my dad
was found dead from hanging himself in his cell. I don't
want you to end up like my mother. I want you to be
who you are, just as you are. The world is confused
enough with all of these standards we place on each
other to be perfect. I already saw you as perfect. Please
don't do this to us. Please understand where I'm coming
from. I'm so all alone. You're all I've got. I'm desperate.

In a daze, I put down the phone. I suddenly knew why he preferred average, passive women to attractive, independent ones.
My mind went on a wild ride, trying to add up his past behaviors
with what he'd confessed to me that night.

And then I noticed the envelope Tyra left me from when she
and Dad were sitting, waiting for me to come home. It was still on
the table there.

Opening the envelope, I removed a single typewritten page. It
was a copy of the letter she'd sent to the radio station about why I
needed the makeover. She'd used a yellow highlighter to mark
the part that read, "It would mean the world to me for your station to consider a woman who has made something out of herself,
is a proud mother, and a beautiful lady. Please consider choosing
Morgan, who always does so much for others, this is the least I
can do for her."

On the bottom of the page, she wrote a note by hand.

Congratulations. I can't think of a better birthday
present to give you than a makeover. You are a gift to

me. You always have been, and always will be. And I
never want that, or you, to change, because I never
will. Happy Birthday.
                                                    Love, Tyra

I had to know that I did the right thing by believing her. Tyra had been my girl for so long. She wouldn't do that to me. No, there was no way she'd have done that to me. She'd always been there in every way. I had to trust her unconditionally. I just had to.

CHAPTER 18

There were two men in my life who'd always been there: Jabril and my dad. I couldn't say that the relationships had been perfect or even functional, but they had been consistent. But my mother fell in love with River Bayley. And one thing was for sure, River Bayley had shown up. And good or bad, functional or dysfunctional, healthy or toxic, he gave up his bachelorhood and took on a woman who he loved. That had to mean something. The last thing I wanted to happen was that he stressed so much that he suffered another stroke, like last year. I'd never forgive myself.

I hoped Dad would answer his cell phone. I was deep into ring number five. He didn't even really know how to work the darn thing.

"Hello." There was his mature voice, sounding confused as hell that this tiny device without a cord would actually ring, awaiting his push of a button.

"Dad, I need to talk to you."

He sounded distant. "Why?"

"Please come over," I requested.

"Why?"

"Please just come."

"You can talk to me on the phone, Morgan. Go ahead."

"Fine, Dad." I laid back in the recliner, elevating my feet. "Did you love me?"

"Why would you even ask me that?"

"Because I need to know."

"If you need to know, then that means you don't know," he replied as though he knew it all.

"I just need to reconfirm."

"What do you think?"

"Dad, can I lead just one conversation?"

His irritation was evident, as was mine. "You're leading this just fine by spewing nonsense at me, Morgan. What is this all about?"

"Dad, did you love me?"

He raised his voice. "Morgan, hell yes, I loved you. All you'd have to do is look at what I did. My actions should be enough to answer that question."

"But Dad, I never heard you say, I . . ."

He interrupted. "I loved you."

"But do you love me?"

His voice cracked from the volume of his word. "Yes."

"Say it." I was firm.

"Morgan, why? Are you trying to find yourself as though you're in a therapy session on *Oprah* or something?"

"I'm trying to find myself, yes. I don't know who I am anymore, and the main reason why has nothing to do with my plastic surgery, it has to do with this person you say is my father."

"I'm quite sure you know more about him by now than I do. Did you check myfamily.com or something?" He sounded very insecure.

"No, actually, Dad, I didn't."

"And why not?"

"Because I needed to talk to you first. I need you to tell me what I don't know."

"I don't know much more than I told you before."

Balling up my fist, I banged it on the arm of the chair. "I need every drop of what you think is not much."

He took a deep breath. I heard the sound of a door close as he downshifted his tone. "Morgan, when I met your mother, she was pregnant. I think barely two months so she wasn't showing."

"I thought you two had been married when she conceived."

"No, she was single when she conceived. We got married a little over forty years ago. I married her six months after we met, a month before you were born."

"Did you know right away, that she was pregnant, I mean?"

"Yes. She told me immediately."

"And it didn't make a difference to you?"

"No. I loved her. Almost at first sight."

"And then what?"

"And then you were born. You were given my name. And you were raised as though you were my daughter."

"Why did she break up with him?"

He explained. "He was her best friend's brother and it caused problems with her friend when she found out they'd been seeing each other, so they stopped."

"Did Mom's friend know Mom was pregnant?"

"No. Her friend was never really able to substantiate their affair anyway."

"Which friend was this?"

"You never knew her. They never rekindled their friendship. Until . . ."

"Until what?"

"Until her friend was diagnosed with cancer."

I continued to probe. "When was that?"

"That happened a few weeks before your mother met with your biological father."

"What do you mean?"

"I found a note from him in her purse. He wanted to meet at a certain time. What I didn't know until I was informed by the police, was that your mom and him were headed to his sister's house so that she and her friend could reconcile."

Question marks swirled through my mind. "Had he and Mom been in touch all of those years in between?"

"No."

"But you thought they had been?"

"Yes," he confessed.

"Dad." My hand opened and flexed.

"I know."

"So he got in touch with Mom and agreed to take her to see his sister?"

"Yes."

"What was her name?"

"His sister's name was Norma Jean."

"Norma Jean."

"Yes. And she died a month or so later."

"So she was my aunt and my mom's friend and I never knew her?"

Silence.

"Dad, did he, my birth father, know about me eventually?"

"Not that I know of. I don't think your mom ever told him."

"So he never knew he had a daughter. He wasn't just some deadbeat dad."

"No, he wasn't."

"Did he have any other kids?"

"Not that I know of."

A scary thought came to mind. "Damn, I could be dating my own half brother out here one day and not even know it."

He did not reply.

My vision blurred from the moisture in my eyes. I rubbed my forehead for clarity, but it would not come. "Dad, how does that make you feel now?"

"Today, I feel like I'm dealing with it. It's been years but sometimes, it's like it's brand-new."

"You've had to live with the fact that I wasn't your daughter all of this time?"

"Yes."

Sure to hit a nerve, I asked, "And is that why you treated me . . . so differently from Olympia?"

"I don't think I did."

I spoke firmly. "Dad, you did."

He waited before he responded. His voice was soft. "I've never heard that from you before."

"I never had the nerve to tell you before. Until now."

"Until now that what?" he asked, sounding monotone.

"Until now that I know the real reason why you treated me like a stepdaughter. Because I was." I leaned forward to lower the footrest from my chair and stood up. This was a great time to pace.

"Morgan, I took on your mother, pregnant and all, and I married her. We started a family of our own and we lived a pretty good life."

I took a stab at him because I could. "Until you got jealous and went snooping?"

"Until I went snooping and witnessed an image that will forever be in my head. I cannot change that night, nor the outcome. But most of all, I cannot change the fact that you are not my birth daughter. That is a huge regret."

"But it always seemed like I could never ever do enough to win you over."

He told me, "I didn't need to be won over by one daughter or another. I needed to be equally loving. I thought I was."

"It didn't feel like you were."

In the background, I heard Sierra announcing, "Dinner's ready." I didn't hear Dad's reply though. "Well, to answer your question, I love you, Morgan. I've been there since day one, and I love you."

"That's good to hear. But do you think you've taken your anger with Mom out on me?"

"I don't know that I've been angry with her. Not since I found out why she met with him."

"She wasn't fooling around on you."

"I know that."

"Dad, where was he all of the years before he died?"

"He was in the service from what I know. And then I think he lived in Germany. He never married. He returned to his hometown in Georgia, and then back to California a few years before he died." His voice was faint. It sounded like he was about to cry.

Ceasing my measured, twelve-step trek across the carpet and ten-step Daddy ass-kicking, I thought I'd better downshift my inquisition. "Dad, I wish I could erase that scene from your mind. I'm sorry you've had to live with that."

He sniffed once, and then twice. He cleared his throat. "I've asked for it. I'm the one who is sorry that you have not felt as though you've been enough. I'm sorry that we kept this from you."

Suddenly, it felt like I took on the role of the parent. "So am I. But everything happens for a reason. This experience has been more of a life lesson than anything I've ever been through. Now I know why you made me feel so unbeautiful. The sight of me must have reminded you of the sight of him."

"Subconsciously, maybe. But I thank you for understanding."

"I thank you for telling me."

"Morgan, I want you to know that your last name is Bayley. Please don't you ever think of changing that until you get married, do you hear me?"

"I do."

"Good."

I entered the kitchen. "Dad, do you think that eventually, you could think about moving back home with me?"

"Why?"

"You loved me for who I was. You were there. You raised me. And I want you to be here for as long as you need to be."

"I've been getting pretty comfortable over here with Sierra," he admitted.

"Like you told me, no man should ever move into his woman's place, but there you are living with Sierra."

"Oh, but it's okay if it's his daughter's place, huh?" he asked.

"Yes, his daughter's place. That's what family is for. It's called unconditional love. Just like the love you've shown me."

"Thanks for still calling me Dad after all of this. Good-bye, Morgan." I heard him yell, "I'm coming."

"Good-bye," I said to his hang up.

I leaned my head down on the white tile of the island in the kitchen. *Do I want to know more about a real father who seems so unreal? Or should I just let it be?*

It was a warm evening. The sky was navy blue and the stars shone like diamonds. Olympia and I used to sit on the front porch of our home when we were younger, trying to identify the constellations, just talking about anything and everything. And we'd always look up high in the sky, amazed by the vastness of it all.

We'd talked about spending some time together so that she could just get away for a minute. Her relationship with Kenyon was good, but it sounded like he was being a little smothering, afraid of losing her again. That was just my opinion and I guess I should have known. My sister didn't seem to want to talk about it, so I knew just the topic to bring up.

"Have a sip of wine, I sure am," I encouraged her as we sat in my backyard at my glass patio table. I enjoyed the sky view, trying to focus enough to locate the Big Dipper.

She looked at the glass I'd put in front of her and turned off her cell phone. "I don't drink before I show up for a catering gig. I have a job at a home in Bel Air later on. What's wrong with your butt today?"

I didn't know she'd noticed. "Olympia, remember all the times that you used to hold me at night when I'd come into our room crying because of something that Dad did or said to me?"

"Yes."

"And you used to witness the times that he'd smack me in the face if I defied him." I said it so casually but the visual was as vivid as ever.

She blinked slowly and then replied, "Yes, but I try not to think back to that."

All of the stars looked alike now. My school-aged astronomy lessons had faded and I couldn't call them out like I used to. Plus, it was easier to tell them apart years ago before childlike problems had grown into adult problems. "Did you ever wonder why you never got the same treatment?"

"I just always thought it was because I was the youngest."

"But didn't he seem particularly angry with me?"

She looked up as well. "Dad was just a trip, Morgan. There were times when I thought I was going to get popped myself. Like when Willis showed up knocking on my bedroom window after midnight. Dad about lost his mind, yelling so hard he was spitting in our faces."

"Yes, from being mad at Willis, not at you."

"What are you getting at, Sis?"

I sat back. "Olympia, Dad, your dad, is not my dad. Not my real dad."

"What do you mean?" She sat straight up.

"Your dad is your dad, but my dad is someone else."

"How do you know this?"

"Dad, your dad, told me."

"Stop referring to him as my dad, he's our dad." She grimaced.

"No, Olympia. He's really only your dad."

She was squinting. "So you're saying that Mom slept with another man who got her pregnant while she was with Dad."

"She got pregnant before she ever even met Dad."

Olympia put her hand up. "Slow down. Now I know if you add up the years, they were married at least a year before you were born."

"No, it was one month before."

She pushed her wineglass away. "Morgan, I don't believe it. And why on earth would he tell you this now?"

"After he saw Jabril trip, it just came out. He'd been holding it in all these years."

"Damn, well who in the hell is this man Mom was with? And where is he now?"

"He's dead."

"Morgan, no."

"He was the man Mom was with the night she died."

"Hold up. That guy, named—what was it—Gary something?"

"You remember his name?"

She looked up into the heavens. "I couldn't forget it. I spent years trying to put two and two together. Dad just told us they were coworkers going to lunch. But I'd never heard of him. He's your dad?"

"Yes."

Our eyes caught up with each other. "Oh, Morgan, I'm sorry. What are you going to do?"

"I don't know."

"Don't you want to know more about who he is and whether or not you have sisters or brothers out there?"

"I don't know."

"So you think that's why Dad treated me differently?"

"I know it is."

She tilted her head my way. "I'm really so very sorry."

"The good thing is, now I know Dad didn't do it because he thought I wasn't as pretty as you." I took a long sip. My glass was now empty.

"Well I knew that you were beautiful."

"He did it because I was the other man's daughter. He could never get over that."

"Morgan, you have to try to find out something about this man. What was his last name again?"

"Washington."

"Listen, I know a woman who works for the DMV. Maybe we can go down there and have her look up his driving records. Even though it's been years now, I'm sure everything is computerized. Let's try to at least find out something about him."

"I don't think so. That would open a whole other can of worms. And I think I need to leave well enough alone. After all, it has been forty years."

"Yes, but you'll always have that nagging curiosity in the back of your mind."

"You think so?"

"Yes, I do. Damn, I can't believe we're not full-blooded sisters. I'm sorry but I'll just never believe it. Maybe it's not true."

"Dad wouldn't make something like this up."

"I say we go tomorrow and check this guy out. I'll call my friend later on. I catered a party for her mom last year. You'll feel better once we find out some information about him, Sis. I promise."

"I hope you're right." The reflection of the moon upon the

water was calming. We looked over and held hands, lounging in the stillness of the night, just like we used to.

The next day, I rode with Olympia to the always bustling Culver City DMV office. We had an appointment at one forty-five in the afternoon. We walked right up to window number eight. Her friend, a young, gum-chewing, tiny-Afro-wearing girl, greeted us like she would anyone else.

"May I see your ID?" she asked me.

I handed her my driver's license.

"Thanks." She looked at my mug shot, and then rolled her eyes up at me. "Hold up, this isn't you. What's your name?"

"Morgan Bayley."

"It sure doesn't look like you. You need to take a new picture."

"I will. I never thought of that," I said to my sister.

The girl looked at Olympia and smiled. "Hi." They played it off.

"Hello." Olympia replied without giving eye contact.

"So his name is what?"

"Gary Washington," I replied.

"And where was he born?"

I tried to remember. "We're not sure. I think he grew up in Georgia."

"What cities?" She was all business.

"Let's say Atlanta or Los Angeles," Olympia suggested.

"No, I don't see anything in Atlanta. Let me check LA." She pressed a few buttons and scrolled down. "Yes, here's a Gary Ronald Washington. He's deceased though."

"How long ago?" I asked.

"Twenty-two years." Olympia and I gave each other the eye.

I inquired, "And where did he live?"

"On Canfield Avenue in Los Angeles. I can't give you his last exact information. You understand."

"Yes." I was fine with that.

"But I can show you his photo if you'd like to see it. It's not as sophisticated as the ones nowadays."

His photo. That was music to my ears. "Okay, I suppose that'll do."

On the sly, the girl looked behind herself, and then peered from side to side. Nonchalantly, she turned the screen our way and enlarged his driver's license photo. And there he was: a fair-skinned, brown-eyed, curly haired man with a wide face, large ears, and big eyes.

Olympia spoke first. "Wow, Morgan, will you look at that?"

"I'm looking."

"He looks just like you," my sister said.

And Gary Washington had one distinctive feature that outshined the rest: his nose was the widest, longest, most offset, overpowering nose I had ever seen in my life. It made my old one look like a button.

"Oh my God. That is your dad, Morgan."

"Yes, that is my dad."

"He has nice eyes," said the girl as she rotated the screen back her way.

"Yes, he has very nice eyes." I looked at my sister, locked that face into my memory bank, and shook my head. Without realizing it, I started to walk away.

"Thanks. We appreciate it," my sister said for both of us.

"No problem. Anything else?"

"No, that's just about it. Good-bye." Olympia flashed a wink.

The girl stayed true to form. "Good-bye. Number 37," she yelled out to the group of seated customers.

Olympia caught up with me. "Morgan, wait up. Are you okay?"

"I'm just fine."

"Well, now I believe it. Now I know. But it's not just his nose Morgan, he has your eyes, your face, your mouth, everything but your complexion."

"I saw that."

She gave me eyes of compassion. "What are you feeling?"

My whole body was numb. My voice downshifted. "I'm feeling as though I wish I'd known, that's all. I just wish I'd known."

"If you'd known, do you think you would have . . . do you want to keep checking further to find out any more about him?"

"Nope. I've seen enough."

We drove the short distance to my house in silence.

She spoke as I grabbed my purse. "I'll see you tomorrow night, right? For dinner?" she asked when I got out of the car.

"Yes."

"Now relax and try to rest your mind, if you can."

"I'll try." Closing the front door, I headed straight to my room and made a beeline to my journal.

> *Journal:*
>
> *Dealing with rejection as a child made me want to scream. But dealing with jealousy and fake stares from men who never noticed me before makes me want to puke. All they see is the flesh that is appealing, and so they want more. That can be just as hurtful as ones who noticed the large nose, yet they decide they don't want you at all. Unless it's behind closed doors.*
>
> *I never seemed to grow into the beautiful swan like Jabril's mom did, not like the glory of the fantasy cartoon. I waited to turn eight, and then thirteen and then twenty and then thirty, but I remained the ugly duckling. Actually, my ugly duckling period lasted for forty years. And so with the help of modern technology, I took fate into my own hands. But had I known that my physical difference came straight from my very own father, that I was just a chip off the old block, and that the man who raised me hated me because of the part of me that reminded him of a man he thought was in his wife's heart, perhaps I would have chosen to stay the way I was . . . different on the outside yet at peace on the inside. It all came together too late, but perhaps right on time. All is in divine order and nothing happens by chance. My makeover led me to a true discovery of who I am. Ugly or pretty, I was made just as I was supposed to be. I was made from love. And who was I to have judged that?*

CHAPTER 19

If Dr. Diamond could have engraved a permanent happy face on my mug to go along with this new nose, it sure would have come in handy that night—the night that Jamie and I had planned a dinner party at my house so that everyone could get a chance to meet him and Cameo. Jamie and Cameo arrived a couple of hours early and Jamie didn't hesitate in getting down with his culinary skills.

"You didn't tell me you had a gourmet kitchen," he said pleasantly.

"I didn't know I had one." I was putting a few dishes away.

"Are you okay?"

I replied, "I just have a lot on my mind."

Cameo entered the kitchen from watching *Waiting to Exhale* on cable. "Can I have something to drink, please?"

"Sure, make yourself at home. Help yourself."

She removed a can of punch from the refrigerator and popped the top. "It smells good in here, Dad." She wiped off the top with a paper towel.

"Thanks, baby." They hugged and she went back into the den. She gave me a parting smile.

Right at seven o'clock, Dad arrived.

I opened the door just before he put his key in the door.

"Where's Sierra?" I asked after he kissed me on the lips and came inside.

"Well, hello to you too. I forgot to tell her until the last minute. She's at a mentoring meeting in Orange County."

"Oh, I was looking forward to seeing her." Before I closed the door, I noticed Olympia and Kenyon coming up the walkway.

"Hey there, everybody," Olympia said while they held hands as they entered. "I miss having dinner over here."

"Good to see you, Morgan," Kenyon said.

We all exchanged greeting hugs.

"You look nice, Olympia," Dad said. He remembered to show me some love too this time. "And you too Morgan. My girls are something else," he said to Kenyon. "Nice to see you again."

Kenyon replied, "You too, sir."

They followed me into the kitchen.

"Dad, Olympia, Kenyon, I want you to meet someone." Jamie stood near the stove with his chef's apron on. "This is Jamie."

"Hi, Jamie. Nice to meet you," Dad said.

"Jamie is Corliss's father."

"What?" Dad asked as if his ears were deceiving him. His squinted eyes flashed a red light.

"Nice to meet you, Jamie," said Olympia.

"You too," said Jamie.

Kenyon exchanged handshakes with him.

Dad did an about-face and walked straight into the den.

Cameo talked to Dad just as he sat down on the loveseat. "Hi. I'm Cameo."

"Hello," he said dryly.

"I'm Corliss's half sister," she told him proudly.

Dad's eyes bugged.

Suddenly, Corliss and Marcus knocked at the door. I could see their images through the side window.

"I think that's Corliss now, Cameo," I said, heading to the door. "Hey there. Hi, Marcus."

"Hi, Morgan. Good to see you."

Corliss headed straight for Cameo and they gave cheek kisses. Marcus was behind her. "Marcus, this is Cameo."

"Hello there. I've heard a lot about you," Marcus said.

"Did you two meet yet?" Corliss asked her grandfather.

Cameo answered. "Yes, we did."

"Isn't she cute, Grandpa?"

"Yes, she is," Dad replied while nodding at Cameo.

"Hi, Corliss," Olympia yelled from the kitchen.

"Hey, Auntie. This is Marcus." Corliss put her hand on his back.

"Hello, Marcus." Olympia waved at him. He spoke back warmly, and then introduced himself to the others. Olympia turned her attention to Jamie. "Looks like you know what you're doing here."

"We'll see. So, I hear you're a caterer," Jamie said.

"Yes, but I don't always prepare the food. I mainly organize the jobs and set up the spread." She sampled some of the jalapeño cheese squares.

"Still, that takes a lot of work."

They continued talking while Kenyon sat on a bar stool near the island. He was knee-deep into the crab-cake appetizers.

Tyra arrived shortly thereafter and gave me a hand as I set out the plates.

It was a buffet-style setup, all spread out in heated chafing dishes aligned on top of the kitchen counter. Jamie cooked up a great meal of garlic basil linguine with salmon and white clam sauce, and a Mendocino salad with lemon dill sauce. It was, literally, the best meal I'd ever had. The boy could burn.

Conversation during the meal was fairly scarce. Most people sat at the dining room table, but Dad and Kenyon sat on the sofa with TV tray setups. They had switched the station to CNN news, and they were deep into their conversation about the pros and cons of war. They seemed a whole lot alike too. But Dad didn't seem to be feeling Jamie. And Jamie didn't seem to be feeling Marcus.

After dinner, Olympia cornered me upstairs in my room when I went to the bathroom to freshen up. She sat on my bed, waiting for me to open the door.

Olympia spoke. "Are you feeling better?"

"I'm cool."

"Morgan, I like him, girl."

"He is very nice, isn't he?"

"And he seems like such a gentleman."

"He is," I replied as I sat next to her.

"Then what's your reservation?"

I leaned back, resting on the palms of my hands. "I don't have any."

"Please, I know you. Is it that he didn't try to find you all these years?"

"No, I didn't try to find him either. I'm telling you there's no problem."

She asked, "Then why aren't you beaming the way we women do when we finally find the one?"

"Who said he was the one?"

"Just the fact that he's here, with Corliss and the family."

"It's not that serious, Sis."

She persisted. "So, is he the one?"

"Olympia, I don't know. You're making this into something more than it is." I sat up and rubbed my hands together. I started to stand but stopped as she spoke.

"Oh, now hold on. You're not still in love with nut-bucket Jabril, now are you?"

"I don't know."

"You don't know?"

Remaining seated, I crossed my legs. "Damn, Olympia, you seem so amazed that I wouldn't be sure after being with that man for so many years. You don't just kick someone out of your heart and mind because they're not in your life anymore."

"Yeah, but you've finally met someone who treats you like a queen. Better yet, the father of your child. And the way you two met up again is unbelievable. I say it's like a fairy tale."

"To you it might be. But to me it's just a man who I need to get to know all over again. Who's to say we'll even be compatible?"

"I know one thing, Morgan, it's not fair to him if you're still stuck on Mr. Stupid. They say the best cure for one man is another. And that other looks damned good to me. He'll get your mind off Jabril in no time. He's a cutie, don't you think?"

"Olympia, he's okay. But looks don't matter to me anymore.

You know, it's really not fair. Jamie gets me on the other side of my makeover. Surely it's easy for him to fall for me, the new-and-improved me with a pretty face and big tits. But he didn't give me all of this attention twenty-something years ago. He hit it and quit it. That's the bottom line."

"I thought he explained all of that."

"He did. But it's still hard to take. Jabril loved me, big nose and all, from the very moment he met me. He saw my inner beauty."

She popped her tongue. "You call that love? Controlling you and talking down to you?"

"I let him do that. I wasn't secure enough to put my foot down." I rubbed my upper arms as though I was cold.

"Why would you want someone who would do that to anyone anyway, someone who you'd have to check?"

"We all have boundaries. You have them with Kenyon. I didn't have any before. Now I do. And I'm not okay with that anymore."

"So, you'd actually consider tossing Jamie and giving Jabril a shot with new rules?"

This time I did stand up. "I don't know."

"He'd never abide by them."

"Never say never. Aren't you cold?"

"No. I'm never going to get you, Sis. I just don't know who you are anymore."

I laughed, grabbing her hand to pull her to her feet. "You're in good company with that statement."

"Just make sure *you* know who you are."

"I do. Finally, I do."

"Morgan, I know you've been going through a lot lately. I just want you to be happy."

"Happy, huh? That's all I want as well."

We proceeded back downstairs, each with an arm over the other's shoulder.

Tyra walked upstairs to use the bathroom as we walked back down. She whispered toward my ear while we brushed by each other. "I've known about Jamie since day one, but I like him for you. And I'm happy for you, and Corliss."

"Thanks, Tyra."

"No problem," she said, making her way toward the upstairs hallway.

Olympia and I walked into the den to rejoin the party.

"Mom, where were you?" asked Corliss, sitting on the sofa talking to Cameo.

"Just talking to your auntie upstairs," I told her.

"Is everything okay?" she asked.

"Sure it is."

"You're so pretty," Cameo said, staring at me.

She was one to talk. "Why thanks. So are you, Cameo."

She looked away shyly. "Your mom looks so young," Cameo told Corliss.

"She is young," Corliss said, triggering my memory in me that I was screwing at the age of thirteen.

I asked Cameo, "Anyway, what's up with your dad?"

"He's in the kitchen, talking to your dad."

"Oh really?" I replied, glancing their way. Now that was a sight for sore eyes.

Marcus walked back into the living room from the kitchen and stood over Corliss, taking her by the hand.

He looked over near the fireplace and spoke. "I love that picture. Is it a sketch?"

"Yes. My mom drew that. It's supposed to be me. It only took her two minutes to draw it."

"I can see that it's you."

"I've never seen the resemblance," I admitted, glaring at it for the umpteenth time.

He stated, "All things are in the eye of the beholder."

I smiled. "That's what my mother used to say."

Corliss added, "I definitely see you. The look on her face is very peaceful, very sweet and angelic."

"I agree," Marcus said.

"Mom's had that picture since I was born," Corliss told her man.

"I hold on to everything," I confessed.

"I hope so," said Jamie as he walked into the living room with Dad right behind him. He hugged me and we exchanged grins.

"Where's Tyra?" Dad asked.

"She went upstairs." I told myself not to go there, until, that is, he went upstairs too. Why didn't he just bring Sierra like I told him to?

One stair, two stairs, three, four, five, twenty stairs. The light was on in Dad's room and the door was closed. I all but tiptoed to the door, brushing up against the door frame as I walked by, staggering as though I was drunk.

"Are you okay?" Tyra asked, startling me as she came out of the guest bathroom behind me.

Damn I felt guilty. I did an about-face. I wondered if saline made people paranoid. "I'm all right, girl. I need to take these damned shoes off while I'm in the house. I needed to see if Dad was up here."

"Be careful," she said with a look. She went back downstairs while rubbing excess lotion into her hands.

Dad came out of his room. "What's going on out here? Has the party moved up here now?"

"No, Dad. I'm just checking on you. We haven't had a minute to ourselves. What are you doing?"

"I was just looking to pack a few more things. You don't mind, do you? I figured I might as well do it while I'm here. I can come back and get it tomorrow."

"So you're not coming back to live?"

"No, baby. I'm going to move forward with Sierra. We're looking for a place of our own. I hope you'll be happy for me."

"I'm more than happy for you, Dad. As long as you're happy."

"And I'm more than happy for you too. No matter what you choose to do." He continued after my smile, "By the way, I did some checking and I found Gary Washington's brother-in-law. His name is Tony Duckett. He's Gary's sister's surviving husband. Here." He handed me a small piece of paper with a phone number.

I took the paper and examined it. "Why are you giving me this?"

"Because I think you should go ahead and find out more about who you really are. And who your dad's family is."

"Dad, who I am on that end is a mystery now and will be even if I call this number. But who my real family is, is right here in this house tonight."

"Morgan, please. Just use it when you're ready."

"Dad, thanks." I handed him back the paper. "I appreciate whatever checking you had to do to get that. But I'll pass for now." I almost told him about the DMV visit, but I just couldn't.

"Morgan, I think you owe it to yourself," he said as though wise.

"Dad, he's dead. Besides, I think I owe it to you to not call. You are my one and only father." I stood on my tiptoes and kissed his cheek.

"Morgan."

"Dad. Enough said."

He put the phone number in his pocket and took my hand. "Thanks."

"I love you."

"I love you too, Morgan."

He led me back to my houseguests . . . my family. We all played board games and cards until nearly three in the morning. Everyone left, exchanging hugs and niceties. Cameo asked Corliss if she could spend the night with her, so she left with Corliss and Marcus. Dad went home to Sierra. Tyra went home alone. Olympia left with Kenyon. And Jamie, well, Jamie stayed a little while.

After closing the front door, I headed to the sofa. "You put your foot in that meal, Jamie. It was excellent." I loosened the belt on my jeans.

He walked over to the guest closet, and then reached into his jacket pocket. "I'm glad you enjoyed it. By the way, I talked to Marcus. He seems like he really cares for our daughter. I asked him what he saw in someone so young. But the reality is, as he reminded me, there's only a twelve-year difference."

"True, but he just looks so much older. Oh well, I've decided to leave that up to Corliss."

"I agree. I think they'll be fine."

A feeling came over me that was a mixture of resentment and appreciation for his caring. But experience prompted me to back away from that subject. "So, it looks like the girls are fast becoming best friends."

"I noticed that." Jamie was now piddling around with my CD player, and then he sat right next to me. He put his arm around my shoulder. "I looked up our Pisces connection and it said that when two Pisceans join together in a love match, there's a union of two sensitive and emotional people. They said that we share honest, efficient communication, a rich emotional bond and a deep spiritual connection." He looked pleased with himself that he was able to recall the horoscope.

"Wow, that's a good thing. A love match, huh?"

"That's what it said."

Suddenly, the song "I'm Ready" played at a low volume. Jamie began to mouth the words. "I'm ready/To love you/Forever."

"Wow, I can't believe you remembered that I love that song."

"I remember everything about you because it's important," he professed, standing up.

He suavely pulled me to my feet and took the lead to begin a cha-cha dance in my den. I followed his lead, snapping my fingers and grooving along. He suddenly stopped and pulled me to him, placing his right hand on the small of my back, and holding my right hand with his left. His eyes were demanding, sucking my glance to meet his. Both of us within three inches of the other's face. Jamie began to grind as if we were slow dancing, but also as though we were warming up for an intimate encounter. I stood more still than he did, but still followed his movement. He then touched my lips with his, smacking the sound of a kiss, and then again, and then again.

All I could think about was this very person, twenty-seven years ago, maneuvering his body up against me in my parents' kitchen. I remembered what it felt like as if it was yesterday. Beneath his belly, his bulge met my crotch area, and it was obvious that Jamie was well endowed, surely just as he was when he was younger and I was a virgin. But now, I was not. I'd gotten past my reservations about sex. I'd explored myself and enjoyed the act of intercourse immensely. But what I didn't feel was a desire for him to experience the new me. Not just yet anyway. I didn't feel the chemistry as he leaned in again, this time with his mouth wide open. He didn't take the time to kiss me way back then, and I just couldn't reciprocate his oral affection right now. I backed away.

"What's wrong?"

I glanced downward. "I'm sorry, Jamie. I just can't right now."

He took a step back too. "I understand. I know it's early. But I've been wanting to do that ever since I first met you again. I've dreamed of it lately, Morgan. But I'm sorry if I overstepped my boundaries."

"No, you didn't. I'm just not ready," I said as Tevin sang about how ready he was.

"I see. How about if we just sit down and enjoy the CD?" He pointed down toward the couch.

A chill filled the room again as I hugged my upper arms. "You know, I really think I just need to get to bed. It is pretty late."

"I agree." He walked to the closet and got his jacket. "Okay, well I'll just get going now. You can keep the CD."

"Thanks."

"We'll take this up again soon. Or maybe we can have that church date on Sunday?"

"Yes, we'll get together again soon."

He kissed my forehead. "Morgan, I am here for you. I want you to know that." He walked ahead of me to the door and opened it.

"I do."

"I had a great evening. Thanks for letting me meet your family."

"Thanks for cooking and for being so wonderful tonight."

He stood under the light of the porch. "Good night, Morgan." He walked away while putting on his jacket. His pace was slow.

"Drive safely."

CHAPTER 20

The next morning I prepared to get the day going but noticed a few dessert plates in the sink so I knocked them out in no time. While the hot water ran over my hands, Jamie was on my mind. In a trance, I replayed the look on his face before he tried to kiss me. It was the look of a man who felt something for sure. I just wasn't sure of his real intentions, and why now?

I really had to make a focused effort to work at changing my routine and making sure that I got a life, that I exercised, got manicures, and got my hair done regularly. It was not something that I was used to doing for myself. I'd been to a hairdresser maybe ten times over the past couple of years. Four of those times were just since the makeover. Today I was willing to put the time in again at Nicole's Hair Nook in Compton. The place was always jumpin'.

It was Nicole herself who was scheduled to hook me up. "Girl, that grape seed-and-avocado conditioner has worked wonders on your hair. It's growing like weeds. Looks like you had that weave put back in." She ran her fingers through my scalp, checking for tracks.

I shook my head and my hair still bounced. "Yeah, my hair has gotten a whole lot thicker lately, huh?"

"Hey, how are you and your man doing?" she asked, always keeping up on everyone's personal business.

"We broke up."

She moved toward my face and dropped her jaw. "That fine-ass man couldn't handle all the attention, huh?"

"It broke apart way before that."

"Oh, my bad. I just assumed you were still together. I remember when he used to drop you off. Are you okay with the breakup?"

"I'm cool. I met someone new." I folded my arms under the peach nylon smock.

"Okay, that always helps."

"But I'll always love Jabril. At least that's how I feel for now."

A lady sitting next to me nearly broke her neck to turn toward me. She sounded surprised. "Jabril?"

Giving her full-on eyes, I jerked my head back. "Yes. Do you know a Jabril?"

"Yes, I mean that's not a common name and all. I'm sorry, my name is Lauren."

"Hi, Lauren. I'm Morgan." We nodded to each other.

"Oh my God, Morgan. I know Jabril. Jabril Montgomery, right?"

Feeling a little uncomfortable, I still had to find out who, what, where, when and how she knew the man who dumped me. "Yes, he's my ex. How do you know him?"

"I met him a while ago at a store when I was buying a printer cartridge."

"Oh really?" I asked, thinking back.

"At Staples."

Now I get it. "Okay, he told me about you."

"He did?" She seemed surprised.

"Yes. He said you were going to hook him up with your agent."

She nodded yes. "And I did. But he never followed up. Morgan, that man loves you."

My instincts were on high. "Oh, so why would he take the time to tell you that?"

"He didn't have to. Women know when a man is stuck on a woman, and he is. Your name came up during every conversation."

Nicole looked at me like this was about to get good.

I probed on. "Just how close did the two of you get?"

She spoke calmly. "Morgan, we're just friends."

"Friends? You've never been to his apartment?"

"Yes, I was, actually, once."

Nicole said, "Uuuummmmmmmhhh."

With my eyes, I gave Nicole a stop sign, still speaking to this woman. "Was that one day when I called?"

She didn't even have to pause to think back. "Yes. But that was just to run some lines for an audition he had. That man is definitely not available. Now, I won't say that I wouldn't have been open if he'd made any advances. I'm not blind. But he was strictly business."

"Well, that's good to know, I suppose. He loves to act. But he's also a man and he sure loves to look."

She waved her hand toward me. "I'll tell you one thing."

"What's that?"

"Why would he bother to look when he's got someone who looks like you?" She checked me out thoroughly, including my feet. And just when I needed a pedicure.

"Watch her," Nicole joked in a soft voice, nudging me.

I replied, "I'll just say that he used to have someone like me."

"Well, I for one don't think it should be past tense."

Oh, I couldn't believe that she was giving me advice. Wasn't she supposed to be the enemy? Watch her was right. "It's too late for that." I spoke as though I was certain.

Nicole chimed in, talking to the other stylist, "Damn, you never know who you're sitting next to in this place."

Wanting to keep the tone as that of two women who had befriended each other, I fought to keep an open mind, forcing myself to think sweet thoughts and not beat her down on the spot. But Lauren sounded pretty cool. I just didn't know if I should trust her as far as I could throw her ass. "No, you never know. It's nice to meet you though, Lauren."

"Nice meeting you too." She turned forward as the round-the-way-girl beautician began to style her hair. And then she gave me a side glance. "You have the most beautiful face. Your complexion is like chocolate milk. What do you use on your skin?"

Nicole nudged me again.

"My daughter told me about using witch hazel and Oil of Olay. Along with a few skin treatments every now and then."

She snapped her finger. "I'm about to go and get me some of that. You take care."

"You too."

Sneaking in another green-eyed view of Lauren through the wall-to-wall mirror, I suppose I was checking her out as maybe Jabril would have, trying to imagine what he saw in her as they stood in that store, bullshitting each other about why they were exchanging numbers in the first place. Before long, she was done and waved good-bye as she tipped the hairdresser. Brown-eyed Lauren looked very curvy. Her complexion was a light shade of brown. She was top and bottom-heavy for sure. Her loose back-side had its own zip code and it shook wildly as she walked away. I wouldn't call her a threat as far as her looks were concerned, but she gained points with me just from being so open and, hopefully, honest. That was the kind of thing Jabril liked. A nice personality. I could see Jabril being attracted to her. Actually, she was just his type. She was not over the top in any aspect visually. But she had this essence and a radiance about her that was very charming. And he liked them thick.

"You'd better go get that man," Nicole said as if she was trying to read my mind.

"I can't."

"Well if you don't, some big-booty girl like that surely will. We women are scandalous you know. We can smell an available man a mile away." She sprayed my hair with a cucumber spritz.

"That's true."

She added, "Sounds like you've got a choice to make."

Now Nicole sounded just like my therapist. I was willing to bet she didn't even have a man of her own. Those are always the ones telling you what to do. I realized I had a whole lot of thinking to do.

I was trying to speak softly—the manicurist sat twelve inches in front of me, giving me a French pedicure. "First of all, I got your message about your mother and what really happened when she died. I'm sorry about that."

"Thanks," Jabril replied, not really sounding surprised, thrilled or phased.

"Are you alone?"

"Yes."

"I never knew all of that was in your head."

"Neither did I."

"Jabril, when we used to talk about our mothers, why didn't you tell me then?"

He could be heard gulping and swallowing. "The fact that she was beautiful didn't matter before. But now, I realize how much her beauty played in the attention she was getting."

"There are some really sick men out there," I told him.

"Well, that's why I never let beauty be an issue with me. And it never will be."

Out of the blue, I announced, "Jabril, I'm going away to think."

"What's there to think about?" He started sounding irritated. Now I could hear a clicking sound. "Just stop thinking so much. That's part of your problem."

"What are you fiddling with?"

"I bought one of those cell phones that takes pictures. It's cool." *I thought he didn't have money. God forbid I dare ask if he got his check.*

"Knowing you, you'll take pictures of every pretty woman in LA."

"Is that how you really see me?"

"No, I'm just kidding." I wasn't. I glanced down at my feet as the manicurist added the final clear topcoat.

"No, I think that really is how you see me," he said, sounding disappointed.

It took all my energy to keep my voice down to a whisper. "Jabril, I'll talk to you later."

"Is that what you called for? To tell me you're leaving?"

"Yes, and also to tell you that I ran into Lauren. You know, your Staples hook up."

He took a bigger gulp and belched loudly. "Excuse me. Where?"

How rude. "At the hair salon."

"Oh Lord." He accentuated the word Lord.

"Oh Lord what, Jabril?"

"Nothing." He started pushing buttons again. The phone's and mine.

"She's very nice."

"Morgan, it's not what you think."

"You really don't know what I think. Hell, I don't even know what I think. But I'm sure you'll hear from her and she'll give you the full rundown. Actually, I'm surprised she hasn't called already." The manicurist nodded her head and walked away after placing a tiny fan on the floor to dry the polish.

"Morgan, I hope you find the answers you're looking for while you're away." His call-waiting beep sounded.

"So do I. Have fun with your new toy."

"Good-bye, Morgan." He sounded as if he regretted the fact that he might have originally been excited that I had called at all. He clicked over.

When I got home, I made a call to my travel agent to ask her to arrange everything. I'd be on a tight budget. I needed to make a few more calls including one to my boss to ask for about ten days off. He was surely going to kill me. It would no doubt be without pay, considering all the time I took off for the makeover. But actually he was very cooperative since he'd just received a check from the investor I recently met with—Mr. Watson, the playboy. He actually came through. Great timing.

I pressed speed dial for Jamie's number. "I'm falling for you," he said just moments after we said our hellos.

"How do you know? It's so soon."

"You know what they say: It's a feeling you feel when you feel a feeling you've never felt before. And I'm feeling it. Every time I see you, I can't wait to see you again. It's a damned good feeling. This is not the feeling of a fling. You and I are going to be in a relationship, Morgan. I'm not going to force you, it's just my opinion."

"My feelings are a little harder to sort through right now. That's why I want to get away."

"Get away?"

"Yes, alone. Just for a little while."

"Well, Morgan, I'll always put your feelings first, almost to a fault. I would ask to go with you but I won't. Do what you think is best. I just want to put a smile on your face every day. I don't see you being out of my life. I'd like to see what happens. Like Jeffrey Osborne sang, I want to 'find one hundred ways' to surprise you. Is that okay with you?"

Oh, he's working me with song lyrics. "Yes, I suppose so. Jamie, can we talk about this when I get back?"

"When is that?"

"I'll call you and let you know."

"Morgan, but I'm serious. I don't want to look any further, I'm telling you. We can make this happen. Don't let our past keep us from having a future."

"Okay."

"And just so you know, I didn't share this with you when I told you about my talk with Marcus, but your dad had a talk with me too. It was man to man in the kitchen at your house."

"What did he have to say?"

"Honestly, he kind of got on me for what happened. Not only the actual sex with you, but about my absence since then. I explained everything to him and he seemed to be understanding, though he frowned the entire time."

"Wow, thanks for telling me that."

"He sort of warned me to not hurt Corliss. And he definitely warned me to not hurt you."

That would have surprised me before.

He continued, "Well, just so you know, I have no intention of doing that to either one of you."

"Jamie, do you feel guilty about what happened years ago?"

"No, not really."

"Not really?"

"No, I don't feel guilty, I don't think that's the right word. I think it's more regret than anything else."

"Regret?"

"That we didn't continue on or at least keep in touch. I just don't want to miss this second chance, so excuse me if I seem a little anxious. But no, I don't feel guilty."

"What if you'd met me again and I hadn't had the surgery?"

"I don't think it would have made a bit of difference."

"You don't?"

"No, I don't. The e-mails between us started before the surgery and we seemed to be off to a good start then. What are you thinking?"

"Nothing, Jamie. I've got to go."

"Okay. Well, don't be a stranger."

"I won't, I promise. I'll be in touch."

Shaking my head, I hung up and grabbed a drink box from the icebox. That Jamie was pretty determined. And Dad actually cornered him and did his protectiveness thing. Usually, it was Olympia's suitors who'd be put through that type of scrutiny. But Dad did check Jabril too. Times had changed after all. I noticed that Dad left a Post-it on the refrigerator that he'd been by to get the rest of his things. I also noticed that he didn't leave the key.

Taking a load off, I sat at the dining room table and called the travel agent again. She had made all the arrangements. The last-minute getaway did indeed end up costing me an arm and a leg. After this next call, I needed to pack.

"I'm sorry to bother you, Corliss, but I'm going out of town for about a week, to Mexico. Will you keep an eye on the house for me since Grandpa's not home? You know, check the papers and mail."

She seemed surprised. "Yes. Where's Grandpa going to be for that long?"

"He's staying with Sierra for a while. They're giving it a try and are going to look for a house together." I sucked tropical orange through the tiny straw.

"That's good. Who are you going to Mexico with?"

"Morgan."

She chuckled. "You refer to yourself in the third person now?"

"Just means I'm going alone."

"Why, Mom? Why now?"

"I just need a vacation."

"To a strange place by yourself?"

"Corliss, the point is that I should have done this before now . . . alone. I'm always with someone. It's just my new way of doing a little soul searching and getting some much needed rest and relaxation."

"Fine. When are you leaving?"

"Tomorrow morning."

"Tomorrow? Does your job know?" She sounded like my mother again.

"Yes."

"Does, Jamie . . . I mean, does Dad know?"

Sucking on the tiny straw, I swallowed and then spoke. "Yes, your dad knows."

"How about Grandpa?"

"My dad knows too."

She downshifted her tone. "Okay, Mom. You know what you're doing."

"Yes, I do."

"Will you e-mail me your itinerary and hotel information?" she requested.

"I will."

"And call as soon as you get there."

"I can't guarantee that."

"Why?"

"Okay, I'll try."

"Who's taking you to the airport?"

"Corliss, I'll be fine." I stood up to slam-dunk the empty box into the trash, feeling so ready to hang up.

"I know you will. I'm sorry."

"No, it's okay. Thanks for caring. How's Marcus?"

"He moved in, Mom."

"Are you . . . no, no questions. I trust your decision. As long as you're happy, I'm happy." I leaned back against the island.

"Well I am happy. I can't believe you didn't ask me why my place and not his."

"No comment." My bottom lip had to be bleeding from the pressure of my teeth.

"Mom, thanks."

"You're welcome."

"I love you, beautiful."

"I love you, beautiful," I replied as a smile spread across my face.

CHAPTER 21

Mexico was magically beautiful, with its white-sugar sand beaches and crystal-clear warm waters. My hotel, called the Bougainvillea Resort, was spectacular. My two-story, top-floor suite had a private sunbathing deck and fully stocked bar.

You'd think I'd have been hitting the hot spots, drinking, dancing, shopping and sightseeing. But, instead I vegetated, tanned, ate, rested, read, thought, reflected, meditated, wrote, and observed. Observed the different types of people—old, young, fat, skinny, tall, short, alone, coupled up, with kids, without kids—all brought together for a purpose: to love and be loved and make memories, in spite of how big their feet were or how many fingers they were born with. All experiencing this thing called life.

Each day, I added notes to my invaluable journal. And by the final evening, I'd compiled enough to have written a book. I hadn't talked to anyone or written anyone, other than letting Corliss know that I made it in safely. I was only there to purge. I felt brand-new.

"Do you mind if I make you a special salad, senorita?" asked the Mexican waiter at the fancy dark restaurant next door. It was my final night. I wanted to treat myself to a special dinner for one.

"Special?" I smiled, sporting a sheer white dress.

"Yes, it is called the Pretty Salad, for a *muy bonita* lady."

My flushed cheeks told on me. "Pretty salad?"

"A Caesar salad with three different types of lettuce, mandarin oranges, grilled chicken, sun-dried tomatoes, and my special dressing."

"Sounds good. I'll try it."

As improper etiquette as it may have been, I rested my elbows on the table and watched him begin his preparation by candlelight. He winked repeatedly and eyed my cleavage while he tossed and smiled. His name tag read Sebastian and he was as fine as the Merlot I was drinking.

"Where are you staying? Here at the hotel?" he inquired while pouring the creamy dressing.

"Why?"

"Just thought you might want some company later."

I'd never been that risky in my life. This would have been a true example of getting my groove back. A groove I never had to begin with. *And so . . . why start now?* I thought. "No, that's okay."

He put the salad plate in front of me. "If you change your mind, I'm here until two in the morning."

Draping my napkin onto my lap, I said, "Thanks for the salad, but I'll pass on the room service." I was so damn chicken.

"Okay, but just so you know, I'm known for paying great attention to detail."

"I'll bet you do." I said a quick, silent prayer. When I opened my eyes, he was staring me down and then cut his eyes away. Poking my fork into a leaf of red lettuce, I took a bite and nodded my approval. He winked, gathered his setup and went back into the kitchen.

Why was it that I no longer had to flag down a waiter, bellmen, or customer-service person? I even appeared to be getting front-row seating. All of those people suddenly seemed to be conveniently at my disposal, whereas before I couldn't even get a salesperson at Neiman Marcus to help me. I'd never been the center of attention. But I was finding out one thing, as shallow as it may seem: being good looking did have its advantages.

After a little while, I left the restaurant, making sure to leave the disappearing Sebastian a generous tip.

"Thanks," I said as an older gentleman held open the hotel lobby door.

He tipped his hat. "My pleasure."

I was walking through the lobby and the song on the piped-in speakers overhead was *Beautiful* by Christina Aguilera.

"Words can't bring you down."

Dang, I wish they'd had esteem-boosting songs like that when I was a kid.

"Ladies and gentlemen, we're about to make our descent into Los Angeles. Current temperature conditions are partly cloudy and seventy-two degrees." The United Airlines pilot sounded cheery and capable.

I usually freak out when I'm mile high, but that day I felt a lot more calm. My mind was rejuvenated and my body was relaxed. My escape to Puerto Vallarta was a complete success, definitely a good thing.

The last word of my journal entry was inked just as the landing gear hit the runway.

I'd agreed to let Jabril pick me up from the airport to take me to get my car, which was parked in a lot only a few blocks away. He'd always been willing and available to greet me upon my return when I traveled on business. It was kind of a nice feeling when he'd offer his services. Early that morning, I'd called Jamie to tell him that I was about to leave but would call once I got settled in.

As was the case when flying, I was in need of a makeup fix, a trip to the bathroom, and a curling iron. But I hurried down to the baggage area to beat the rush.

"Do you work for the network?" a gentleman asked, glancing down at my BET bag as he walked alongside.

I glanced down at it too. "Oh, this bag? It was a gift from a friend." That friend was Jabril.

"It's nice." He viewed it again, and then gave me the once-over, checking out the area of my midsection exposed above the waistband of my low-rise jeans and below the bottom of my midriff

T-shirt. "I work for Turner Broadcasting and I noticed those type of bags while I was in Las Vegas at the television conference this weekend."

"No, I wasn't coming from there." I remained tight-lipped.

He commented, "You look like an actress or a model. Are you?"

"No, I'm not." I shifted my bag to my other shoulder.

"What do you do, if I might ask?"

"I'm a program director." I tried to be vague.

"Oh, okay." We walked fast. "Are you single?"

"Yes." I smiled inside.

"Would you mind exchanging numbers so that we can get to-gether for a drink? I live in Atlanta but I'm in LA quite often." He flashed his major dimples.

"That's very nice of you but I don't think so."

He seemed as though he was trying to figure out the real rea-son for my denial.

"Do you live here? Because distance doesn't matter to me."

"Yes, I live here."

"So are you single but just not available? Or just not interested? I'm a big boy, I can take it," he joked, cracking himself up. His voice was deep and he had a sexy-ass laugh.

"It's just that I don't think I have time to make new friends."

"That's a shame. I'm the head of diversity at Turner in Atlanta. Not like that should matter, but to be honest with you, you'd think I'd have it going on, but I'm still unlucky at love for some reason."

I wasn't buying that. "That's too bad. You seem like a charming man. I'm sure love is just around the corner."

"I hope so. Well, how about if I just give you my business card and maybe one day, if I'm lucky, you'll decide to call me? I'd also like to hear more about this program you direct." He extended his hand and I reached out to take the card.

"Hey, baby. There you are."

I heard a voice coming from behind me. I did an about-face, tucking the card into my pocket.

"Surprise," said, of all people, Jamie, standing with a beautiful large bouquet of candy cane, red and white roses. "You got a tan."

"Ahh, Jamie. What are you doing here?" *How do you spell nervous?*

"Nice to meet you," the man said, excusing himself as he put two and two together. He looked over toward Jamie and tipped his head.

I replied to the gentleman, "Yes, you too. Take care."

He walked over to the other side of the baggage carousel. He stood next to a man who was standing with his arms crossed, watching. The man was Jabril. He looked right through me with a dazed-type stare. Yet as usual, it was mixed with a hint of anger.

I turned back toward Jamie, speaking from the corner of my mouth. "I didn't know you were coming." My heartbeat was booming under my new breasts.

"That's the point," he grinned, like he was actually proud of himself.

"I've already arranged for a ride to my car."

"Well, I'm here just in case."

"No need. My ride is here." I pointed to Jabril who was fast approaching.

"What the hell is he doing here?" Jabril asked as he stopped within an inch of me.

Jamie asked, "Who's this?"

"Jamie, this is Jabril."

They did not greet each other.

"You needed two rides?" Jabril asked, seeming confused and sounding sarcastic.

"I didn't ask him to come," I told Jabril.

He jumped on that statement. "You heard the lady. She didn't ask you come. Nice flowers, dude. Now go and find someone else to give them to."

Jamie handed them to me. I took them. And Jamie looked happy that I did.

"Why would I do that? They're obviously for Morgan."

Jabril put his arm around me. "Because my Cookie is taken."

"Not from what I heard. I hear you walked away from your Cookie months ago."

"Yeah, but in actuality, I never left. I haven't left in years. Unlike you."

"Yeah, well I'm back now. Both for her and my daughter," Jamie snapped.

"You're about oh, let's see," Jabril glanced at his watch, "twenty-six years too late."

"Not from what Morgan tells me. Isn't that right, baby?" Jamie stared at me like he was still in junior high school. Suddenly he was starting to look very familiar.

Stepping out of Jabril's hug, I raised flat hands in each direction as they sandwiched me. "Look guys, you both need to calm down. Jamie, I don't appreciate you showing up out of the blue. You never know what can happen when you do something like this."

"I thought I was surprising my lady," Jamie exclaimed.

"Your lady, my ass," said Jabril.

"Jabril, please. Jamie, I asked Jabril to come so . . . so, please leave."

Jamie shrugged his shoulders. "No problem. If that's how you want it I'm cool. I'll let him play taxi for now, but I'll call you later on tonight."

"If you do, bro, you'll get me on the phone."

"I doubt it," Jamie replied with certainty.

Fast losing patience, I broke it down. "Look, both of you. Cut all of this testosterone-battling, test-of-wills crap out. I just came back from a relaxing vacation and I'm not in the mood for your selfishness. I'm not sure what I'm doing. I don't even know what I want from me, let alone from the two of you. But for now, I need you to leave . . . both of you. I'll catch a darn airport shuttle. This is not worth all of the drama."

"I'm not letting you catch a shuttle, Cookie." Jabril spoke as though his wants and needs were still my priority. But damn he smelled good.

Strength felt like my middle name. "You can no longer let me or not let me do anything, Jabril."

"You know what? I'm here because you asked me to come and

pick you up. I'm not the one who showed up unannounced," Jabril said, darting his eyes at the competition.

Oh, I did not want him to get it twisted. "No, you offered and I accepted. I didn't ask you and you're one to talk about un-announced."

Jabril spilled his words. "You know what, you need to make a damn choice, here and now. I have told you how I feel and you know I've always been there. Not like this dude who tapped it, and then ran off without even looking you up for decades. And now he sees the same thing all of these other dudes out here see: tits, ass and a pretty face. You should have sent him on his way as soon as you found out who he was. Corliss's father or not."

Jamie jumped in. "Morgan, in spite of all of the lip flapping here, and as uncomfortable as this might be, I agree that you need to make a choice. I'll be comfortable with whatever decision you make. I'd just like to know."

Jabril stood firm, crossing his muscular arms across his burly chest. "Oh yes, perhaps this little threesome was meant to be. Make a choice."

Suddenly, all was crystal clear. "What I want is for you to stop telling me what to do, Jabril. You have never stopped trying to control me. I told you I'm not the same woman I was when you met me. I'm stronger and I'm not afraid."

"Afraid of what?" Jabril asked.

"To stand up to you, Jabril. I love you, but not more than I love myself. It's over. I don't want to move forward with you. So there's your answer. Now please go."

"Yeah, man, you heard the lady," Jamie taunted.

"And Jamie, I did not ask you to come here. You just show up out of the blue and yell, 'surprise,' like you've got it going on like that. And I am definitely not the same as when you first met me. I want you to go too."

Jamie was silent but Jabril spoke.

"You're missing out, Cookie."

"No, you missed out when you didn't support me through my decision."

Jabril replied as though it would make a difference. "Okay, baby, you're pretty. There, I said it. You're a hot-ass girl. Now can we get things reconnected so this chump can leave?" His expression looked so insincere.

My stomach turned. "Good-bye, Jabril."

"Whatever, I'm out." He took one step.

"Oh wait, not before you give me my house key." I put my hand out.

He did an about-face. "I don't need your key anyway. I'm about to go and get a key to Lauren's house since you made your choice. You know, the Staples woman, as you call her."

A look of indifference consumed my face. "That's so you."

He took the key off his ring, pushed it into the palm of my hand, and walked away.

Jamie spoke more calmly but with less certainty. "Morgan, are you sure about this?" I could smell his manly perspiration and feel the heat of his breath.

"Yes."

"How are you going to get home?"

"I've got it covered. My car is not far away."

"Will you at least keep the flowers?" he asked.

"Good-bye." I was through.

"Fine, but I want to be able to see Corliss."

"She's not a child, Jamie. She's a grown woman. That's between you and her." I walked away.

"Morgan, I love you," he exclaimed to my back.

I turned with a runway pivot. "You love who?"

"You," he replied.

"Jamie, you love the new me, but never took the time to get the know the old me. You love my image, not my essence."

Jamie stood and watched as I headed toward the baggage carousel. I spotted my bright red bag and ran up to grab it, swinging it to the side and nearly grazing the woman next to me.

"Hey, let me get that," said the man who gave me his card earlier. "My name is Michael."

"Hi, Michael."

"Looks like you do have your hands full, huh?" he arranged his bags as well.

"Not anymore," I said with double meaning.

"Is everything okay?" he asked, looking over at Jamie.

"It's fine. I've got it, thanks."

He tried to garner a face-to-face exchange. "You have beautiful teeth. My goodness." He looked mesmerized.

"Thanks."

"Do you need a ride? I've got a limousine picking me up." His bodyguard-looking driver walked up and took his bags.

Turning around, I noticed that Jamie was finally headed toward the exit door.

"No, I'm fine."

"Are you sure? We can drop you off. It's not a problem."

"Believe me, I can make it alone."

"I'm sure you can, if that's what you want."

"That's what I want," I assured him.

"Okay, but will you consider calling me one day?"

"I'll think about it."

"I'd appreciate it." He started to walk on. "You look to be pretty popular, huh?"

"All of a sudden, I guess I am." I pulled my bag toward the exit.

"Must be nice," he spoke loudly.

"No, really it's not. Take care now."

"You too. What did you say your name was?" he bellowed.

I turned back and said, "Morgan."

"Morgan. Nice meeting you."

"Good-bye."

Walking with my luggage on wheels, a large shoulder bag, and the big bouquet of flowers, I approached the blue shuttle area. A lady stood nearby. She was an older woman. Her age lines were deep. Her salt-and-pepper hair was pulled straight back into a one-inch ponytail, which made her features more prominent, especially her round, wide, bulbous nose. She had deep-set eyes, an overbite, and a large, high forehead. She was empty-handed. Not even a purse.

Her presence was strangely undeniable. "Has anyone ever told you you're beautiful?"

"Who, me?" she looked around, placing her right hand over her heart.

"Yes, you."

She spoke with a demure softness. She looked toward the concrete. "Not lately, ma'am."

"Well, you are."

"Thanks." She parted her bee-stung lips and exposed every one of her teeth.

"Here, these are for you," I said, offering her the bouquet of roses.

She looked up, extending her hands. "But why?"

"Because every woman should enjoy the feeling of being given to. The feeling of beauty that matches our internal beauty too."

Her demeanor changed. "My God. Thank you so much for those words." She sniffed a red rose and took in the fragrance. She looked pleased with the scent. "These are so beautiful. I'm speechless." Her eyes started to well up with a glassy haze. She moved closer and gave me a bear hug.

"Thanks, Morgan," she said in my ear.

The world came to a standstill. "What?" I broke away.

She repeated herself as I watched her lips move. "I said thanks again."

"Oh, I thought you said my name. My name is Morgan."

"My name is Norma Jean."

Comfort enveloped my skin. "Hi, Norma Jean."

She explained through her surprise, "You know what, people usually don't even notice me."

"That's hard to believe."

"Bless you."

"Have a nice day, Norma Jean." What do you know? That was my mom's friend's name who my dad told me about. The one who'd died of cancer. My aunt.

"You have a nice day too, my child."

Barely taking half a step, I had to inquire, "Norma Jean, do you wear Shalimar?"

She glanced up from admiring the beauty of the roses. "Why, yes."

"I knew it," I told her as we parted.

From her strong embrace, I could smell my mother's scent lingering in the air and on my shoulder. I stepped in the half-empty shuttle bus and the door closed. As I took a seat, I turned to look out of the window. Norma Jean had vanished.

It felt good to give her those flowers and put a smile on her face. It should always be a great deed to give. But as for the charming man's business card, I decided to just keep that for myself. First checking my pocket to make sure I still had it, I placed it securely in my wallet.

My thoughts journeyed back to the words I'd spewed onto the pages of my journal less than ten minutes before the plane landed. Traveling to Mexico was one trip that was well served.

Journal:

God made me perfect in every way, no matter what genes I was assigned through an egg and a sperm. I was made in His image and likeness and that can never be wrong. They say to be made over is to be redone, improved and altered. Perhaps similar to being born again as a disciple, as though the previous me died in some way. They say as a society we tend to boost things that are bothersome and that breeds a lack of self-acceptance. I admit that I fell into that trap. And so now . . . I am pretty. But now that I am redone, made over and altered, by my own choice, that means I'm a product of Morgan's makeover. So, I must live with my decision and make the best of it, being the best me I can be, from the inside out. I suppose it's never too late to learn to love yourself again. Perhaps that's my true makeover. God, please show me evidence that

*it's okay to move forward as I am, with or without a
man. I ask this in your name, Amen.*

After putting my spiral journal back into my shoulder bag, I un-
consciously crossed my legs and my arms. Peace owned me so intensely I could smell it. It actually had a fragrance.

Eyeballing the familiar Los Angeles surroundings, I looked forward to going home to my empty nest, alone. It felt as though it
was my turn to live, finally. In no time at all, the shuttle dropped
me off at Zone 12, right near my car, which was parked in Lot C.
Carefully, I stepped down, adjusting my bags, trying to remember
the exact spot where my car was parked, when I heard a startling,
high-pitched honk. Peering over with caution, I saw a car I'd never
seen before. It was an older, sky blue Ford Escort. Two young,
baseball cap-wearing men were in the front seat, both looking my
way.

Speedily rolling my luggage along, I made sure I had my keys in
hand. My third eye was at its height. Suddenly, I heard one of the
men speak.

"Damn, man, look at that. I'll bet you'd hit that if no one was
looking."

"Hell yeah, dude. I'd hit that, hoping everyone was looking,"
the other replied, sucking his teeth. "Looking good."

Breathing outwardly with intense relief, my hasty strut downshifted. Things really hadn't changed that much after all. And
some things, I supposed, never ever would, no matter what.

MAKE ME HOT

MARISSA MONTEILH

ABOUT THIS GUIDE

The suggested questions are intended
to enhance your group's reading
of *Make Me Hot*.

DISCUSSION QUESTIONS

1. Author Marissa Monteilh recalls that being 5'10" since she was very young, combined with the fact that she couldn't break the 100 pound mark for the life of her until she was in her twenties, led to some very cruel name-calling well into high school. Memories of the taunting rose to the surface as Marissa wrote some of the early scenes in *Make Me Hot*. Have you experienced similar teasing as a child? If so, how did it shape your early level of self-esteem? Did some of that pop up during an adult? Did you have someone in your life who reinforced your worth?

2. At the beginning of the novel, Morgan Bayley describes her boyfriend of five years, Jabril Montgomery. What does her acceptance of him tell you about her? What does her need to please her father tell you about her?

3. After a night of passionate lovemaking, when Morgan tells Jabril about her decision to have plastic surgery, he decides immediately to end the relationship. Do you see this as a control tactic on his part, or do you think he really loved her as she was? Was he justified in his decision? Would you support a mate who decided to have plastic surgery?

4. After living with her extra-large nose for nearly forty years, is it your opinion that Morgan would have decided upon plastic surgery if Jabril had not been searching Beautiful Girls.com? How would you feel if you were in her shoes? Do you think society puts pressure on women to fit a certain "pretty" mold? Do you think the molds are different for black women as opposed to white women?

5. When Morgan showed up at Jabril's home after her makeover, she wanted him to take her back, but he resisted. Can

you relate to her need to win him back? Do you think she was simply trying to work through the fact that he rejected her? Would you have tried to get him back or would you have moved on?

6. Throughout the first half of the novel, prior to the surgery, Morgan appears fairly passive, then afterwards, she appears to stand up for herself, getting into conflict with her ex, her father, her best friend and her daughter. Do you think her attitude changed simply because she looked hot and gained confidence, or because the people in her life really needed to be confronted? Try to examine each character one by one as it relates to this.

7. Morgan's daughter, Corliss, started dating Marcus who seemed to be suddenly attracted to Morgan once she had her makeover. Would you have been okay with your daughter getting serious about an older man who she tried to set you up with, especially if the man wasn't interested in you at first, and then suddenly appeared to be?

8. Morgan's best friend, man-hunting Tyra, makes mention quite a few times about her need to get with an older man. Do you believe she had a real attraction to Morgan's father? Do you think they really did get together?

9. In a major scene from *Make Me Hot*, Morgan's father, River Bayley, comes clean to his daughter after years of what she perceived as treating her as though she was never enough, unlike the way he treated her baby sister, Olympia. Do you think Morgan should have forgiven him for the years of indifferent treatment?

10. Rump-shaking Lauren, Jabril's Staples woman, tries to befriend Morgan in the beauty shop. Could you have handled a conversation with someone who very possibly could have

been the other woman? Would you have trusted her or would you have told her to get lost?

11. Jamie ended up desperately wanting Morgan after nearly twenty-seven years, in spite of the fact that he never tried to find her. Should she have given him the time of day? Did he really love her?

12. Throughout Morgan's ordeal in this book, did you feel sympathy for her in any way? If so, was she was better off before the makeover or after? Did she have realistic expectations?

13. *Make Me Hot* presents an example of which factors might lead a woman to decide to get plastic surgery, and it shows the deep need for self-love. In your opinion, should plastic surgery offer a quick fix to physical dissatisfaction? What are your views on extreme makeovers? If you could have plastic surgery on just one part of your body, what part would it be and why?